The
IMAGINARY
LIVES
of
JAMES
PŌNEKE

Tina Makereti

Published in 2019
by Lightning Books Ltd
Imprint of EyeStorm Media
312 Uxbridge Road
Rickmansworth
Hertfordshire
WD3 8YL

www.lightning-books.com

British Library Cataloguing in Publication Data
A catalogue record for this book is available from the British Library.

Printed by CPI Group (UK) Ltd, Croydon CR0 4YY

ISBN: 9781785631528

ARTS COUNCIL OF NEW ZEALAND TOI AOTEAROA

Randell Cottage

For Lorry

He speaks English so well, that at first we took him to be some English boy dressed in savage costume — some intruder from a masquerade. We were, however, mistaken. He reads and writes English as well as any boy his age, and is particularly fond of joking. In fact, we have seen many English boys much more stupid, more ignorant, than this specimen of the New Zealanders.

— *The Daily News*, London, 6 April 1846

But maybe being entertainment isn't so bad. Maybe it's what you're left with when the only defence you have is a good story. Maybe entertainment is the story of survival.

— *The Truth About Stories*, Thomas King

Listen, miracle of the future. You strange possibility, my descendant. I know you are embroiled in your own concerns, but hear me. I've seen so many miracles in my short life, things I never dared imagine possible, and just as much pain. Here, in this place and this time, I am nothing but what I can conceive, what I can imagine. Why shouldn't I make a message for you and you receive it? You use machines I cannot even imagine, I know, since even in my time there are machines I once could not have imagined. So think of me with you now, as I think of you. Perhaps you are a mix of all the different peoples I have seen. Perhaps you are even something new. You are magnificent; I can sense it. For all I know you might wear a coat woven from insect wings and draw energy from the sun. You are my greatest imagining. So listen.

I have a story for you. It will seem, as you read, that it is a story about me, but the more I write the more I think it is not

5

about my life or my time at all. Mr Antrobus told me so often of progress and emancipation and the evolution of humanity, but some small voice inside me wondered, what if progress is an illusion, alongside these other great Imperial illusions I have come to love and hate in equal measure? What if, in the end, all that exists is the show and the cost of a ticket? No. Let me take you behind the curtain.

I apologise. I grow tired and distracted and abstract. The hour is late. The candle is low. Tomorrow I will see whether it is my friends or a ship homewards I meet. But I must finish my story for you first. My future, my descendant, my mokopuna. Listen.

ONE

I am not yet seventeen years of age, but I have a thought that I may be dying. They don't say that, of course, but I can read it in their many kindnesses and the way they look at one another when I speak of the future. Perhaps I do not need their confirmation, for surely I wouldn't see all I can in the night if I weren't playing in the shadow of death. So when they come and ask about my life, I tell them all. What else is there for me to do? I don't feel it then, the brokenness of my own body. I feel only the brokenness of the world.

From here, in the shadows, I can see a piece of London's sky and the roofs of countless houses. The curtain is flimsy, and I have asked Miss Herring to leave it aside, for I am so high in this room and the sky is my only companion these many hours. At night, I see the beetle making his slow, determined way between cracks. I smell the city rising then: black smoke, the underlying reek of piss and sweat, the sweetness of hung meat and fruit piled high in storage for the morning, its slow rot. My own. The street waits, and the beetle crawls, leg over leg, down the brick side of the house. From his vantage point, I see it all: every detail in the mortared wall, the coal dust that covers it; the wide expanse of London Town, lights shimmering along the Thames and out into a wide panorama more delightful than even the sights of the Colosseum. I wish I could tell you the air is fresh here, but no, it is stench and smoke and fog rising, obscuring the pretty lights. Yet I love it, love this dark and horrid town, feel the awe rising even beside the dread. It is a place of dreams.

Sometimes I follow the moth who finds her way on swells of air, a ship catching currents established lifetimes ago, knocked sideways by the draught of a cab passing, the hot air expelled from a gelding's nostrils. The moon is different here, not a clean, clear stream but a wide and silty river. She lends her light all the same, so that I might see the faces that pass. And they pain me, it's true, for every face is one I know, and I cannot say whether they are living or dead. I see all the misses and misters of the streets of London, and the ones of Port Nicholson. The worst of it is when I see the tattooed face, or hear the music of the garden orchestra, see gaudily dressed couples dancing circles, the spectre of shows pitching illusions into the air: tricks of light, mechanical wonders, wax figures bearing features I knew only for the first few years of my life. I couldn't even remember my mother's face until I was confined to my bed, and now I see her every night, a doll animated by a wind-up box. The acrobats then, and my friends from the card table. Warrior men and women of my childish and dark memories, from before I learnt about the world of books and ships. My shipmen, both loved and feared. They don't speak, my friends and enemies and loved ones, but I know they are waiting; I know the streets below

8

are teeming with them, even when the hour grows late and all decent men should be in their own beds.

It is as if I travel through all the old battles each night until I reach him, and though I know not whether he still walks the solid Earth, I always find him. Billy Neptune, even now grinning and ready to make fun. He is the only one who sees me.

'Hemi, good fellow,' he calls, 'back to your bed! What is your business out here amongst the filth of the streets? Not the dirt, mind you, I mean people like us!' At this he laughs his short, booming laugh, a sound that breaks open in my chest like an egg spilling its warm yellow centre.

'What is it like?' I ask him every night, or, 'How are you?' But he doesn't answer.

'Ah, Hemi,' he says. 'What games we made of it, eh, my fine friend? What games.' And he goes on his way, and I go on mine, circling the restless world.

⊚

These past few nights I seem to have gone further than before, and this morning Miss Herring commented that I looked more tired than I had yesterday, when I had seemed more tired than the day before.

'Are you not recovering, Mr Poneke?' she asked. 'Should I ask Miss Angus to bring the doctor again?'

The doctor has been three times already, and though he works his doctoring skill on my body, I'm afraid he does not have medicine for what ails me.

'No — all is well, thank you, Miss Herring. Only, I do not seem to sleep at all, and travel the world in my imagination through the long night instead. It seems as real as you standing right here this morning.'

The maid shook her head and smiled, as she always does when I use her name, for I am the only one who addresses her formally, and no one has yet found a way to correct me in this habit.

'Mr Poneke, I believe you've travelled to the very ends of this Earth. You must have many memories of adventures beyond what's normal.' She hummed as she made to clean the fireplace and reset the fire. I suppose Miss Herring and I enjoy an uncommonly open interaction, one that she would not enjoy with more formal masters. But I am not a master, and my position in the house has always been unusual, and I have a great need of companionship, spending so much time alone in bed as I do.

'It is a dark night I go out in, and I am liable to see ghosts.'

At this she drew in a sharp breath and blustered about, leaving as soon as she saw Miss Angus arrive with the soup she brings each day. Miss Angus enquired after my health, and I repeated what I had told the maid, save for the part about ghosts.

'Sometimes I wonder — if I had a way of telling my story, perhaps it wouldn't haunt me so. What think you, Miss Angus?'

'It seems like as fine a way to pass the time as any.' Miss Angus sat with her sewing in the chair she'd set up by the window for such a purpose. She is endlessly patient with me, endlessly considerate. It is a comfortable room, and easy to talk. And so I did, describing how only three nights before I had begun to leave the London of my dreams. I was tired of all the shadows of the city, I said, thinking of my personal ghosts. Instead of my usual wandering I sped to the wharves, and there I took a ship and walked among the men as they worked. I did not tell her that all my ghosts found me on the ship, that I had simply moved them along with me. These crews of my old life took me over the oceans, faster than ever before, until we were again in Barbados.

From there, each time Miss Angus came to attend me, I told her of a different night's travel. Sometimes we stayed aboard ship, or were tossed again in the wreck of the *Perpetua*; other times we returned to my wandering days in New Zealand. Despite never straying from the tasks in front of her while I spoke, Miss Angus seemed serene and even entertained by my foolish stories.

After a week of such adventures I feared I may have confused Miss Angus with all my tales of roving about the world. I hadn't told them in any sort of order — it does not happen that way in the telling of a tale, and it is hard to keep my mind straight when my existence is so still. Time makes its own game when life is so slow and painful, my entire world now nothing but this bed, four walls and window. I cannot even rise to relieve myself, and so all modesty goes out that window with my mind, though I find the telling alleviates the dreams somewhat. Occasionally Miss Angus frowns and asks where this or that island is, what I mean by a foreign word or shipman's phrase. My descriptions are of no use to her, I fear. She has no reference point beyond the river, no experience of the world beyond London's centre. The strangest place for her might be the land of my birth, which had no grand buildings, no trains, no exhibition halls or galleries, no palaces, barely a newspaper or carriage when I left it. I was just a boy, half wild and fully lost, and the world around me an unmapped forest. I knew there was trade and ships — of course I knew that — but I could not imagine this world that seems to be made up almost entirely of those things.

In my earliest memory there is green everywhere, leaves and leaves of it in a great pile, my mother working beside me, and, when I look up, more. It is the wide umbrella of the ponga

11

tree I see, its many brothers and sisters encircling us. A kind of speckled light is thrown over everything as it breaks through gaps in the trees' canopy. My mother works the flax until it is soft, and folds it into her many layers. I cannot tell you what it is that day. Often she made whariki — the mats we used to line our homes or sleep upon. Or kete — those were quick and easy to make, and sturdy, for gathering our food or carrying things from one place to the next. Some long winters were spent working at a cloak — I remember this because the muka fibres were so fine and I was not to touch them even though she let me play freely with the broad green leaves before they were stripped down to soft strands.

No, this day it must have been a kete, something easy and light, I think. It must have been warm, for I remember no cloth or cloaks hindered our movement. Even so, the undergrowth smelt like wet dirt and rotting leaves, the kind of smells that signal not decay but new growth. It was my game to imitate my mother's work by lifting and folding leaves one over the other, though mine did not stay together or transform into a whole as hers did. Even Nu, my sister, tried to help, but I had more game than goal in mind, so my failures gave me as much pleasure. When I wandered away she came after me, calling in a high voice, or scolding when I took too long. She tried to work at her own weaving when I was settled. Sometimes kaka parrots came down to make off with our scraps. Sometimes tui birds yodelled at us like singers from the opera. We talked to them as if we knew their language. Perhaps we did. It was just the world. We listened and tried to call back, my sister entertaining me with her imitations while our mother worked.

I do not know how old I was, but I cannot have been more than four or five. Everything for me was sight and sound and flavour, the grubs beneath as fascinating as the pretty leaves above. The forest litter, rot, all of life. The delicious squirming and leaping of my small-child's body. Our simple entertainments. Sometimes we wandered away to join the other children while our mothers worked together. Nu was my constant companion; I couldn't tell you her proper name now. If I was hungry she found a morsel for me to eat, some dried fish or meat from the night before, fern root to chew. She never let me out of her sight.

I remember all this because what came after was so sudden and preceded by such stillness. It was the birds who first went quiet. Nu was dangling from the branch of a tree overhanging a little creek we liked to play near. All of us children were making our noisy way across, and my sister thought she might do so without touching the water. I tried to copy but fell to the riverbank, then pretended I was happy to watch her swing above, almost as if she could touch the tops of the trees. Looking up, always looking up at my sister.

At first we didn't know what was missing. We were being loud enough for our mothers to hear us, and the sound of nothing came over us slowly, swallowing our voices one by one until we too were silent, straining our ears, listening.

I don't know how long that moment of silence was, but when I think back I am suspended there. Everything slow and quiet and wrong. Then a loud noise came in, a sharp cry that shattered the still. Sound rushed towards us then, our mother's cries: 'Tamariki ma! Rere atu! Come away now!' All of it at once — scooped into my mother's arms, but where was Nu? Where was Nu, my big sister? And my mother ran and ran and put me down under branches and then there were the sounds of weapons on flesh, and something else, too, sharp and so loud it sounded like the world had split in two. I stayed hidden because I was small, and silence had now been pushed into me and planted there. And no one saw me even though my mother lay down and looked right at me. She couldn't see me, though. I understood this when she looked and looked until her eyes became clouds.

๑๑

I woke to Miss Herring stoking the fire again, and bustling about the room as if the fire had been set under her own petticoats. 'What is it, Miss Herring?' I asked, and she made a hmph sound that seemed to be another way of saying I had done wrong.

'It may not be my place to say,' she said eventually, not looking directly at me. 'But you must watch what you say to Miss Angus now. She left this room in quite a state this afternoon.'

'Oh dear. I seem to have got carried away. Maybe I shouldn't speak so freely.'

'Of course you must, Mr Poneke — speak freely, that is. But these are not always things for delicate ears, are they?'

'No. Quite. I will not speak of it again.'

The maid stepped towards the door, then back again, swaying like one of the great animals in their cages in the zoo and getting redder in the face as if she fought some internal battle concerning her thoughts.

'Please, Miss Herring…'

'Mr Poneke.' Miss Herring is a year or two older than me, but she speaks as if I am her senior. 'I think it is good for you to …unburden yourself, so to speak.'

'But, as you have shown, my words are offensive to Miss Angus's ears.'

'Perhaps she was only unprepared, or perhaps you might watch how much you say in the unburdening.' Her countenance

14

had relaxed somewhat. 'I may have an idea, if it's not too bold.'

She didn't allow me to respond before she was gone.

The next time Miss Angus came she brought paper and ink and fresh quills. Of course I had a small supply, but she must have procured some fresh for this purpose. I was to write my burden down. Miss Herring had suggested it, and she'd agreed. It would exercise me, and give me something to do. I had not so much as lifted a hand since I'd been brought back to the house, and I had to agree the time for idleness was over.

And Miss Angus asked that, when the time came, I might sometimes read my writings to her while she sewed or mended. She might be shocked, I warned her. There were things I could hardly believe and wanted to forget myself. To which she answered she had seen a preserved two-headed monkey at the Egyptian Hall when she was just eleven, and a woman swallow swords and fire when she was fourteen. Worst of all, she had heard the tales of two hangings from the cook when she was a child and she knew the world was simply full of such horrors, which was why we should put our faith in the sweet Lord to keep us safe and sane. Besides, I could always keep the worst to myself, since I now had the paper to keep it.

I did not feel adequately endowed to argue with this.

◎◎

I will write to you, my future, and sometimes I will write to the ones who look after me here, and sometimes to the ones who have passed on. If I try always to write for Miss Angus, everything will have to be genteel and kind like her, but my life has not been that way. As I tell you about the land of my birth it will, I know, seem like a picturesque scene to you, for it seems that way to me now, and I do not know whether it is the Artist's pictures that throw shade on my memories, or whether it really was that pretty. My earliest memories certainly do seem green and innocent. It is something to hold on to that any time in one's life is so. The sound of guns put an end to all that.

My father was a chief. I did not know this when I was an infant hiding under a bush. After the quiet came again, sometime after, when hunger gnawed away at me but silence still kept me hidden, I heard the sound of men coming through; I heard them calling in rough voices that turned soft too quickly when they found us.

'Mihikiteao! Nuku? Hemi? Aue, hoki mai koutou!'

Hemi was my name, I knew that, and so I peeked out. As soon as I moved, great arms came down and lifted me around my stomach, and I vomited in fear. But the arms took me to the man I knew as Papa, and he wiped me clean and held me. 'Taku tama,' he said. 'Taku potiki.' And I knew these were his tender names for me. The man who had brought me now showed my father where my mother was, and he held me close and shook, with sadness or rage I could not know. I was so frightened I retched again, but nothing came out.

Later we found Nu, and she could no longer call to me; she would no longer watch over me. The men buried the women and the children. And I stood at the graveside, mucus and tears running down my face and into my mouth.

My father took me with him, but I was too small to keep up, and I imagine I must have been too burdensome for the men to carry as they searched the land for the murderers of my mother and sister. I was with them only a few days before my father found some people for me to stay with. We came upon a white house on our own lands, and my father said it was the Missionary House and I would be looked after there, and I remember nodding solemnly and with great importance as if I

16

knew what this meant. It was only when the people came out of the house that I gasped and shook and ran to hide behind my father's legs, for they were the first white people I had seen.

'These are my friends, Hemi,' my father told me. 'They have been great friends to your father, and they will be great friends to you.'

I heard these words, but I couldn't move. The people looked sick, their colour gone. Could they see from those eyes? What shape were their bodies under the strange clothes? Where were the ladies' feet? I rested my forehead against the back of my father's patterned thigh and peeked out from behind him. I remember I felt hidden, my arms wrapped around his leg, even though some part of me knew I could be seen. It did not matter, he would protect me forever, I thought, but my father's legs never stopped moving, and I could not stay in their shadow much longer. He pushed me forward.

'You will be safe here, taku tama. If I leave you with our people, who knows what may become of you? These Mission people are not part of our fight. They bring solace with their Christ and their wonderful things. Look at the cow! Look at the butter churn! You will learn here, and when it is all done I will come back for you.'

I did not know what 'cow' or 'butter churn' were then. Can you imagine? But father had gestured towards a big animal on four legs like a kuri, and even though she had terrifying proportions and sharp-looking growths on her head, she had the softest, biggest eyes I had ever seen. I did not know what the churn was, but white people and cows were quite enough learning for one day. I had no inclination to get closer to either of them.

I was a small, half-naked child, and it was easy enough for the missionary lady to take me by the hand and for my father to leave swiftly with his men, and for the world to seem emptier than it ever had. Where were the trees? Where were the birds? All around the house was cleared, though a wall of forest encompassed the place. This was my new home, then, and I was too exhausted to fight once Papa was gone. They took me and washed me and put me in white people's clothes. I had never been so uncomfortable in my life, everything held and bound and scratching against my skin. For weeks I would wander as far as I could from the house, and they would find me with my clothes half off and half tangled around my limbs. But the white men's clothes were too ingenious for me to engineer an escape until I was already used to them.

After that my father would come whenever he could, which was not often. He was my sun. His arrival signalled for me a glorious break in the tedium of mission days. But whenever I saw him I also thought of my mother as she'd stared at me with no sight, and of the lovely sister who was no longer there to watch over me, and it was like a dark hole opened and I almost tripped into it. I think I feared my father and the feelings he brought with him even as much as I desired the bright glamour of his company. For he was exciting, my father. He was a presence — physically imposing, yes, but more than that. To hear the warm depth of his voice as he spoke his endearments to me was to hear the night talking to the day. I know others were drawn to him too, though the missionaries did their best to keep a pious distance. His arrival was preceded by a heightened nervous energy throughout the Mission — all of us keen to catch a glimpse, or hear stories of his most recent skirmishes. And of course I had an honoured place in all of this, for I was the only one who came within touching distance of his great person.

Sometimes he came to eat with the Minister, and listen to the sermon, but he would not enter the white house. I can see now how important he must have been, for the Minister came out to him and sat with him, even upon the ground. I came to his lap and traced my fingers along the tattooed lines on his legs until I was too old for such intimacies. He coddled me, not even slapping me when I pulled at the hairs and made him wince. But I was not to touch his face. Even I knew that. The moko there fascinated me, and he told me how my ancestors were all in those designs, how every line and curve told the story of our whakapapa, and how this was the most sacred of knowledge, written on his face, written in his flesh and blood and the ink of our land. Papa, how you indulged me, and how I have failed you, for I can no longer recite those genealogies, nor have I earned the right to wear them. I am so far from our whakapapa now, though I know you would tell me it runs in my veins the way the sea runs over the Earth, and there is no distance I could travel to disinherit that which I am. This I know you would say, though I don't know that I can make myself believe it.

Perhaps you can forgive the foolish boy I was for my fears and insecurities. I pay for them each time I think of you. Once I was finished with the fun to be had on your knee I would be away again playing with the other mission children, safe in the knowledge that you would return, and return again. I was not a true orphan then like the rest. You had serious conversations to have with the adults, and such things bored me, but you were a good distraction for the whole house, and all us children took advantage of it. After service we managed to avoid the chores while the main meal of the day was prepared. There'd be plenty to do later. In the meantime we would run and chase and play stick games and pretend. Most often I got to be chief in our make-believe games, for I was the only one with a parent still alive, and such an impressive one. Except when Maata Kohine decided she was in charge: she had more natural authority than me and was stronger, too.

The only thing that fascinated me as much as your moko, Papa, was the other writing I was learning. You were keen on it too, but it came to me so quickly and I had not the other responsibilities that were your burden. For you did not come back as often as I would have wished, and the tribal battles kept you constantly moving. I didn't understand that world, except that you wanted me away from it and safe. And you were happy to see my love for the Book, the Word, and the ways of the pen. You said these were implements that would help our people be strong in this strange new world. Now I think that sometimes when you talked like that it was with a mix of admiration and horror. I know this feeling well, especially here in London. I might have even known it then, for though it was weighted greatly towards admiration, that same equation still played a part in my feelings for you. You were a formidable man. You were a fearsome man. Your voice told me you were a gentle man. You were my sun. And then you came no more. If I had known, I would never have left your knee nor lifted my fingers from the tracing of your moko.

Two

I was eight or nine when news came of my father's death. They told me nothing except that he had been killed in battle and eaten by his cannibal enemies. So the chasm opened again, only it was there all the time now and I was in it, not dancing on its edge. I could not see or feel the way out of this hole. Looking back, I can see I was too inexperienced to know what was happening to me. I only knew that though the Mission continued to serve up food and drink and the Good Book, I found no flavour in anything. Even after the time of mourning was supposed to have passed, the world seemed lifeless to me, but I didn't think about why.

I suppose it might have meant that I should be chief now, too, but chief of who? Our people, the ones who had survived, had scattered or made other alliances. It had been a long time since any of us had been at peace in our homelands. There was nothing to go back to, and I was ignorant, more educated about the Book now than about my own people. The Minister found ample use of this example in his sermons, admonishing us to turn away from the ways of our forefathers and follow the Word of the Lord, of Peace and Joy and the Christian faith. But he could not take from me the language that was already under my skin. No, I had not the spiral markings that my father had worn, but I am sure the same ink runs through my veins.

Following my father's death, the Minister also preached that it was the Lord God who had taken him. He proclaimed that, though we cannot fully know the ways of the Lord, and though we were right to mourn, the death of our parents made it possible for the rest of us to be saved. For each time one of the heathens fell, their children were welcomed into the bosom of the Mission and the grace of our Saviour. I had been at the Mission a few years, and knew the English language better than my own tongue, and loved Jesus as much as any of us. I had been the best of the students, not because I was smarter than anyone else, but because I had loved the Good Book as much as any stories told to me by my sister or mother or father. What better tales were there for a boy's imagination than David against the giant Goliath, or the many strange beasts of Noah's Ark saved from the deluge, or Daniel and his brave taming of the lions? Though what lions were and where Jerusalem was were mysteries. Such details didn't matter when faced with the magical stories of Jesus, who could produce loaves and fishes enough to feed all gathered. What miraculous gifts for a single man to possess! Would I let Him into my heart? If it meant understanding this power, of course I would. Forgive me for my blasphemy, but you will understand that Christ was a magician to us children: a man of wonder and magic.

But now it occurred to me that there was something in the Minister's preaching that I did not like. The Minister had given me to believe that it was my Lord who was at the centre of my trouble. If my father hadn't brought me to this place, would he still be alive? Was he such a greedy God that he needed the death of my entire family to make me His own?

I had been a proud boy, proud that I was the son of such a great chief, and of the respect accorded to him even by the adult missioners. Perhaps I thought that one day I would stand with him, and fight with him, and return to the ways of my forebears, armed with all my knowledge of the newcomers. Perhaps it was nothing so clear as that. I began to fight with the other boys, meting out a steady stream of black eyes and bloodied noses for little or no offence. The Minister's wife and her niece, who did most of the teaching and had the work of looking after us, could no longer control me. They gave me extra chores, and forced me to sit long hours in the corner, facing away from the other children. Eventually they took to beating me, though my misbehaviour only increased, until one day I grabbed the very stick they wielded against me and tried it out against the Minister's wife's own hand. I missed, of course, and hit her voluminous skirts, but that didn't stop her wailing in overwrought terror. She asked why I behaved so when all they wanted was to correct me and make me the best young man I could be. But I was no man, I was only a sad boy, and no amount of instruction could teach me how to care for anything any longer, let alone their silly rules. The Minister, a mild man for all his emphatic sermons, was forced to deal with me.

And so he did, with a cane, and with more sermons, beseeching me to behave for the sake of my soul. I challenged him for a while — some weeks, months even. I stopped reading and writing and doing my sums, and that took away what was left of any joy I had. I no longer knew what the Mission did for me. I did not know what the world outside offered, but I knew what was lacking in the place I was in. If I was anything like my father and mother, if I was any use at all, I would be able to survive in the forest now that I was older. I should return there, and seek my people or at least people like them. I thought I knew something about the world, and I did not.

I doubt it would have been a surprise to anyone when I disappeared one night. Something had to happen, one way or another. I was either going to return to my former placid, scholarly self, or become the wild thing I seemed determined to evoke. I don't know if they came looking. I slipped away after everyone was supposed to be asleep, so no one would have noticed my absence until morning. I'd had a warm bed and good food and learning amongst honest people, which was more than many of my kind could say at the time. But I thought I knew better, thought I could make something of myself in my father's name. It didn't occur to me that he put me in that place for a reason; that I was already in the place that might allow me to make something of myself.

Of that time I remember only that I was deeply unhappy, and that unhappiness made me reckless. What followed was a long time of hunger and searching. I'd taken a bundle of food — what I thought I'd need until I found some people and some work. I suppose I imagined I would return to my scattered tribe and reassemble them under my chiefly name. A boyish fantasy. I decided to walk in one direction, marking the trunks of trees, low, until I found a settlement or a road. I still knew which plants and roots were edible in the forest, but did not know how to snare birds and had no weapon with which to hunt.

Hunger is a sharp-toothed eel in the belly. Once it sets in, it is hard to think about anything else or feel anything else. My memories of that time are coloured by the hunger. Loneliness, fear, sorrow — these all must have accompanied me each day, but I remember only that terrible hunger, like a fever, washing over everything.

@@

I counted five days and six nights before I found something like a village and more than a fern root, the juicy baby leaf at the centre of a tree fern. A boy surviving on so little for so long. I thought I might begin to go mad with the need to see other friendly faces again and have conversations that weren't rambling and pitiful mumbles to myself. Always too cold or too tired or too filthy. I wanted to play. I wanted to eat. I wanted to lie in a bed. I almost didn't care how I might achieve those goals.

Almost. New Zealand was an untamed place then. I dare say it is an untamed place still, though I hear they are bringing the land and the people under Britain's control more each day, that the forests are being swept aside and civilisation built with timber, if not brick.

A boy not yet ten years of age understands the dangers of being free and unprotected in the world, even if he cannot name them. Many of those dangers are connected to men, of course. He could be lost even when he supposed himself found. By this time I had realised my mistake in running from the Mission. So as I walked towards a settlement that was only a dozen-and-a-half makeshift homes gathered loosely around a general store that was itself half-tent, and a public house that was fully shack, my hunger pushed me on, though my fear held me back. I walked at a steady, determined pace, and with each step I decided to take on the character of these determined steps, so that I should not appear meek and needy, but somehow convincing in my bravado and cleverness. I thought of you,

Papa, of your bravery and great strength. I had none of that, but I prayed for your courage to inhabit me. I knew by now that I was quicker with the quill than any of my mates, that I could make them laugh with ease, and that in what was left of my reserves of character there was something of an entertainer. I would make these people laugh and sing and forget their miseries (for I knew by then that we all have those), and in exchange they might feed me and offer me a warm corner.

I miss that arrogant youth! By the time I reached the village I strode with such purpose, my chest puffed out with the enormity of my confidence, that people began to chuckle just to see me. I chose the public house first, where there were several men and two women. All looked my way curiously as I entered.

'Good day!' I exclaimed, and bowed deeply. 'Hemi at your service. Songs sung, letters penned, stories told! I can tell you tales that'll bring tears to your eyes. I won't just make the hairs on your neck stand on end, I'll make them fall out! Even better, I'll make you laugh until your belly aches.'

The lady of the house peered over the wooden boxes that made up her bar. 'Well now, look — a little black boy with a nest on his head and a cheeky posh way of speaking.'

'Black, no, just a fine shade of brown like the great totara of the forest. Offer me a bath and you'll soon discover my true colours, and that my nest untangled becomes curls that are the envy of many fine maids.'

'Eh, you cheeky little brat. Asking for a bath from Emily Jenkins, eh? That's worth a shilling if she makes it her special.' This was a wide man with a moustache who had to stoop so as not to lodge his head against the ceiling.

'You shush, John Low. Little Black Boy can earn himself a bath and a meal too if he's as talented as he makes out.'

I already had them if I could keep my wits and bravado about me, but really I had no clue what I should do next, so I climbed on to a chair and began to bellow a song I'd learnt from Maata Kohine, whose father had been a whaler. We'd sung it in secret in the playground, sometimes under our breaths. The swinging, jolly rhyme of it had seemed ungodly beside the long-vowelled hymns we were given to sing on Sundays. It had been deliciously coarse on our tongues.

Mr Willsher sold to 'Bloody Jack'
Two hundred of flour tied in a sack
And a Maori carried it all on his back
On the beautiful coast of New Zealand.

By the end I could see I had everyone's attention, but one little ditty wouldn't get me far, so I tried another. I blessed Maata and her sharp tongue that day.

Come all you tonguers and land-loving lubbers
Here's a job cutting-in, and boiling down blubbers
A job for the youngster or old and ailing
The agent will grab any man for shore whaling

I am paid in soap and sugar and rum
For cutting in whale and boiling down tongue
The agent's fee makes my blood so to boil!
I'll push him in a hot pot of oil!

I can't quite believe I was so audacious, but as I sang I stomped my feet and swung my arms and leapt off the chair to dance myself in a little circle, my arm cocked at an angle as if I were swinging around an invisible partner. Then Mrs Jenkins hooked

27

her arm through, and we swung around together until I was out of breath and she had to do the swinging. I was dizzy and light-headed, but I took it as success that there were a few grins from the men and a hand to help me up.

'Get the boy some soup and bread, Missus. If he can write as he says, we might make use of him for more than entertainment.'

This was Mr Jenkins, who was much shorter than Mr Low, and had no hair upon his head or face that I could see, not even eyebrows. Mr Jenkins was shorter than his wife, too, though his wrinkles told me he was somewhat older. His eyes were the colour of the coldest part of a river, and I tried very hard not to let their frigidity seep into me as I held his gaze.

As I ate, Mr Low lit a pipe and towered over me, puffing and watching me through the smoke. I dare say I ate fast enough for my story to come clear — I couldn't help myself at that point. I was almost dizzy with elation that food — warm food — was now in front of me. Mrs Jenkins gave me another bowl of soup soon after the first disappeared, but no more bread until morning, she said, in case I made myself sick.

'Go on then, Black Boy,' said Mr Low when I was done. 'Tell us why you're here by yourself, no mother or father or brother to keep you.'

So I told them about the deaths of my mother and sister and father, adding all the details I could think of to make the story colourful and exciting and draw them in. I believe I may even have fulfilled my promise of interfering with the position of hairs on their necks by the time I was finished. I don't think my family would have minded that by talking about them I secured the goodwill of strangers, a roof and some food. But I didn't talk about the Mission, except in a blurry way. It was there I got some education, I said, but the wars between tribes caused even neutral, peaceful places trouble, and the Mission had burnt to the ground one night, all the people scattered and scared of who might have caused the fire. I became hopelessly lost and couldn't find my way back, I said. In truth, now that I had food in my belly I was stubborn again and did not want them to return me to my prior life.

By the time I was finished I had gained more attention than with my songs. And probably more sympathy, too. The other men slapped me on the back and gave me half-glasses of their beer, until it became a competition to see who could make me drink the most. I was a boy who hadn't reached his teens and had never had grog, so by the time I reached four half-glasses I was quite ready to fall off my chair. That's when Mrs Jenkins stepped in.

'No more!' she commanded. 'Time for bed, Little Black Boy.' She helped me up, and took me to another shack behind the makeshift public house.

'We sleep in there, visitors in here,' she told me. 'We'll get you a bath in the morning, though I don't know why we bother, the filth that comes through here. The filth that lives here, for that matter.' And she went and left me to my own devices.

@◎

The bath that Mrs Jenkins promised turned out to be a tin tub of cold water with one pot of hot thrown in to warm it beyond freezing. I didn't want to get in, but Mrs Jenkins suggested she would need to do the job if I didn't, so I complied. Using the rough soap she'd left for me, I scrubbed as quickly as I could and dried myself off with a rag before putting on my same old dirty clothes. I'd not yet earned myself any new ones, or laundry service. When I came back into the public house, Mrs Jenkins clapped and teased me.

'You're no black boy after all, are you? Just a wee brownie.'

No one called me anything but Brownie after that.

I suppose I became a kind of village mascot. I would do errands, take messages, help with gardens, dispose of rubbish and vermin. That first day, Mr Jenkins set me down at his desk and had me write some of his letters to suppliers and debtors, just to see what I could do. I suspect he began renting me out for odd jobs and letter-writing, though I never saw any money pass hands. I myself was given only warm meals and a roof over my head, and I felt like that was all I needed. I didn't miss affections, which were hardly present at the Mission anyway, and Mrs Jenkins was kind in her way. She always made sure I was to bed before the men (and occasional women) got too noisy, and she always made sure I ate.

I did miss children my own age, and brown faces like my own. There was a reason the name Brownie stuck so well. My companions had no Maori amongst their number, and evidently viewed my kind as a menace who lived beyond the ranges to the south. I was the first they had been truly friendly with, but they attributed my skills to my Mission education, and saw my skin colour as something of a novelty. In my later travels I found this was not the case in most villages in my country. It was more common for brown faces and white to mix and trade freely. After all, Maori are still the chiefs and landowners of most places, and being perturbed by the colour of their skin will not assist a man who wants to do well in trade.

Of course, the misunderstandings and occasional skirmishes between peoples who spoke such different languages (and I do not refer only to the words that came out of their mouths) created isolated communities. The people in the village of Hollycross, for that's what it was called, were distrustful of all and quick to violence against any they judged alien to their type. I think even then I recognised the irony of my position. The only thing that saved me was my naiveté, my bravado and my eloquent writing style, for old Jenkins made regular use of my hand whenever he needed to appear persuasive and clever to his correspondents. I don't suppose my writing was comparable to that of an older scribe, but it was certainly neater and more eloquent than Jenkins's own misshapen scrawl. In general, I was pleased to be used so. I was the village pet, I was sure of that, and safe only so long as I was employed.

I had become tougher from my time wandering, and knew I must grow up fast now that I was responsible for myself. The effort of earning my keep while holding my childhood at bay meant most of my time was occupied by the tasks that lay directly before me. But I was still a child. One of my early-morning routines was to assist Mrs Jenkins with her preparation for the day: sweeping up from the night before, washing down tables, collecting up cups and bowls and utensils, seeing to the few livestock. My favourite task was collecting the eggs. The oddly intelligent hens cocked their heads to peer at me, calling to each other in warning tones about the egg-stealing intruder who was upon them again. I liked to tease them, it's true, and pet them, if they let me. They got used to me eventually, and soon became more attentive to the grain I brought than to protecting the products of their labours. But I also liked the task itself, collecting the eggs one by one, some still warm to the touch, each a small prize for looking.

And that is where Emily Jenkins found me one day, my fingers moving over a warm shell, closing it in my palms, bringing it to my cheek, each day the same question: was there a baby in there, just beginning?

'I wondered why you were taking so long,' she said, looking down at my hands.

I looked up and her eyes widened. She even took a step back. I didn't know what I had done.

'I forget,' she said, 'that you are just a child.' She held out the wide pocket of her apron, and I placed the eggs in.

'I was like you that way once.' She nodded towards my hands, now empty. 'Gentle. Just a baby.'

I pulled my shoulders back and frowned. I was no longer a baby.

'No. I understand. Not a baby. But soft. There is a part of you that is soft. You're very good at not showing it. It's in the best people, that softness.' She looked down at her own hands — they were rough and red — and when she looked up her eyes were wet.

'Mrs Jenkins? I'm sorry, I didn't mean to—'

Her face changed. Whoever was there a minute ago had gone away. 'You can't let the softness out too often, Brownie. They'll use it to hurt you. Put it away, even if you miss it. Must be that the time for such things is over.' And then she turned and left so swiftly I couldn't ask who she meant by 'they'.

∾

Thus passed the better part of a year. Mrs Jenkins didn't again show me the self she kept hidden, but she did watch over me, just enough to ensure I came to no harm. It was autumn when I'd arrived, and in that sullen place I weathered the long, grey winter, an icy spring and at last the arrival of raumati's sun. I was given reason to start walking again soon after that.

Daylight lingered until long after supper even in that early part of summer, so I would spend the evening outside, basking in the last of the day's warmth before retiring to my bed and bundle. I knew a pub was really no place for a child, and though the patrons tolerated my presence well enough, it was clear that I should make myself scarce when, after the sun went down, the drinking took on a more earnest and dedicated tone. But one evening I was not to be left to myself. Two drunkards, Petey and Maguire, had been ejected from the premises, most likely because they were arguing and cursing loudly, and taking swings at each other with very little accuracy. This was not unusual for them, and I had learnt already that it was best to avoid their violent moods.

'Oh, bloody hell, Maguire, stop your jabbering for once in your sad, whisky-sodden life.'

'At least I can afford whisky, you rat-infested pile of rags, always skiving off my earnings and not paying me back.'

'Are you calling me a thief, Maguire, you bastard?'

'I'll take that as a personal affront to my dear mother, who was married to my father in a church. You owe me an apology.'

'An apology, my great white dirty arse!'

They swung and kicked, but didn't make enough contact to slow each other down. I was finding it quite amusing, for I was off to the side and well out of range. A couple of other men had come out to watch.

He was almost upon us before anyone noticed him, and I suppose that's why they took fright. We'd graduated to laughing out loud now that Petey and Maguire were trying to outdo each other with the most foul and repulsive insults.

'Dog-lover!'

'I don't lie with dogs, not when I've got your sister!'

'No, you're too busy eating the shit of the dog you bed.'

'You're right, I don't want your sister — she's too busy on the floor with you.'

You must forgive me. These are the things such men say. And in latter times I've had reason to adopt such language myself.

Such jibes kept me in good stead when it was my turn to drink too much and make a pathetic fool of myself on the ships.

But then we were all suddenly aware of him, only twenty or so paces away, carrying a musket, hand weapon tucked in his belt. He was smiling at us in an open manner, but this only made the whorls of his facial tattoo even more alive — and, to my friends, possibly more sinister. He addressed me in our own language then, and told me he was from a place called Waitara and forced to come to this white man's town to buy provisions. He could pay.

Petey and Maguire and their audience turned to me. I didn't seem to be able to make use of my tongue. They were glaring at me as if they'd only just been made aware of my alien heritage.

The man took a step forward. 'E tama! Kia tere — w'akautu mai!'

It was all that was needed.

I don't know who pulled out their weapons first, but by the time I understood what was going to happen there were two guns trained on the man. Maguire was hopping from one foot to the other, Petey was swaying, but one of their audience, a man whose name I no longer remember, was steady and sure with his weapon. Our visitor had two choices, neither of which guaranteed his safety. Had it been me I would have put my hands into the air and backed away, but this warrior did not seem to consider that an option.

He was fast, much faster than anyone was prepared for, and was almost upon Petey when the first shot rang out. That first one didn't take the warrior's life, but disabled him so that he was forced to the ground, trying to hold back the blood that came profusely from a wound in his thigh.

He looked at me again. All he wanted was some food. He'd thought he could approach because I was there. He spoke again, steadily and clearly, words meant only for me. He was a warrior doing warrior's work.

Then he was up with his weapon, disabling the addled Maguire and Petey with a few clean strikes. There were more gunshots. I felt the ground sliding under me then, the whole of the world shifting. Momentarily I could not grasp what had happened, or how, but the hot appearance of blood at the toa's chest and the tang of gunpowder smoke made everything clear. It was the second time I had watched someone die.

Perhaps it happened then. Perhaps it happened with the first death I had seen, or my father's. It is hard to tell now when I see the world through the gauze of so many later events. But I wonder if that was the first time I really saw the darkness that sits in the hearts of men and is so beyond us to control. I should have stood between them. I should have spoken up — I was the only one who could. I could speak with both sides, yet I didn't. I hadn't wanted to give them reason to feed their hostility with my blood. My weakness filled me with revulsion. I had been too scared to speak, and now a man lay dead because of it.

I was old enough now to see what death is, and to feel it, and to be stricken, but I could not show any of that, for the fear stayed, a cold stone low in my belly. I swallowed the feeling that rose up my throat and threatened to bring my last meal with it. My limbs twitched with the effort to keep them from shaking. I wanted to sink to the dirt, to be comforted like a baby. But I remembered Mrs Jenkins's warning. Though the people of Hollycross had shown me kindness, or at least tolerance, and though I had begun to relax in their world, I was just a boy in a village full of strangers who suddenly had reason to question my allegiance. Why had the tattooed man spoken to me? What did I know of him? They eyed me when I shrugged away their questions, and I knew I was in trouble. Everything had changed as suddenly as the toa's heart had been stopped by that smooth, sure weight of steel. So I held in my sorrow for this fallen stranger, I swallowed the shock that now told me I should leave this place that could not abide other people who looked like me. I did not know what they would do with the poor man's body, but when I saw his hand weapon where it had fallen, I swiftly gathered it to me and hid it amongst my own possessions. I knew these people should not have the precious item, and I wondered if I might use it to protect myself. It now seems curious to have done such a thing, especially considering where my next steps took me.

The following morning I gathered my few possessions and farewelled Mrs Jenkins stiffly. We were not to be left alone, so there would be none of the softness she had warned me against. But when her husband raised his voice at me, she told him to hold it, the fierceness of her gaze quietening even the drunks. She bundled some provisions for me and pushed them into my hands. 'Once a Mowri always a Mowri' was all the publican could say to his wife. She shook her head and returned to her bar without looking at me again. The only one who seemed visibly moved at my departure was Mr Low, who stood watching until I was half the way out of town.

The road ahead was empty. I was not yet out of boyhood, and despair blackened the edges of my world.

THREE

I was alone, wandering again, avoiding colonial settlements and native. And even though I had found little love in my last home, my fears grew with each step I took away from it. There is nothing quite so bad as loneliness and hunger, the wretchedness of a child utterly without friends. I knew I was in for more of that now, and more of the dangers of the road, and I wondered whether I should have stayed despite my fears. Even a rag bed in a publican's shack was better than not knowing when you might eat or rest again. Even the intolerance of a white-people's settlement was better than no people and no village.

Looking back, I see it was not so simple. At the time I had only felt the pain of fresh displacement. From where I lie now, it seems like I left a piece of myself behind every place I went, and a boy so young is too ill-formed to go around leaving pieces of himself behind. Each time a home was lost, so also was some flesh sliced from my frame. I took Mrs Jenkins's words with me: the harshness of the world would have no patience with any part of me that wasn't hard enough. And so I would be tough, I thought, and if I couldn't be tough I would at least play my part well, and hide the rest.

I knew that I had to find people, perhaps people more like me. I had subsisted in that narrow community, but it had not been a living: my ties with them were broken so easily. But walking into a new village was not an easy thing to do, especially after I had seen a man cut down for simply being on the wrong side of the mountain.

I walked west this time. During my stay in Hollycross I had had my wits about me enough to establish where on the map I was, and where I might go if I needed to leave. I suppose part of me was always readying to move on should necessity dictate it. I was headed towards the coast, to the southern part of a district called Taranaki. I knew I might find food along the shore more easily than in the bush. I also knew there would be more people that way, more of my own kind perhaps, and I thought they would at least not shoot me on sight, not until they found out who I was anyway. Yet there were no guarantees. I might not be the right kind of New Zealander, my tribal affiliations might not be the right ones to keep me safe, and this made me trepidatious.

In the end I was in luck, for I was not three days from Hollycross when a whole village of people found me. Yes, that is what it was — a whole walking village. From the shadows of the bush I watched for many minutes as they passed, the poor light of dusk making it easy to remain hidden. There were all different kinds of people — young and strong men and women in possession of weapons at the front and sides, children and elderly people at the centre of the group. Some were very alert to every sight and sound, and I became afraid that they would catch me spying; others walked as if beaten, heads down, pained at every step. They were wandering and defensive like me. I thought they might not mind the addition of an orphan.

I waited until the last group of elderly was passing, with children up ahead. The direct approach was the only way, so I stood tall and walked towards them, not full of bravado the way I had when I approached the white-people's village, but with what I hoped appeared to be humility, for that is what it was. I was at their mercy — I needed their approval. The old man at the front saw me first, and raised his stick in my direction. He worked his jaw for some time before he spoke, however, standing stock still so that everyone around him stopped and looked, too.

'No 'ea…' he said, opening and closing his mouth as if to make his tongue work. 'No 'ea te tama nei?'

Everyone waited for someone to speak for me. He had not asked me anything directly, but launched his question into the air as if I had not yet the authority to speak for myself. My own language was unfamiliar to my mouth after years of occasional use at best, but I understood. Where had I come from?

I saw that if the group continued to stand still it would not be long before one of the sharp-eyed sentries was among us, wondering who the troublemaker was. I opened my mouth to speak.

'E koro, no te nga'ere tenei tama. 'e tama ngawari ia.' It was a pregnant woman who spoke before I had uttered a word. She said I was from the forest, and harmless, and then she asked, could they let me follow? She would keep an eye on me, and there were others who would ensure I was no trouble, and she could use another pair of hands. The old man said nothing, but rolled his eyes and lifted his chin in assent, turning back to his path to begin the long, slow procession again. I was not a threat, but he did not care to know my story.

So she handed me a bundle and I walked. At first I walked alongside the group but several paces away, head down, to show I knew I did not belong, I had no rights. But as the night stretched on I came closer in, especially when the terrain dictated it. I saw that whoever they were, I was not particularly special. We were all displaced. They didn't have the energy to ask me my story as we walked, and did not offer theirs, though the younger children seemed as happy as children are under any circumstances, running up to me in a game, teasing me with pukana faces, throwing stones or poking me with sticks. The older children considered me sullenly.

We were close enough to the coast to hear the sea, but close enough to the forest to enable quick retreat. As we moved, some of the group went ahead and lit fires along the shoreline for some distance. From afar it would look like there were a great number of us, with many fires, and that we were strong enough to feel comfortable making our presence obvious. In fact, there weren't many toa among us. The old man chanted an invocation, which sounded like a song so ancient I was not sure I had ever heard anything like it. From time to time his words seemed to come to a natural resting place, but when he stopped the chanting did not end, for other voices took up the call, some more like song and some more like prayers. This did not stop as we walked the whole night through, but as we reached the deepest, darkest part of night before dawn's light began to change the sky, the only voice I heard belonged to the old man.

By the time we stopped to eat and rest, I was as tired and sore as I had ever been. Again I showed my awareness of my station by sitting a little apart and asking for nothing. After the elders and young children had eaten, the woman who had spoken for me earlier brought me some rough bread and dried eel, with some kind of relish of native berries. She did not say anything, but touched my shoulder and left to attend others. As dawn's light drew in, people settled down on bedding of whatever they carried or could find, and rested in sheltered areas, the young and strong taking turns to watch. I woke often, as one does in unfamiliar circumstances, but at least sleeping by day kept us warm.

We were walking again before it was fully dark, chewing on the remnants of the previous morning's food. I lifted some kete — baskets of tools and food — to lighten the loads of those I had been walking with the night before. They acknowledged me with a nod, but again no one said a great deal to me the whole night, intent as they were on the walk. By the following dawn we found ourselves at a cove of rock pools where paua and kina were abundant, and many of the young people dived, again and again. I helped by hauling their catch up along the beach to where others were pounding the meat of the black shellfish, making it tender for cooking, or breaking open the sea urchin carefully so that the shell could be used like a bowl. The flesh, still shivering with life, was treated as a great delicacy. The elders and children had their fill first, but there was plenty for the rest of us too. I was unused to the rich flavour, and could take only a little. The feasting made everyone more relaxed, however, and the cove seemed a safe place to rest and eat. The older people began to tell stories, starting as they always do with whakapapa.

Yes, my reader, I can see the question behind your eyes. What is whakapapa? It is a magnificent cloak that connects each person around the fire to each other person and the places they are from. It is kinship to the mountains and waters and lands. It is who one is, who one is connected to, who one's ancestors are. But if whakapapa is a cloak, then why did I feel unclothed while the people began their stories? No one could take my whakapapa from me, even if I did not know it well enough to recite it aloud. It was in me, just as my father's mana was part of me. But my lips remained closed, and as the reciting and storytelling went on into the night I felt more and more the need to curl into the shadows. These were their stories of belonging, not mine. I properly understood this word 'orphan' for the first time then. To be orphaned is to wear a plain cloak, one that is still woven with many strands but has lost its outer layer of tassels and its inner layer of warmth. My cloak had lost its fine distinguishing features. Only the most knowledgeable would be able to read meaning in it, and then only by close examination. I felt a fear of any examination and what it might find.

But these people had left their places far behind, too. They recited their whakapapa with fervour — the old places were further away than they had ever been; only new mountains and waters and unseen dangers lay ahead.

'We are all children of the maunga,' said a tall, strong-looking man who could not have been more than twice my age. 'But now we walk away from our ancestor. We walk away from our burial places and our home places. We tangi for our old home, but we look for a future in a new home, where we have allegiances that will keep us safe, where we can make new homes and new burial places. Our new homes will be in Te Awa Kairangi and Te W'anga-nui-a-Tara, and soon we will live a more prosperous life with the Pake'a trade that the great harbour of Tara will afford us.'

This was not the first migration, he acknowledged, but one of many. They would go where their people and more distant kin had begun to establish territories.

'Kia ka'a tatou. Kia maia. Be strong in your mind and your person. We are the last of many to establish new rights in our new home. Our kin will welcome us. And if battle is required of us by those who are not our kin, we will fight as we have never fought before. We have that in us. We will make those who challenge us shrink back in fear and those who welcome us glad they have us as allies.'

The other children of the camp had come closer to me as all this talk went on. Their burdens laid down, they now had the opportunity to find out who this stranger amongst them was. I must have looked the way I felt: exposed, vulnerable.

'No 'ea koe?' Where was I from, asked the tallest of them. I shrugged and did not make direct eye contact. Sometimes it is when one rests that one feels all the things that have been put away in order to survive. I was tired and had no pretence of bravado left in me.

'Little boy from no place…'

'No whenua…'

'Ara, te tutua!'

'He tutua koretake!'

Koretake, koretake, koretake, they chanted. Useless. I did not argue with them. It was my price to pay.

◎◎

It seemed impossibly far away — a settlement in Te Upoko o te Ika, at the place we called the head of the fish, the southernmost tip of the North Island of New Zealand. I wanted to believe that when we reached this place, these people would have a new home and I might have one with them. Though I also knew, because I had been walking alone so long in my short life, that there could be no easy resting places for anyone on such a journey. Each place already had a people, and they would protect their home grounds. They might not take kindly to our arrival.

This was all debated at some length. And then, as the time came for rest, the speeches turned to song. I cannot describe the deep comfort I took then from the waiata. It had been a long time since I had heard songs like this and been surrounded by faces of all generations just like my own.

The children had long ago left me alone, since I did not produce any pleasing reactions to their teasing. But I knew the parents and elders could not ignore my presence forever, or at least they could not give the appearance of ignoring me, without eventually asking who I was. The time had already passed when proper introductions should have been made. I can only credit these strange protocols to the odd circumstances of our meeting. Having decided I was harmless enough, they had neither the energy nor the will to make much of my existence in their company. But now that everyone had enjoyed some rest from their long days on foot, they turned to me.

'E tama, no 'ea koe?' This time the question was offered with no malice. It came from a woman who accompanied the old man. She was one who chanted the invocations of protection with him through the night. The old man was close by but did not look up — though, looking back, he must have been listening intently. The woman who had helped me that first day was busy settling her children, but didn't hide her interest in my answer.

'It is a good question,' I said in our language, 'for I have been lost a long time. We came from that direction, inland.' I pointed. 'And my father's name was Te Rakaunui, and my mother was killed when I was not much older than that boy there.' Here again I pointed. 'Then my father died only a few years after that.

44

Before he died he put me at the Mission. Sometimes if they wanted to make themselves superior to me, the other children would tell me that my father was eaten by his attackers. I don't know if this is true, but one day I left.'

Everyone was silent for some time. I seemed to have said too much. Then the old man pulled himself up to face me. 'Your father was a chief whose exploits were known in every corner of the island. He was no friend of ours. I do not know who killed him, but it could have been our kin. What happened to him after that could be as your friends told you.' He drew his hands along his walking stick, and for a long moment I focused on his swollen knuckles, the claw-like grip. 'Now I see the anger behind your eyes. But we let you come among us because everything has changed now — we are all on a path whose end we cannot see. If you had tried to join our group elsewhere, our warriors might have left your corpse for us to walk past. Instead, we hand you our things to carry. This is the world we live in now, the old rules slipping away, chaos interfering with our ways. The debt is paid. Your father died, but you live. Continue to help us and we will let you live with us. Or leave. The choice is yours.'

His words made me angrier than I remembered being for a long time. There was so much in me that had been scorched by all I had been through, and as time went on it became more mixed and muddied until I could not separate one horror from the next. Now I felt the soot of it under my skin: the unfairness of this life that would leave me no person or place to cling to. What good had any of it done me? I took the weapon I had been concealing, the patu that came from the man slain at Hollycross, and raised it above my head, animating it by making my wrist shiver with something we call wiriwiri, letting my anger flash through widened eyes just for a moment; then, finally, I lowered it to the ground.

'I have seen more death than I would wish,' I told them. 'And I do not desire to see more. I took this weapon from the body of a man who asked for food and was killed for it. I lay it at your feet. I lay my anger down with it.'

A woman came rushing forward and fell upon the weapon, embracing it and weeping loudly.

'It is Rua! Rua Kanapu is dead!' A great tangi started up then, a great wailing, and I was filled with wonder at what had brought me amongst these people.

'Do not lay down your anger, boy,' the old man told me. 'You may need it.'

He turned to the mourners, raising his voice in karakia once more. There would be much praying that day.

FOUR

It was another week before we arrived in Port Nicholson and took up semi-permanent residence on the northern side of the settlement, in areas that had already been claimed via intermarriage and occupation by tribal affiliates. There had been wars like the ones that had killed my family everywhere, I heard. The old rules and alliances had been swept aside by the musket and the power it brought with it. The peoples who lived here before our group arrived and asserted our mana over this land had been pushed out by defeat in battle, or integrated by various means to become low-ranking members of the new tribal group. My position was somewhat like this. It wasn't my group or my mana at all, but this was the only 'our' I belonged to now.

All of this was in living memory, within the same generation who now occupied these places, so our claim was not yet unbreakable. We had to be vigilant, stand strong in this place to maintain our authority. Our place. Our authority. I was never fully part of that equation. Like the others who were now fitted awkwardly into the tribe, I was tolerated, and given work to do, and allowed to participate as long as I was useful. But my position was humble. I wasn't angered by this. I did not belong to these people. If I were to follow custom, the best I could do was marry one of them to ensure my own children could claim a place.

At first I worked in the gardens and with the livestock. Soon after we arrived, Ana Ngamate, the pregnant woman who first spoke for me, gave birth to her sixth child. Ana's husband was often away, so my help was of great use to her. Though she worked right to the day the baby came, after that she spent many weeks with her new child in a house just for them. Other women could visit her, but she was otherwise left alone. The rest of us took on her work, and somewhere in all of that I found myself attached to her family more than any other. I watched Ana Ngamate's baby grow big enough to run, and then another baby was born. These two were special to me, and often left to the care of Ana Ngamate's eldest daughter, Kahurangi, and me. I was happy enough in these occupations, as they kept me busy, but in this new life I seldom saw quill, paper or slate, nor book, and I missed them.

Many of our people had a great fervour for reading and writing in those days. Perhaps writing even more than its counterpart, for books were rare, while writing allowed us to speak over great distances to each other and to people of other lands and imagined times, just like I speak to you now. Writing implements were not easy to obtain, so most correspondence was left to the ones with the skill and leadership responsibilities. The rest of us encountered the written word most often when the Minister came through every few weeks to make his sermons and share his biblical stories. After the sermons he would speak with our rangatira and, if needed, take their chiefly opinions, or sometimes their letters, back to his own side. I watched with great longing whenever the Minister arrived or left with his bundles of letters and his books, which he sometimes gave away to these high-ranking tribespeople.

Ana Ngamate recognised my desire. She had watched me writing the alphabet for her infant son as soon as he was able to copy the patterns I made in the dirt with a stick. One day she saw me throw my stick aside in frustration.

'Why do you stop?' she asked.

'Why should I bother? The writing is only temporary. It means nothing in dirt.'

'It means something to Tama and the other children.'

'But I wish to make longer sentences. Sentences that aren't taken by the wind or Kahurangi's foot.' Kahurangi loved to tease me and take anything I thought of as mine.

'Find yourself something to write on, then. I've seen others make use of korari leaves. Or harakeke.'

'Leaves. With what?'

'Sticks make the marks. Scratch the letters. They will stay.'

'I don't know.'

'Others do it. You're not the only one with a fever for writing. Show the children. All of them. Soon it will be a competition to see who can find the best materials and write with the most eloquent hand.'

And she walked away, because Ana Ngamate always knew when to make her exit.

She was right, of course. We wrote on anything we could find: carved our letters in tree bark, passed secret notes on those leaves, scratched shells against rocks to write chalky messages to one another. The women and older girls began weaving their words into baskets and mats. Somehow my status lifted, for no one could match my quickness with the written word, but I made it my business to share my gift rather than flaunt it. I was made a teacher of sorts, for I was patient with the younger ones, and everyone wanted this gift of writing. We saw that among other things it had great potential to make our thoughts known to the Pakeha, and to understand his. Eventually, when the Minister noticed my work, I earned my own Bible. My first book. Still, no matter whether I knew that volume by heart, or covered an entire tree with my markings, I was unhappy. Everyone else seemed content enough: the rhythms of our days, the making of families, political alliances, good foods and trade. There was enough to keep up with in everyday life. But not for me.

∞

The Englishman arrived in our midst on a day that was hotter than any we had experienced that year. We were coming into our sixth summer in the area, and the heat signalled the spring storms were likely over. We were all in a lethargic mood, though this was a busy time in the gardens. Ana Ngamate had been several hours every day at her weaving. She was working on a finely woven cloak for her husband, who had returned from the south wounded but successful in his campaign to consolidate his claims to lands there. He did not like me, I knew, for he never looked at me deliberately nor spoke directly to me, except to issue orders. I had begun sleeping out whenever weather permitted it: there was no space in the whare for me now that he was back and I was getting older.

The foreigner was a strange sight to behold when he strode into the village wearing his wide-brimmed hat, a maroon waistcoat shimmering alongside its matching necktie. His light frockcoat was cut in straight lines and angles which made him seem very refined, though it was far too hot for so many layers of clothing. I fantasised about wearing such things, but knew if I dressed thus on a similar day I would perspire abundantly and ruin them. This gentleman exhibited none of these worries — he cut a fine figure and held himself erect as if unaffected by the external conditions of the world. There was an air about him, let me say a volume of air around him, as he glided buoyant into our lives. I think I was taken then, immediately, by the way he seemed so unaffected by us even as he placed himself directly into our village. White men did not visit us every day, and rarely unless they knew us. We knew the missionaries and a few traders in the area — one or two had been allowed to marry our women and still lived close to us — but this gentleman was something new. He had with him two guides, Mowhai and Kina. A crowd gathered around him.

He set about drawing almost at once. One would think he might introduce himself more formally in some way, but he simply greeted us all through Mowhai and Kina, who led him around each of us gathered for shaking of hands and hongi — our customary pressing of noses and sharing of breath. Then he set up his tools and materials and began his bright little sketches, his hand darting over his paper and producing lines and shadings that materialised into images quickly. We had seen writing, and illuminations in very special books, and of course we had our own arts, but we had never seen the way a world could remake itself from fine lines that flowed from the fingertips of an English artist. The Artist, the Artist! the group exclaimed when Mowhai gave us the word. We had our tohunga whakairo and raranga and moko, our own experts in the fine and sacred arts, but we had no equivalent term or equivalent occupation. After this we referred to him only by this revered title, rather than the name he had given us on arrival. He was the first of his kind we had met, and we thought it unlikely we would meet another.

The likenesses he produced surprised and delighted us. He began with our buildings and implements, and when he had our attention he requested our weapons and weaving be put before him so that he might copy them. We brought the things that could be shown, but kept them out of his reach. The most precious and dangerous of our belongings stayed hidden, as did the most precious and dangerous of our people. Finally, he asked that he might draw some of us, starting with the eager children.

Now that I have a more practised eye with such things, I can see that the likenesses were not as strong as we took them to be at the time. The Artist drew a group of young women and girls, and I don't think I've ever seen so many coy looks and blinking lashes. We thought it a magnificent jest, and when he was finished there was some commotion, the girls blushing as we cheered and teased them about their images.

Everyone wanted their image made, and we jostled for his attention.

'I would be honoured,' he told us with the aid of young Mowhai, 'to sketch as many of you as I can. But I must rest a while and take some refreshment. We have been walking all this long day and have not eaten for some hours.'

So we set about bringing him the best delicacies within reach. We had fresh camp bread, and the sea was not so far that we could not obtain a basket of mussels with some haste. Ana Ngamate even ordered a preserved bird to be brought from the stores — I believe she had her eye on a likeness of her girl.

I brought the food and watched quietly from a distance, as I was accustomed to doing. The Artist and his servants ate hungrily, and were quiet for some time. I wondered how the boys came to be in his service. It seemed a good enough place to be, unless you had family to miss. The boys ate well, and their master seemed to have simple requirements: his things carried, his words translated, guidance as he walked. Eventually, as their appetites were satisfied, they told us from where they had come — all the way from the far north, down the east coast of the island, to where we were now. The boys spoke to us in our native tongue, but after he had rested a while the Artist rejoined the conversation.

'Ask them who I should draw next,' he said. 'I don't want to make the mistake of taking down the image of a servant before his master again. Please find out who the chief is here.'

Of course I didn't need a translation.

'Sir, there is more than one. I know they will be ready to meet you, otherwise they would have driven you out by now.'

The Artist considered me. His gaze was penetrating, haughty. Perhaps he did not like the implied threat of force. In our culture, this appraisal would have been considered rude. But he was not one of our own. I was used to the direct ways of white men.

'Your English is very good, boy. What is your name?'

'Hemi. I am named for the James of your Bible.'

'Ah yes: "Every good and perfect gift is from above, coming down from the Father of the heavenly lights, who does not change like shifting shadows." James 1:17. And what is your family name?'

I mused on his question. Given the choice now, I think I would give my father's name, but at that time thoughts of my father produced in me an ache I was not prepared to entertain in the company of other men. I did not want his name spoken aloud in reference to my own person, for fear of what emotions

53

might rise to the surface. I was a boy who was as lost as any of our people then, but I'd been found, too. My fortunes had turned out, thus far, to be more on the high side than the low, considering the fate of all my direct family. I was a free person, despite my occasional servitude. And Te Whanganui a Tara, or Ponekeneke — Port Nicholson, the place we had migrated to by night — was the place that had given me a home. I could sense the wheels behind my fortunes turning as I spoke to the Artist; I could feel the portentousness of his contemplation of me. In that moment, I was a new person, just as the land around me was a new place — made from the old world and the new.

'James Poneke is my full name, but people in these parts prefer Hemi.'

'Well, I shall call you James, for I am not from these parts, and James is a very fine English name to have.'

The others in our vicinity looked at me unkindly, as if I had made myself too important or too prominent with this exchange. I could not stop, however. I saw my chance. My English was at least as good as Mowhai's, and I had not yet seen the sullen Kina make himself useful. Risking my own wellbeing, I told the Artist I would take him to the chiefs, that he might offer to make their portraits. There would be plenty of time afterwards for him to create scenes from common items and people.

I was lucky. Our leaders decided to entertain the Artist, and donned their cloaks and finest taonga in order to appear at their best. Ana Ngamate's husband wore his newly completed kakahu, and Ana Ngamate was asked to stand between him and his uncle: an old warrior chief, a young warrior chief and his wife. The next few days followed this pattern. The chiefly families of our village all took their turns with the Artist; he made his sketches, then made what he called 'facsimiles' of these to leave with the families. He would take the rest with him to England, he told us, to show what great chiefs there were in New Zealand, and how rich we were. This would be a good thing, paramount chief Te Puke agreed, for sometimes our white companions did not respect our ways. A treaty had been signed only a few years before, yet traditional ownership to land was already being disrespected, and the surveyors were moving into areas they claimed were needed by the Queen for her people. Perhaps if the Queen could see us, her new people, she would tell her men to respect us in land dealings. They were hopeful, and convinced of the effect that contemplation of their great ahua, or grand appearance, might have.

Later in the afternoons, when the day began to slow down, the Artist would sometimes bring out his paints and make his pictures even more fanciful by the application of colour. One afternoon as I watched, lazing in the shade by our freshwater stream, some impulsive streak in me stirred. I could think of nothing better than to be in his service, and I would do almost anything to make that possible.

The Artist always had one of the two boys with him as he worked, but this day he had both. Kina was now striding towards me with a half-gourd.

'Gathering water for his brushes,' he said, bending his head towards the Artist.

'He doesn't usually need you both.' I tried to sound casual.

'Ae. Not much else to do.'

And it was there in my head instantly. I could see a way.

'You should go and talk to Kahurangi.'

'Why?'

'I've heard her talk about you.'

'Really?'

'I'm sorry. I shouldn't have said. She would be so angry if she knew I'd told you. I think — I think if you speak with her, but

55

don't reveal that you know. Just be sweet to her. I think that might bode well for you.'

He grinned. Widely. Stupidly. He was a boy only a year or two older than me, and inexperienced with girls. An easy target. I didn't have his heat for it yet, but I'd seen how these things worked. From that day, Kina was no longer an obstacle to my desired course of action.

I offered my help to the Artist whenever Mowhai was elsewhere occupied; and because my presence was so constant he barely missed Kina. The Artist seemed to enjoy my company, or at least make use of it. He asked about my upbringing and my education. He wondered about my family, and when I told him I was completely alone save for my adopted tribe, he even seemed somewhat moved. Sometimes he would ask me what I knew of the Bible or Greek philosophers or, one time, mathematics.

I will admit it — I allowed his interest to affect me. I may have walked a bit more upright, may have maintained eye contact with my peers for long enough to call into question my desire for self-preservation. I became the Artist's favourite, even while at the edge of my thoughts I understood this was a dangerous position to take. What would happen if the Artist left without me? I would be in an even worse position than before.

When he allowed me to tend his fire in the evenings we talked of many things — usually the Artist would interrogate me, and I would do my best to provide answers. He wanted to know how we lived here, how our families and villages operated, the nature of our most treasured belongings. For this last question I told him about our chief's carved house, taonga made of pounamu, weapons of whalebone and hardwood. But it struck me that these were not our greatest treasures, so I stood and gestured in one direction or another as I spoke.

'To the east, that mountain, Matairangi, to the west Te Ahumairangi, to the north Whitireia. Here the harbour Te Whanganui a Tara and our fresh water Tiakiwai. Beneath our feet, the whenua, and there —' I pointed to a whare from whence a child cried — 'our mokopuna. Our most treasured possessions. All around us.'

Perhaps he thought this a romantic notion, though he did enjoy the landscape and spent much time making pictures of it. But he seemed most interested in our houses and our dress, the prettiest women and most chiefly men.

'And what of you, yourself, young James? What do you treasure most?'

I had nothing to speak of.

'I have little status here, and few possessions. But I am well fed and well used, and as secure as any of us in these strange days. I think what I treasure most is my education, which allows me to speak with you in your language, and allows me to write whenever I have the opportunity and the tools.'

I told him of my desire to see more of the world, to be a fully educated, modern man. And of my doubts that such opportunities would ever be available to one such as I. He was philosophical.

'You only have one life in your possession, James. Why not make it of your most magnificent imagining? In my opinion, one cannot possibly have anything that one has not first imagined for oneself. This is how we bring our most profound and creative inventions into being: first we conceive an idea, then we express an idea, and finally we perform those acts that are required to make the idea reality. Perhaps one needs to think on an idea and discuss it at length before arriving at the third stage, but these are the three elements required to make anything happen.

'For example, I am here, in New Zealand, of which, before I arrived, I knew very little. A year ago I was assigned a position in a counting house in London, which earned me a good wage and set me on the path to excellent prospects. But in my heart and in my mind was a different imagining: I wanted to try my hand at making a life of my greatest joy. Painting. And I wished to travel the world. And I could see a way to bring those two desires together. Even though I caused this to happen, it still seems like a delightful surprise that I find myself in such an exotic location, so far from home, making pictures and speaking with natives like you.

'So make it happen, boy. I see you have it in you.'

I felt myself glowing under his gaze. He saw me. And it was not until I felt myself respond to his steady gaze that I understood: this was the feeling I had been missing, this feeling of having been seen and understood, even as I did not yet understand myself. In truth, I do not know whether the Artist's gaze contained within it all the attributes I gave it, for I saw in his eyes all my unspoken desires and more. He seemed to contain within his person all the glory of a future in far-off, greater places. When he laughed and tousled my hair and returned to his work, I remained beside him, deep in my own thoughts, which seemed suddenly to spread out in all directions, a wave cresting over a horizon, blue and fathomless.

From that day I was his fervent student. Perhaps Ana Ngamate understood my future lay not with her people, for she did not call me back to my work as often as she might have. Her leniency was indulgent, and through this, even as I dreamed of leaving, I understood her love for me. But I could not tie myself to it. I saw my goal was within my grasp, though whether this was a good education in England or that other, more ineffable feeling I had encountered under the Artist's gaze, I cannot say. It became my mission to make myself indispensable to him. This presented a problem: how does one make oneself essential to a man who has everything in the world? When I could, I encouraged Kahurangi and Kina in their courtship, mentioning this or that the other had said or done. Kahurangi became kind and gentle, two attributes she had never displayed in my presence. Kina was suddenly more manly and clever than I had yet witnessed.

When I was alone with the Artist I did my best to make him think that I, also, was more clever and witty than I truly was. I worked hard to be quick with words, to offer conversation that might make me a good companion. Each evening I would bring up a story or theory I had read about at the Mission, or discuss some story from the Bible. The Artist would sometimes gently correct my pronunciation or interpretation. I see now how impossibly naïve my chatter was.

'I have heard about the Age of Reason, also called the Enlightenment. This is when men decided that everyone was equal and free — that reason should rule. Yet I understand there is a system in England like ours: some people are rangatira or chiefs, some people are mokai or servant-slaves. How does that fit with this idea of Enlightenment?'

'We don't have slaves! Not any more. That's progress, James. We move steadily towards enlightenment, and reason is our guide in such movement.'

'But whose reason rules? And what of the Bible?'

'Perhaps God's reason should rule, and for that we look to the Bible. These are good questions, but they are ones that might be answered more thoroughly through study and contemplation. They are not something I can explain to you over one meal.'

My questions seemed to have wearied him. He kaka waha

nui! I had said too much. But the Artist's voice was kind.

'You are a clever boy, but there is much about the world you do not know. That is the way of things, of course, especially when you are so far from the heart of the Empire. I have seen many things in my travels, many places and peoples that surprised me. I have found them all interesting, in their own way, even the cannibal and the ignorant nomads. But I have seen nothing that comes close to the grandeur of England's great capital, save the grandeur of God's own creations — the great oceans and mountains and skies of the world. If you saw that, James, you might gain a sense of the scale of the things of which we speak.'

We sat for a while. I could not think what to say to the Artist of my ignorance and my heart's deepest desires.

'I have enjoyed our talks, young James. To know that our scripture and our civilisation have extended right into the heart of islands so very far from our fair shores. You have shown me well, and I thank you.'

This was gracious of him, but there was a note of finality in his voice. He was signalling his withdrawal from our conversation. Would that I could go to the heart of things as he saw them — this word 'Empire' seemed the source of all the glory and knowledge in the world.

'Sir, you have been very kind to me, even in my ignorance.' I would show him my urgency. 'I have made myself available to assist you whenever my duties allowed it under false pretences. I have kept you talking and explaining things to me under false pretences also. When you came to our pah with your notebooks and paints, and your magic pencil, I admit all I wanted to do was get closer to your books and tools. You are a scholar, an observer of men. This is what I wish for more than anything I have yet experienced in my life. I miss the ways of the quill. I miss reading and learning. My ignorance shames me. I wish to study. I wish to bring the scholarly riches of the Empire back to my people one day. But first I must make myself like an English gentleman. This will never be possible for someone as lowly as me.'

I admit it now, though I'm not sure I was aware of it then: this last was a dramatic flourish to obtain pity.

The Artist contemplated me as he gathered himself together to retire.

'We plan to leave in two days, and already Kina has asked to remain here. I was going to deny him, but why take a reluctant traveller when an enthusiastic one has become available? We will travel north up the east coast of the island and then on to the ports where I will obtain my passage home. Come with us, if you wish, James. If your desire is education, the worst that could happen is that you'll learn more of your geography and find more possibilities for learning.' He had a way of cocking his head to the side when he was planning something. 'But I may find good employment for you further afield, with education as the prize.'

Surely not? Surely I had not just received the invitation my heart so desired. But there it was: the unmistakable possibility. Now that the offer was there, I wondered on it. Another leave-taking. Another venture into a world I knew to be unconcerned with how well I made my way through it.

FIVE

My mokopuna, listen. Just as I see you stretching out in a line before me, my future as yet unmanifest, so, from my bed in London, do I see a pattern stretching back to the day my whole family was cut down around me: a series of exits, a series of opportunities to be born anew, a series of enactments, each of them carrying a sense of possibility — except for the last time, but we will get to that soon enough. I could create who I would be from the raw materials around me, and some of those materials came from my origins and some came from the new world the Pakeha brought with him to our land. So farewelling Ana Ngamate and the children was bittersweet. I was never theirs but they had sheltered me, even loved me, and I had loved them in return, as much as that was possible for the unsatisfied orphan boy I was. When I announced my leaving, we ended up on the ground, me and all the children in a pile, tears and anger and embraces so tight I did not know where any of us began or ended.

'Make me letters,' I said, when at last I pushed them away. 'I will take them with me to Auckland, perhaps further. What would you tell people at the other end of the world?' And so they ran off, and as usual it was competitive — the best leaves, the most beautifully formed letters. The younger ones brought me carefully formed single words or faces etched into bark. The older ones brought me their names and the names of our special places. Ana Ngamate brought me a carefully worded letter on paper. It said, in Maori:

> To you, esteemed Chiefs, Greetings,
>   We entrust our son to you. Look after him for us. He will work hard. He wishes to learn everything about this new world and the ways of the Pakeha. He is a good son.

It was signed *with great love.* In that moment it took most of my strength not to change my mind and remain. Perhaps I was utterly wrong. Perhaps my true home was already right in front of me. But this home had never satisfied the thing I yearned for, and I knew I had to take the opportunity the Artist offered. We embraced, one by one, all who knew me, which took some time. Even Ana Ngamate's husband clasped my hand and pressed his nose to mine. There was much crying. At last I came to my adopted mother, and we held each other for a long time. When we parted she placed a pounamu-jade hei tiki around my neck — a most precious gift, a pendant I should wear always.

'It will keep you,' she said. 'We will be with you.' But she could say no more.

◎◎

And so I found myself walking north, carrying the Artist's belongings and equipment alongside Mowhai, who knew the land much better than I. We travelled up through villages along the coast, stopping and making pictures where we could, and accumulating more goods — examples of the arts and technologies of our different tribal groups. Wherever we stopped the Artist followed the same course of action, immediately taking out his artists' materials to disarm the local people with the magic of his pencil. On the few occasions when the locals were not to be seduced by a white man's pictures, we swiftly moved on without causing offence. Once or twice we came to a township big enough to have a port for shipping, and Mowhai and I were offered relief from our ever-growing bundles, which the Artist sent home to London. Despite this, he enjoyed his accumulations so much that we often had a brand-new load the following day.

Each time we stopped I took the opportunity to make use of the Artist's scraps, writing down what I remembered of my lessons or new things the Artist had revealed to me. Sometimes I would try my hand at sums or the writing of letters, which never seemed to convey with any accuracy what I wanted to say. I found my hand had very much suffered from its lack of use.

In this fashion we made our way up the island, and found ourselves at last in our capital city. Here the Artist announced his intention to purchase return passage to London, and Mowhai announced his intention to return to his people in the Bay of Islands further north. Unsurprisingly, the Artist had too much luggage and offered Mowhai one of his less fashionable suits as an addition to the agreed fee.

'You have served me well, for I am preparing to return home in one piece, which was not a certainty when we began.'

'Ma pango ma whero ka oti.' Mowhai drew the Artist

towards him, and pressed his nose to the Artist's nose in a farewell hongi. 'I am pleased with my new cloth.' For our part, we hadn't had much in common, hadn't become close friends even though we had shared the same burden, but now Mowhai took me firmly by the shoulder and pressed his nose to mine as well. 'Go well, orphan.'

He seemed pleased with his takings from the adventure, and was swiftly gone.

'And what of you, James?' the Artist said as he counted out half of what he had given to Mowhai to my own hand. I had never been paid money before and closed my fist tight around it.

What of me indeed? I had nowhere in particular to go.

'If I have proven myself a worthy companion, perhaps you will take me with you to London? Perhaps through my assistance so far I have earned passage with you?' I opened my palm, revealing the paper and coins he had just placed there.

'Of course, the young scholar. I had hoped you might still be interested in seeing more of the world. You have earned your way there, and more, I suspect. We can offer you little but an English education and a home until you are able to find your own way in the world. What do you think, boy?'

I thought this was the most wonderful thing I had ever heard, and told the Artist as much. The money remained in my hand, and the Artist reached out and closed my fingers around it again.

'There may be many ways we can help each other out, James. In London I will make my drawings into etchings to be exhibited and made into books. Many of our royalty and aristocracy, our own rangatira if you will, will be interested in images of the rangatira of this land. But London is a busy place, with many shows running all the time. My show will need an extra enticement — something our visitors cannot encounter anywhere else.'

It was all an abstract amazement to me. I had only a vague notion of what he meant by shows.

'James, what do you say you join in? A living exhibit! A chief's son — my drawings made real! I have been thinking on this during the last few nights of our journey; I must prepare for the success of my exhibition. You are a handsome and clever fellow, James, and my countrymen and women will find a specimen of the native people of New Zealand fascinating, I'm sure. It is quite the fashion to see natives of many lands in the shows of London. I had hoped my collection of artefacts would be enough, but this will be even more magnificent. What a crowd we will draw!'

I like to think that I was not taken by his flattery, but I suspect I was. I was certainly caught up in his excitement. I gave him my widest smile and nodded. Why not? It was a strange but intriguing proposition. And in exchange I would have the opportunity to experience a London education. It was known that our people sometimes went away on the ships, but school in London? I had not dared to believe such a thing would be attainable for me.

'What do you say, James? Your passage, and an introduction to English education, if you play a part in my show?' The Artist held out his hand to me, as if we were to shake as equals.

I placed my hand in his.

◎◎

I will not bore you with tales of our journey. I was not a good seaman and spent most of the time in our cabin, unless I was losing my stomach over the side. Forgive me, the bile rises even to remember. British ships rock and list from side to side so! And I was confined to the floor of the Artist's cabin which, he told me, was more comfortable than the other classes. I should think myself lucky, he suggested, though I was too miserable to think at all. After some weeks I was able to hold down more than water, but I was weakened and useless by then. Much of the long discomfort of that first passage passed in a blur. I think I would have been at the mercy of anyone who had wished to take advantage of my state, but the Artist made sure I was cared for, just as I am cared for now, and for that, and this, I shall always be grateful.

We were ten nights at sea before we made our first stop in Sydney, a busy port. We were there only to unload and collect our cargo, but we spent two days and two nights in the town, and I was much relieved for the time away from the sea, which I had begun to view as an enemy. Was London like this? I asked. The Artist only laughed at my naïveté. Indeed, he said, but nothing more. He knew he would not be able to explain a city like London to me through such pitiful comparisons.

At first I saw only the sharp brightness of it all, my eyes and nose becoming attuned to the sights of well-dressed men and well-built houses, the richness of goods being loaded and unloaded — great cargoes of sheep and steers, fruit I couldn't give name to, bushels of flax rope and sacks of potatoes. The settlements I had seen before Sydney had consisted of only a few houses, perhaps a hotel or church, some tradespeople setting up business and doing quite well from it. Nothing that approached a real city. In Sydney there were warehouses and factories and, beyond the shipping yards, streets of multi-storeyed buildings made of stone. Carriages and horses were as common as people on foot; glass and steel glinted in the heat. I gazed somewhat rudely at the ladies' bright skirts — a treat for the eyes after the monotonous blue-green-greys of our journey. Despite all this, the thing that amazed me most, the thing I hadn't expected, was the way the town was covered in words. Everywhere I looked I was offered the gift of reading: *Ironmongers*, said one store, *John Sparks Royal Hotel*, said another; *Wool Warehouse, Draper, Hardware, Youwell Millinery & Dressmakers — Can Serve You Well, Galvanised Iron, C. Clarke & Co., Importers*. This is the world, I thought. And I did not know whether to be excited or terrified.

But it wasn't the world. It was two days before I saw them. Blackfellas, they were called by the locals, and they lived in the shadows. They weren't welcome where they could be seen, unless someone was telling them what to do and how to do it. There were men of many colours on the ships, men from many places in the world, and even the white men sometimes had skin burnished from the sun and tide. So yes, I am ashamed to admit, it took me more than a day to sift the native people from newcomers like myself. How could I have been so foolish, I thought. Of course there were tangata whenua here — people who belonged to this place, people who were here first. You wouldn't think it the way the sailors squawked at them and gave them the boot if they could get one in. I hadn't seen because I had been too busy looking at other things, too seduced by the dazzling new world of the white man.

The Artist had been through their communities on his way to my country, making his pictures just as he did in New Zealand.

'They have their charms,' he told me the evening before we were to leave. 'They know a thing or two about how to live in very rugged country. Yes, they certainly have their wisdoms, though I must say their culture, in my opinion, is not as refined as the New Zealanders'. Oftentimes they have only crude, makeshift shelters, and they have far fewer carvings and crafts. Once cannibalism and polygamy are fully driven away by Christianity, and once English education is spread by adventurers like you, James, I suspect the Maori may be the next best thing to a European.'

It shames me now, but I could not identify why his words disconcerted me. I only felt sad not to have greeted the people who belonged to that place. I tried to ask why no one spoke of them. Why no one spoke *to* them. Why no one acknowledged them, or asked their permission to walk where we now walked.

'Do not worry yourself about such things, James. They are not proud like your people, and not as interested in us foreigners. This is not so unusual, the more populated a city becomes. Here, even more so. I dare say there is an official will to ignore their existence. In some parts, this will has a dark way of making itself evident.' He paused. 'You might even say, in some parts it is thought expedient to eradicate that which one claims does not exist.'

We considered his remarks for some time before he chose to speak again.

'If he survives, I don't know if the Aboriginal will ever really benefit from our education and religion to the extent possible. Just look at them, next time you have the opportunity, and consider the differences.'

But I did not have another opportunity, and I see now how I should have insisted. I wanted to believe, with all my being, in the benefits of the English education I was to acquire, but I was disquieted by the Artist's words. Even worse, we left the country without me ever paying my respects to the people I had seen there. They had been much driven out of the areas that were made into cities. I could not imagine such a thing happening to my own people.

Altogether, we were seventeen weeks at sea before we saw England. This is too long for any boy to have his feet so far from land. I know my people were great seafarers and navigators, but somehow that inheritance bypassed me, for all my bookish cleverness. The Artist schooled me on our journey, and eventually I could hold myself straight during storms, though I never ceased to hate the ways of the ship, especially when we were too long gone from the green shapes of islands on the horizon. On a ship the body grows weary even when one has done nothing but rest all day, and food loses flavour after just a few weeks — not that I had the ability to enjoy the food at first. By the third month, all food is a bland and salty scratch down the throat. Limbs ache and eyes fail to focus on anything worth seeing, accustomed as they are to the wide and dark blue and the sharp shards of sunlight reflected from waves.

I kept my mind occupied with thoughts of the great city and school, annoying the Artist with my incessant questioning. Eventually I noticed that the boys my age who worked the ship occasionally looked at me sidelong, nodding in my direction and making some joke between them. I considered this for some time before I understood my idleness offended them. I would have been more of a hindrance than a help to them anyway, but all they knew was that I did not lift a finger and that I kept apart from them. It had not been deliberate, but I had earned my passage with the Artist, and he had paid our way, and I was not the worker they suspected I should be, at least for the journey.

It has been less than two years since I was on this, the first of my ships. Now I speak like an old man and I feel like an old man. It is because I have seen so much. More than a lifetime of wonders, and of horrors, I think. Miss Herring was right — the writing has been a relief, for my restless spirit does not wander the streets while I hold quill in hand. I need rest, and must try for sleep. Though how can I, when we are so near my first sighting of London?

SIX

We arrived in the city of London in March 1846. We had entered the Thames from the great wide of the sea, and as we drew near to the city, the ships and buildings began to gather together more thickly. At times I wondered how we navigated through as the estuary narrowed and became the river proper. Every size and style of boat made its way haphazardly to its destination, and all seemed to understand the rules of their game. There were near-misses: small craft turning speedily away from the crushing weight of the large and lumbering. I sought out views of villages and gatherings of people on the shores, but the closer we came the more my view was obscured by the many masts and sails.

At first, I admit, I may have felt a little disappointed. In my mind London shone like polished pounamu, was clean and bright like the prized feathers of the kotuku. There would be no dirt there, I thought, no hard labour of the kind we were accustomed to, just people thinking fine thoughts and having fine conversations, if the Artist's descriptions of his hometown were true. Instead, what crept up on me felt like a sickness. As buildings gained height and solidity, brick upon brick reaching higher and further afield than I had ever seen, I felt overwhelmed by the city's vast size, not shining, but brown and black and grey, and built so far up into the sky — how to not get dizzy at such heights? This was my first view of London — a beast of smoke and stone, populated by insects running, following on. As we came in, the city swarmed, overtaking the river and the fields beyond. Still, the size and multitude of so many sails and buildings also grew a great excitement in me. I felt my heart in my chest and my stomach swirling as much as my vision. Oh my, how it filled me with dread and excitement.

Closer in I felt the air change. The sky closed. As we approached the main docks, I feared how the city went on and on. There must have been more people than in all of New Zealand and Australia too, and it didn't seem natural, all of them living atop one another, all eating and cooking and making fire and defecating and dying in this one place, because I could smell that, too. The great river Thames carried with it the stench of a latrine and the potent hint of putrescence. It was an assault on my senses and a shock to my sensibilities. No river in my land would be treated thus, for water carries all life, and no person would dare transgress that with bodily pollution. This by itself was enough to churn my stomach. The crewmen seemed excited as they worked, and laughed about what delights awaited them at home. But I was not sure whether I had entered a realm of gods or demons.

The impossibility of it crowded my senses. Why so many windows and so few doors, and why were all those windows closed upon the world? Those houses. Those factories. Row upon wretched row. The streets thronging — how did anyone find their way in such a horde? How could they all be fed? How could they all speak to one another? The sound, even from where we sailed on the wide river, was a rumble like the far-off signal of a thunderstorm. But this was constant. Some part of me knew this sound would infect my very dreams for the rest of my life. I do not think I overplay my impressions — I hold this memory as distinct as the episode of my mother's dying. For some long moments I almost believed I had arrived in the Hell of the Missionary's Bible. To reassure myself I tried to imagine the people on the streets were just like me and people I'd known. This trick had limited success. Amongst the well-robed I saw figures so gaunt and poorly dressed I wondered how they remained upright. I did not understand the rules of this place.

Perhaps I had come into some sort of fever as we arrived, for it was a kaleidoscope, a panorama. But then a kind of wonder overtook my horror. The dome of St Paul's had come more clearly into view, no longer a wide smudge among the confusion, but a perfect dome, grey-green, crowned by something so yellow I had to look again — gradually I grew certain it was a cross atop a golden ball. It was some minutes before I understood that the cross was real gold, the stuff of so many legends. I had not seen it before, and did not expect it to shine even from so far away. Sometimes a thing does not seem important or even possible until you see it for yourself, and then you understand why people speak of it as they do. That cross of gold had been sitting above the great and smoky city for over a hundred years, and yet it still shone its beam to people like me who had come so far. There it was amongst the chaos: God's perfection made manifest by men. It filled my chest with awe, and I thought I glimpsed, if only momentarily, why the tribes of England flocked here. Was it possible to glimpse the divine in the commotion and insanity of such a place? Were my ears too underdeveloped to hear the music within the roar? I knew I was not yet the equal of this mystery, and I made it my business to understand.

The men around me were too busy for such contemplation. Even the Artist, who had no ship work to do, was engaged busily with sketching and writing notes. He must, I supposed, have had thoughts of homecoming, feelings that threatened to overflow should he not capture them with his pencil. So I was alone in my scrutiny of this strange new world — and here a rush of excitement surged up under my fears. Here I was, an orphan Maori boy with a cheeky mouth who made too much of himself. I had arrived in one of the grandest, richest cities in the world, where Queen Wikitoria sat upon her throne and sent her men to the far reaches of the Earth to make it her dominion. What a Queen she must be, if her authority extended so far and was carried by so many. I would not have been surprised if she herself were the size of St Paul's, with a golden crown atop her radiant head.

I saw something curious then. As we came in closer to the docks I noticed a number of children in the mud further along where the tide had moved out — some nearer to infancy and some nearer to adulthood. The mud sucked in their little feet and shins, but they bent elbow deep in the stuff as well, searching. I was reminded of the tidal gatherers at home, digging for pipi or toheroa in the sea's generous tide. But this was not a place of food gathering. The mud was too black and rank for that. The smell that rose up, even from our distance, caused me to cover my nose. The children bent and searched, bent and searched, and rose up in a cheer when one of them withdrew her paw with an item clutched in it — an old post of wood, a rag or a ring of metal. They deposited this with some glee in a bucket, then continued their search. I thought I could hear their voices, high-pitched and hopeful, rising above the rumble and shout of so many men and women, but I couldn't figure what they might do with their wretched treasures. Could one of those voices have been mine, if I had been born in London?

And so the ship docked, and the men about us were made even more busy, and the Artist instructed me to gather my belongings, while he found a boy to carry his. It was all I could do to maintain focus and composure, the world around us was such a haze of industry and noise. I would have been lost immediately had the Artist not continued to issue instructions in the manner to which he was accustomed, and he soon had us ensconced in a carriage with his many cases and my feeble pile. The accompanying feeling of apprehension made me quite ill to my stomach — I was to meet the Artist's family now, and it was imperative I make a favourable impression, for I was quite without other means to make my way in this city. Yes, I had been a clever urchin in the small villages of my home country, but here, I feared, I would be swallowed by the crowd as easily as those small children's feet were swallowed in the mud.

As we made our way through the streets, the strange feelings that threatened to overwhelm me grew only more strong and conflicted. I must have provided an amusing sight to my benefactor: my eyes as wide open as I could make them, my face pressed to the small window that allowed some view of the city. It was a bumbling, uncomfortable ride. After one particularly sudden crunch of the wheels I almost wished myself back on the boat, whose horrors were at least known. The Artist was not a wealthy man in London, he told me now, though his father might be considered such, since he owned a carriage- and ship-maker's yard. As a merchant he had done well from the obsession with transport and offshore trade in recent decades. I was not then capable of discerning the distinction, but the Artist seemed to be offering some explanation of what I should expect. All I know now is that he meant to indicate they were comfortable and generous. More comfortable than most, it would seem.

This city was so unknowable to me; I could not imagine on that first day a time when I might make it my own, or understand how any of it worked. From my small, shaky window I saw a heaving, thunderous beast hand in hand with an exquisitely fashioned goddess. For every awe-inspiring tenement and statue of astonishing craftsmanship, there was a hole in the ground hundreds of yards wide and deep, filled with filthy men on scaffolds, tools in hand, or a crane high above everything, with men climbing into the sky upon half-made skeleton houses. Walls crumbled to pieces across slick roads from newly painted houses. Children and the elderly were on every corner, cross-sweeping, or calling their wares, running with deliveries or grazing for what could be gleaned from beneath rich men's feet.

It would take many more days walking the streets of London for me to discern one tribe, or class, from another, and the rules of each. In that moment I felt only ignorant and vulnerable to the whims of a creature of such immensity. I did not think I would ever know her secrets. Yet again, and at exactly the same time, I felt the greatness of the city inside me like a fierce and rising storm, and I wanted some of that strength for my own.

☉☉

'Here we are, Poneke!' the Artist said, pleasure evident in his voice. I was facing a building many levels high but even more levels across — it reached to the end of the block, in fact. This was a palace, surely, a building of such immense proportions I thought the Artist's family must be very, very rich. As I turned to gather my things I saw that we were surrounded by many large buildings of the same sort — I counted four or five windows to the top, and noticed there was another level that descended beneath. People lived, I realised, below street level also. Some of these grand façades were made from stone, some from brick. All were imposing — so square, and flat and sooted-grey from the smoke that pumped from the chimneys — yet there was something serene, even reliable in their uniform window frames and doorway embellishments.

In the centre of this square of tenements was a small park. It was surrounded by an iron fence, but appeared easily accessible and was burgeoning with trees and flowers.

'It is the opposite of my home,' I observed. 'There the trees are the grandest and most numerous features, and you might only find the occasional small house or village among them. Here, man has tamed Nature.'

'Why yes, James.' The Artist seemed pleased with my observation. 'I suppose you are right. This is the way of things in our modern age, as perhaps it should be, don't you think?'

I did not know the answer to such a big question. I was inclined to agree, at that time, with all that was said, for I was unsure of my own mind.

'Your home is very grand,' I said. I felt unable to move from my spot on the pavement.

'Come along, James, we won't hurt. I suspect it is only my sister and the servants at home. Father will be at his office and my brothers are away on their own adventures.'

'But such a big house,' I blurted, 'for so few people? And so many doors!'

'Perhaps, although there are only enough rooms for our family of five. Not what we would think of as extravagance here. Ah, Poneke!' He'd followed my eye all the way up the street. 'We don't own all of this — just one set of rooms for our family. Did you think the entire building was ours?'

I felt foolish, yet I still could not discern his meaning. This all became evident, of course, as we entered the house and I was shown the extent of it. The building was divided and shared by many. A fact you will find obvious, but which I had yet to learn. It was like that continuously in those first weeks — what everyone took for granted I could learn only by stumbling my way through.

Finally the Artist was home. He had sent word to his family by the post that morning, as soon as we docked, but it had taken the rest of the day to unload and make our way to the house, so that we arrived only an hour before dinner. A maid, who I would eventually come to know as Miss Herring, opened the door for us. I removed my hat and nodded my head but did not greet her, as the Artist had gone past her without acknowledgement and I thought it best to follow his example. The front door opened onto a passageway that led on one side to a staircase and on the other to two rooms. We were taken immediately to the back of these, which was furnished with a table and sideboard, sewing desk and writing desk. A pretty young lady stood as we entered and welcomed us, running a little to embrace the Artist. She had on a light apron, but was finely dressed, with wider skirts than I had ever seen in New Zealand and Australia. Her hair was styled in a very particular fashion, with what seemed to be a quite severe division down the centre, and curls tamed in neat bunches on each side. Her form was so tightly bound and upright that I had the distinct impression of a tree with a tall, strong trunk and branches that fanned out to the softest leaves.

This was Miss Angus, whom we did greet with much emphasis and warmth. Since their mother had died, the Artist had intimated to me earlier, his sister had taken on full housekeeping duties for their father.

'Here is my friend and helper, James Poneke, dear sister. He is a Maori from New Zealand, a chieftain's son, and the most civilised example of his kind that I could recommend to you. Young Poneke is interested in an English education, and I have agreed to furnish him with one if he should condescend to assist me in my exhibitions.'

She appraised me and smiled tentatively.

I bowed, and, using my best English accent, said, 'How do you do? I am very pleased to meet you.'

'Why, his English is perfect!' said Miss Angus. 'And he is quite lighter in complexion than I might expect.' Here she suddenly looked flustered. 'My apologies, Mr Poneke. I am well, thank you, and pleased to make your acquaintance also. I hope you are not offended by my manner — one doesn't meet chiefs of New Zealand every day, or know how to speak with them.' She dipped in a small curtsey.

I had never been called Mister before, existing as I did on the crux of boyhood and adulthood, nativehood and civilisation. I found I enjoyed the sensation.

'At last you are here!' She looked to her brother now, taking his hands in hers. She seemed a little overcome as she let go, smoothing her apron and skirts repeatedly. 'I have been making this for the drawing room in honour of your return.' She turned to indicate a little screen, beautifully embellished with flowers and vines, in front of the fireplace.

'Why, Amelia, it is quite beautiful!' The Artist was indulgent, and more openly joyful than I had ever seen him.

'Nothing like your own work, of course, but I did my best to emulate the flora you enjoy.'

They talked for some minutes about the day, the journey, their father's imminent return from his offices in the city, but we did not linger over this conversation, as it was evident there was much preparation still needed before dinner.

They showed me to this room, which has always been reserved for guests and travellers. Then suddenly I was alone for the first time in many, many months, on solid land, in the grandest house I had ever entered. My hosts had given me an entire room to myself, though I could see space for at least ten to sleep on its floor. I looked out the window, smaller than those on the lower floors but a magical portal to me nonetheless. Outside I could see a corner of the little square, and the upper floors and roofs of the other majestic houses of the neighbourhood. We were not far from London's centre, but it was quiet here, save the few passersby or, very rarely, a horse or two, with carriages. I wondered at the good fortune that had brought me here, to see so many things I could not see in New Zealand, and to learn of so many wondrous ideas. I could see how the people of England would want to spread their magnificent wealth throughout the world, and how one day my own country might be full of such streets. Perhaps I could be an agent for that enlightenment. A great hope bloomed in my chest, where it sat alongside the puzzlement and darkness of my first impressions of the city. In those first few weeks, these two were constantly side by side. In hindsight I see how contradictory my feelings were, and how I was stretched between one extreme and another; no wonder I felt sick in my stomach much of the time, as if I were still sailing an unsettled sea.

I washed at the little basin that had been provided to me, and changed into the clothes the Artist had sent to my room. The servants of the house were there behind everything, for it was they who set my room and brought me items or took them away for cleaning. I did not know how I fitted between them and the masters and mistress of the house, so I decided to treat them as I would my hosts. Miss Herring was the only one who responded in kind immediately. I rarely saw the cook, or the manservant who aided Mr Angus in his daily life. They were willing to help as needed but hardly acknowledged me, for I was simply another job to do, and I suspect my status as an in-between, swarthy imposter made me an object of suspicion.

The dining room was on the ground floor at the front of the house, and was furnished in heavy burgundy fabrics, with a wide mirror above a fireplace. An immense table stood at the centre of the room. The Artist introduced me to Mr Angus before we sat, and after I made a little bow and greeting he nodded to me vigorously.

'It is a great pleasure to have you here, a great pleasure!' He was very well dressed in a tan suit, with a glint of gold chain at his pocket. Something about him exuded comfort and confidence, and this helped me to relax in his company. Or perhaps it was his accent — his vowels were not as long as his children's. He had not grown up in London. Had begun life in the country north of here, and carried something of a country manner with him, as he was fond of pointing out.

The table was already set with a succulent array of items, many of which I had never seen, though after so long at sea I would have been impressed with even the simplest fare. We began with soup, then lobster cutlets, potatoes, a joint of mutton, cheese and celery, and brandy bread pudding. Such a feast I remember to this day, even though I am now much accustomed to the generosity of the Angus house. Mr Angus liked a good table, and a good claret to accompany the meal, and soon set about interviewing me at length about my people and my country.

'Poneke,' he said, 'what foods are best to eat in New Zealand? What are the marriage customs of your people? Do you take many wives, as I've heard? You seem like a fine, sensible fellow; are there really cannibals amongst your kind?' Miss Angus tutted and frowned at these last questions, and Mr Angus apologised and withdrew them, though I could see he very much wanted to know the answers. He immediately seemed a kind man, and the exuberance with which he ate, drank and asked questions made me feel only positively towards his inquisition.

There were many days after when he, a cigar in one hand and fine whisky in the other, would find me in a quiet corner of the library and I would do my best to satisfy his curiosity. That first evening, however, we attempted to contain our discussion within more palatable boundaries. I told him about sea urchins, crayfish, pigeons and other fine foods of my home, how we married in much the same way as other people as far as I knew, how we were adopting Christian values with regard to matters of life and death.

'What do you seek in London, James? An education, my son has told us, but what does that mean to you?'

I liked Mr Angus a great deal for asking this question as if it did not have an immediate and obvious answer.

'I want to know the world,' I said. 'I want to see everything in it, and become worldly, and educated, and therefore...' Therefore what? I did not know. 'I am sorry, I know not where this must take me. I only have a great desire for education and improvement.'

'Well!' Mr Angus boomed, beaming his great grin towards

each person seated. 'This is why, my dear family, I am so against slavery and some of the more brutal forms of colonisation in the Antipodes. Look at this fine example of humanity at our own table! All he wants is education and improvement, and won't we make sure he has the chance for it?'

There was a murmur of agreement, and the Artist smiled in a way I had learnt to recognise as meaning he was pleased with himself. Evidently I was a project of interest and pride.

'And will you pursue our God as well, boy?'

I have to admit, God had not been on my mind a great deal recently, but I knew enough of the Bible to know it contained all the best, and worst, of mankind.

'God is everywhere,' I answered. Suddenly, like the Artist, I was pleased with myself, for I remembered a sermon I'd heard long ago. 'And I do expect to find him here, of all places. My first sight of St Paul's Cathedral told me the greatness of God has a place in this fine city.' I did not mention the other things I had observed on arrival — it seemed the game here was to perpetuate fine sensibilities, not dirty the conversation with descriptions of street grime and mudlarks.

Mr Angus and Miss Angus seemed well satisfied with this answer.

'Father, shall we take Mr Poneke to see the sights of London on the next fine day? I am sure he would love the sights of the rest of the world too, such as we might find at the Panorama. Oh, and if we are to go to Regent's Park, there is of course the zoo and the Colosseum! One cannot but be amazed at the breadth and wonders of God's creations in our own neighbourhood — they are quite astonishing, Mr Poneke! We go every year, more than once, and I never cease to be amazed.' This was the most I had yet heard Miss Angus speak, and I observed she was lovely in her exuberance. Without waiting for her father to respond, she asked her brother if he should care to accompany us.

'It would be good for James to become accustomed to exhibitions and London's crowds, indeed for James to become accustomed to a great many things about our world. I'm sure it would be a delight for him to accompany you both, but I must prepare my work for exhibition, and shall be busy between this and making arrangements with an exhibition hall. We are thinking of creating a book as well!' Here the Artist looked brightly at his father, and I observed a shadow draw itself over his features almost immediately. Mr Angus, for his part, maintained a neutral expression, and took up his daughter's exclamations about the virtues of Regent's Park and the entertainments therein.

When you hear the rest of my story you will understand the gratitude with which I consider my good fortune at coming into this house. The Anguses have surely saved my life, if not my soul, with their kindness. They are the very best of people.

But Mr Angus was not so unfailingly kind to his son, and the Artist could not be seen to have offered his father anything but a mirror of the treatment he received. I noticed it at that first homecoming dinner: there was an absence of questions for the accomplished young man on his return. No one asked about his travels except in the most light and trivial manner. Miss Angus enquired upon his health, his tiredness, the pretty sites of other countries. Mr Angus asked only about the costs, the prices of things in the Antipodes, and the manner of transport the Artist used, its comfort and proficiency. He had a great interest in such things, as this was his business, and an interest in antipodean commerce for different reasons.

It was not my business to become involved in the private interactions of the family, but in those first days I could not avoid noticing some of the personal affairs of the house. I soon learnt that Mr Angus had, in fact, organised the Artist's first job at the counting house, and that the Artist had absconded as soon as he had the opportunity and the sponsorship to follow his artistic ambitions. Mr Angus's disapproval was evident but not heavily enforced. He had patience enough to wait until the Artist wearied of his unlikely and difficult profession, and he had other children who were more obedient. The Artist was tolerated, but his work was ignored. I was lucky that the family did not view me as 'his work', though the Artist oftentimes seemed to do so.

For my part, I found everything fascinating: the design of the staircase and window latches, the daily rhythms of the house and its working inhabitants, the alarming but ingenious technology of the privy. Most of all, the magnificent library. The house itself contained many treasures, though my companions thought these ordinary. I was sure that I was making many mistakes in etiquette, and I was determined to learn how to avoid them, so I made a study of everything that happened. Thus, the several days of rain that followed my arrival were not a disappointment. My senses were already overwhelmed, and when I wasn't taking in the sights and sounds and smells of the place, I was engaged in reading from that generous collection of books in order to stave off the queer pangs of anxiety that came upon me should I think too hard on how far I was from home.

SEVEN

Papa, I'm ashamed to say I mostly forgot you in those first days in London — there was so much to see and absorb. And yet the ache never left me. That unmistakable thrum in the background, the rhythm to my hungry and seeking heart. How strange that even though I had felt unmoored as a child in New Zealand, the sights and sounds of this strange new city now made everything I had left behind seem more comforting and dear to me. I suddenly had a strong sense of myself as a native New Zealander, as if being abroad gave me claim to the whole of the country that I had not felt when I was there. Whole days would go by without my noticing, sometimes whole weeks, but that ache would always return unbidden: as I walked along a crowded street, as I bought a posy for Miss Angus, or an eel pie for myself, as I searched the park for familiar plant life. I'd feel it descend on me like a wave then, and I'd look around and find myself in a wholly alien land, and wonder how I got here, as if I had just woken, still a little boy with two living parents from whom he had somehow walked too far. Maybe I didn't attribute those jarring feelings to you every time, but now, with hindsight — glorious hindsight, what things it could save us from.

It took a week for the skies to clear. When at last they did, we all resolved to make the most of the fine weather. The Artist had taken a cab as soon as he'd finished his breakfast, but Miss Angus was still keen to go on our proposed sightseeing excursion. Even Mr Angus took the morning away from his office so that he might accompany us to the zoo and the Colosseum, which were within a short walking distance of the house. I had thus far ventured only to Dorset Square, the little garden around which the houses were gathered, so I was pleased we would see all of Regent's Park as we made our way there.

I had already become quite weary of the coal dust that filled the nostrils of every person who ventured outside. There was a constancy to it, so that I thought I might grow accustomed to the accompanying fumes, but I never have. I wondered at the Londoner's ability to ignore the soot that coats every surface, wall or building — even those he feels some pride about. I mention this not to complain about what every citizen lives with here, but to contrast how surprising it was always to find the smog lift almost immediately on entry to one of the parks. One could imagine the bellowing smoke-stacks of the city had never existed, at least for the duration of a walk. It was a sweet relief.

On this fine day, I found it difficult to contain my exuberance for the green everywhere, and trees, and birds, and so much terrestrial life. It had been many months since I had seen a forest, and I couldn't help myself going from tree to tree, examining each plant and feature. A small red creature, bigger than a kiore but smaller than a dog, with a great bushy curled tail, darted around the trunk of a tree. The thing was quick and delightful as it dashed along the branches, then settled, sniffing and looking about. I laughed out loud.

'It's a squirrel, James,' said Miss Angus as she took her father's arm and both looked on. I ran from one side of the path to the other, exclaiming at these everyday creatures found in almost every tree. My companions seemed to enjoy rather than scorn my childish enthusiasm. Still, there was something I couldn't quite grasp. The park was very beautiful, yes, serenely ordered, easy to run one's eye over all the rows of trees and carefully trimmed bushes. The flowers were arranged in delightful patterns of shape and colour. The overall effect was enchanting. Why, then, this other feeling beneath, an unease? Why the fear that came unbidden and unexpected?

At last we arrived at the London Zoological Gardens, and paid our sixpence to enter. If I had been excited at the start of our day, I was now truly amazed. Every bird and beast defied my imagination, for I could not have conceived of the many different colours and shapes that Nature had assigned them. In my lifetime I had seen a dog, a goat, a horse and a cow. I had not forgotten my suspicion of that first great mammal, and here I was again, a boy who knew nothing of the world. We gazed at the tropical birds first, then the otters and the monkeys. The intelligence in the eyes of those creatures was beguiling. They came as close as possible to the cage netting, and spent some time picking lice from each other's fur, looking up from time to time to make a face. We must have been as strange a sight to them as they were to us.

'Do you think them intelligent, James?' Mr Angus asked me, and I considered them afresh. One of the creatures had come to perch on a branch not two feet from us. I lifted my hand to smooth back my hair, and the little one made the same gesture. This must have been coincidence, but when I did it again, the miniature man followed suit. Soon we were engaged in a game of copycat, or copy-man perhaps. The monkey copied a good portion of my movements, but was easily distracted by its mates.

'I can see they think,' I said. 'And feel, and deduce. Just look at the one with the baby clinging to its back. There must be some intelligence there. I don't know if it is the same as ours.'

'Indeed not. There are some who would say we verge on blasphemy to even suggest such a thing. Some who would say they can't possibly be conscious in the same way as us.'

'Ae. Yet it is there. Plain enough to see.'

'Perhaps you are correct, James. Perhaps it is all a matter of different ways of thinking, or God's higher plan, of which we know little.'

As we met each creature the Anguses explained its origin and purpose, as much as they were able. The tree animals, and amphibians, the earth diggers and jungle beasts. Every creature seemed so well suited to the habitat it was made for, and this filled me with curiosity at creation and the Creator: so much vaster than I had known, so much more inventive. The giraffe astonished me most — a mythical creature I had hitherto seen only in books. She rose up as tall as a tree, taller. I was a tall boy, but I would have barely reached her knees. Beside her was a creature more like a horse in dimensions, though this beast had black and white stripes and a mane that stood on end. I couldn't make sense of any of them, not in their artificial holding pens, and I thought their homelands must be so very different from places I'd seen.

All this amazement was tempered by the miserable sight of the big cats, confined as they were in their cages, pacing back and forth behind the iron bars. I had held in my mind so long the majesty of the lion, whom I had first encountered alongside Daniel in the Bible, and I had heard the tiger was not only bigger but had a more brightly patterned coat than the King of Beasts. There were no kings in the cages I saw — only poorly looking creatures with scruffy coats. They were certainly massive and strange and pitiful in their ruined beauty, but I did my best not to think what it must be like for them if they had any measure of intelligent perception. Beneath everything I could sense their held-in tension, the long-drawn-out pain of their days in captivity.

Finally we returned through the park to the house for lunch, and my eyes traced those straight paths and cleverly designed gardens once more, and I began to understand my earlier unease. There were no cages here, yet the natural way of the forest had been tamed and contained to such an extent that the effect was similar. I yearned now for the smell and shade of forest grown up fully around me, the crunch of dead leaves underneath, the vines growing up around thick trunks, branches fallen and eaten away by grubs. I yearned for the encompassing density of trees, the feeling that I was small and insignificant but somehow protected, somehow part of something greater than me. In this place everything of Nature was subject to the will of man's designs. I couldn't settle the churning of my insides. It felt like a slow twisting of bone, pushing my inner structure out of alignment.

'Young man, it sounds like homesickness!' Mr Angus exclaimed when I tried to explain my quietness.

'It must be very hard to be so far from home,' Miss Angus agreed.

I knew they were right, though the sense that seemed uppermost in my mind was not that I was far from home but that some natural order had been upset, or ignored, and that there would be a price to pay.

'Perhaps, Father, you should take Mr Poneke to Hyde or even Richmond Park?'

'Indeed, these might soothe your soul, James, but I fear even our largest parks may be different from the forests you hold in your heart.'

I suspected this was true.

෨෯

Of all the things I have seen since, perhaps my first exhibition was not the most fantastic, but it is implanted in my imagination with so many firsts, and with the flavour of London itself. Londoners know the Colosseum well — anyone with a shilling or two will have seen the famous panorama of the city inside. So you may understand, as we entered and began our ascent by way of the hydraulic lift, how awestruck I was. When we were at last at the top of the viewing platform, the point the Artist, who had joined us for the afternoon, asserted was the best place to experience the phenomenon, I was astonished to be able to see all of the city laid out before me, in all directions. It took me some time to register that the platform emulated the very dome of St Paul's, with its sacred ball and cross at its pinnacle. I knew not by what magic this thing had been made — the immensity of it was beyond belief. Light filtered down to us from the sky and air moved in and out of the dome, so that the vast canvas (for that is what it apparently was) was animated by shifting light and shadow and breeze. I fancied I could see the river flowing, people living down there in this wondrous city; there were carriages, and smoke, and windows opening to the lives of others. The details were so fine and minute that my senses wanted me to believe the illusion was real.

'The Panorama is not what it once was,' the Artist told me. 'It has faded in part. The touch-ups have worked well, but there is only so much life in the old thing. My word, as children we gazed at it so enraptured.'

Miss Angus considered me. 'Like you, Mr Poneke. We were just like you as children.'

'We can bring you again at night. The new night show is apparently impressive and worth the return.'

I feared the Anguses would grow tired of my gazing, though I felt I could have stayed for hours. I wanted to fill my eyes to the brim — I suppose that makes no sense. There was an intense hunger in me, but I pulled myself away from the scene after some twenty minutes, for I noticed my hosts were becoming distracted. We then made our way down to the Glyptotheka — the Rotunda and museum where dozens of sculptures representing classical forms are gathered. Again I gazed in wonderment, for now I was surrounded by the finest, most elegant forms of famous figures. Cupid, Psyche, Achilles, Chaucer, Nelson, these were all pointed out to me. It was an ever-changing tableau, apparently, with new sculptures added and sold as required. I thought them most natural and fantastic representations.

'Oh look, Prince Albert! And Sir Francis Bacon too.' Miss Angus was well acquainted with the collection and treasured the appearance of new faces. The gathering of greats created a tranquil sensation, surrounded as they were by silk curtains and decorative embellishments.

'These are Doric columns, James,' said the Artist, 'and this, a frieze — a panathenaic procession of Elgin marbles.' He named the figures represented — gods and demi-gods — and I recognised some of the names from classical stories I'd read under his tutelage. I had missed his instruction and his company since we had arrived in London.

'Whenever you come to one of these exhibitions, James, it is a good opportunity for improvement. Here you have the chance to come face to face with the gods, both heavenly and earthly. Every face has a story behind it. We are fortunate to be so close to such a vast range of shows.'

We sat for a while on velvet-covered seats. I tried to turn towards my companions, for I was disconcerted by the many gilt-framed mirrors encircling the room, at eye height now that we were seated. I could not turn too close to Miss Angus for fear of making her uncomfortable, and so, while sister and brother discussed the merits of the new decorations and sculptural forms (she admired the sculpture but found the decoration too overt; he had criticisms for both), I found myself averting my gaze from my own reflection. It was not that I did not like what I saw. I know who, and what, I am. But I had never seen myself beside the pale form of an English couple before, and I had not been aware of how marked the difference in our appearances was. If you are around a people for long enough, you will begin to see yourself in them. I had begun to lose a sense of my exterior self, though I still carried my own stories with me. I think I must have identified too closely with my hosts, and I was not ready for the strange experience of being both knowable and unknowable at the same time. I was their friend; we knew and liked each other well. But there were aspects of me, written into my skin like a sailor's tattoo, that they would never understand.

I know I speak like an Englishman. I know I play my part well. But in those first weeks I became aware of myself as a member of a privileged class, as well as a Maori boy in a world that was foreign to me. I occupied those two worlds simultaneously, and it is hard enough for any man simply to occupy one. In that moment I felt the oddity of it — the place I now found myself in, where artificial materials had been made to emulate the whole of the world in all its majesty and beauty. What these men of industry could create with their arts and inventions and technologies! They had the ability to recreate the world in such a way that it was almost unnecessary to seek out the real thing. They were, indeed, made in the image of God, creating their own facsimiles of God's creations, and taking pleasure in all of it. For this is what everything I had seen this day was — pleasure. Nature tamed and forces harnessed to promote man's own mastery of the knowable universe. It was magnificent, and I was an immediate slave to the brilliance of it. And yet none of it was real.

If you detect distaste in my tone, it is perhaps because later events have coloured my telling of this tale. At that time there was no hesitancy in my fervour. All doubts and fears were soon replaced with a kind of passion for the inventions and entertainments on show in London, and whenever it was deemed convenient and proper my hosts took me to some of them. I put my unease aside and became somewhat of a hedonist to the joys of the shows. It was easy enough to do with such substantial distractions at our disposal. Such entertainments were frequented by everyone from royalty to the poor, so that I was able to observe all the different peoples of London, even as we were seemingly engaged with the exhibits themselves. Indeed, all of the city is an exhibition, and I had only to walk the streets, gazing upwards as I did so (and only just avoiding walking into others). The beauty of it is a spectacle; paired with its noise and filth and crowds, it is a delightful conundrum.

◎◎

The promise between the Artist and myself was that I would have the opportunity for schooling, but he himself was too busy to tutor me. He consulted with Mr Angus, and they sent me to a small private boys' day school in Marylebone, a neighbourhood close to our residence. There Mr Jones taught us classics, French, writing, English grammar and composition, history and chronology, geography and the use of the globes, practical and mental arithmetic, algebra and trigonometry. In truth, I endured these classes with less enthusiasm than I had imagined I would hold for my English tuition. I found I did not have a great deal in common with the spoilt boys who attended the school, and I made no effort to impress them. They tended to treat me with silent contempt once they discovered I was immune to their taunts. Perhaps it was that I no longer really felt like a boy at all, and that their ideas of superiority were so limited to their small realm that I felt myself wholly separate from them. Already the city and my wider practical education beckoned. I longed to abandon my morning classes, and soon discovered that the Artist was happy to support my delinquency whenever the opportunity arose. He needed me for the exhibitions. My attendance at the school did not progress beyond irregular, and as the spring days lengthened and grew warmer, I was content to learn that my formal lessons would soon be declared over for the year.

Respite, meantime, came in the form of Miss Angus who, often accompanied by Miss Herring as chaperone, was my afternoon companion at least once or twice weekly. The Artist was usually busy with his etchings and writings, and seemed to consider me taken care of now that I was established at the house. He was a curious man. As I became acquainted with other English people, I began to understand that his aloofness was not simply a characteristic of all Englishmen but also a unique aspect of his own obsessive and fastidious nature. Once he had a goal, nothing would keep him from it. His pride would not allow it. Miss Angus intimated to me as much during one of our walks through Regent's Park. She was evidently proud of her brother's achievements, but somewhat chagrined at what she described as his single-mindedness.

'Do not feel abandoned, Mr Poneke. My brother's manner does not mean disregard. Some days he simply cannot see past his own goals. But he is my only brother still at home, and he knows he has my instant forgiveness for his absences.'

On this day there were stilt-walkers in brightly patterned costumes on the paths, and dancing dogs dressed in white frills further along. We threw them our pennies.

'And it has been most delightful to have your company. It almost makes up for my dear sibling's neglect.'

I often felt that, despite the genteel manner with which Miss Angus spoke, she was making fun of us while appearing to be saying something else entirely. It may have been in the way she smiled, her eyes telling one story while her lips told another. I had learnt not to direct our walks or conversations in any way — it had already become clear to me that there was an unspoken code to Miss Angus's life, one that I could make no sense of. Should I make suggestions, I was sometimes met with sudden silence, averted eyes and the redirection of conversation. Miss Angus was not the only one to do this. Her father and brother were apt to guide me away from my mistakes, and I once witnessed Miss Herring's eyebrows raise in alarm when I suggested a meal at a public establishment as we passed — a discreet indication that I had transgressed some unwritten rule.

From these silent admonishments I came to understand that ladies were guided by a set of regulations for each circumstance that menfolk were not beholden to. Miss Angus began her day planning the running of the house with Cook and Miss Herring and the valet (if he was not out with Mr Angus) in the morning room, where she also sewed or painted or wrote her many letters. She always seemed busy, and was always present at each meal I attended in the house, while the men were sometimes absent. In the afternoons she might take calls in the drawing room on the first floor, or make them herself, though this was an infrequent event, and she intimated to me that she was much more inclined to pass the time in reading, or attending the ferns she had established under glass in the drawing room, or making the colourful paper peep-shows she had become quite famous for among her circle. She gave these as gifts, but their primary purpose seemed to be her engagement in making them, which gave her many hours of occupation and pleasure. The house owed much to her eye for beauty and proportion.

But she had one weakness that my presence allowed her to indulge.

'I do so enjoy all the different exhibitions,' she told me. 'And Papa has always taken us to them, since we were children. There was nothing quite like the magic lanterns, or embroidered monuments of the world, or Napoleon's carriage, but the great paintings and sculptures are my most fervent obsession. Can you imagine how long each must have taken? And how monumental the skill behind them? Each year there are new delights — the automaton, steam-powered machinery of all kinds, wax figures with the power of speech, yet I don't think any of these quite outdoes the classical works —' Here she shivered visibly. 'You know, Mr Poneke, sometimes I wonder how it is deemed proper for us all to attend, ladies and gentlemen alike and the different elements of society. This, in itself, is perhaps a kind of magic.'

Indeed, I indicated my own wonder.

'It is educational. This is what they tell us, and so we must go, we are encouraged to go. But you know, Mr Poneke —' She looked at me sidelong, her eyes narrowed as if assessing my face. 'I do not know how we might measure the science of each show versus its...versus the strength of its amusement. For I find such things endlessly amusing.'

I laughed. The more time I spent with Miss Angus, the more I was able to detect her witticisms. I learnt much from simple quiet contemplation in her company. And it helped, immensely, to learn from her the ways of society, and the shows, of which I would soon be a part. The library, which was generally Mr Angus's domain but which I had been invited to investigate, contained an entire collection of her peep-shows — the ones she made for her father, she told me. Most were modelled on a show or exhibition she had seen; one was the zoo, and two showed simple neighbourhood scenes, including the house and square. There was nothing simple to these paper marvels, however. Each was composed of many layers of a scene constructed in such a way as to create the illusion of depth. The first layer might be a frame of shrubbery or curtains, with a small aperture through which one peered in order to take in the full scene. The next layer contained foreground figures, then each successive layer contained other figures, buildings, trees or other salient features. By viewing the peep-show from the correct angle, everything was presented with the correct perspective, the layering effect giving more of a lifelike sensation than a simple drawing on one layer might produce. I liked to peer into each, as if secretly discovering a story that was not my own.

EIGHT

The Artist woke me early to get ready. I had been in London only a handful of weeks, but already we had rehearsed, and my wardrobe had been chosen. There was a finely woven kaitaka cloak that the Artist had obtained on the east coast of my country, a taiaha that had been gifted to him in the north, and some feathers I had kept with me since I first left New Zealand, as well as Ana Ngamate's pounamu that I always wore, usually beneath my Englishman's clothes. New Zealand and the life I had once lived already seemed so far away it had lost the semblance of reality in my mind, and here we were preparing ourselves to show all of London what my home country was like.

After a light breakfast, during which I could only nibble a piece of dry bread and the Artist drank only tea, we took a cab to the Hall. I carried the cloak so as not to appear conspicuous by wearing it on the street, but the Artist's new assistant for the show carried all of our other belongings, including the taiaha, which made us conspicuous anyway. We talked little, each one of us nervous or busy with his own thoughts, until we came close to Piccadilly and the cab driver stopped to let us out.

In my land, we are likely to have two experiences of the sky above. It is either obscured by forest, making its presence known only through a shadowy light, or, if we are high on a hill pah or walking through the tussock plain, it is more vast and more encompassing than any land formation. I have seen skies that are bigger even than the sea, and been thankful that my feet were planted on the good earth. Sometimes those skies are so blue I wonder if I am looking into Te Kore right there, the great nothingness from whence everything comes. Here, in this land of the genteel and the modern, I have not yet seen skies so big. The buildings rise and rise until all the sky allowed to us is the sliver above the road, between one side and the other. But let me tell you: that day as we moved through the city I looked around at the magnificence of the fine buildings, the clamouring shapes of things, the lovely roar of London talking and walking and wheeling past — the horses' footfalls, ragwomen, *Oranges, 2 a penny*, pot-repairmen, costers with their wheel- and donkey-barrows, *Buy a pound of crab, cheap*, voices rising up from all over the world, turbaned and pale- or dark-skinned, *Mussels penny a quart*. Steaming cloth bundles and heavy black pots carried aloft through small gathered crowds. I could smell fish and yeasted bread even amid the horse dung and road dirt. *All large and alive-o*. The thick stench and high spirit of it all. *New sprats, o*. That day I had the same feeling as my home sky gave me: as if I could be swallowed by it all and lifted high above and beyond my life.

I took a great breath and let my eyes close for a moment before I heard the others move on. Then I was hurrying forward.

Soon we passed through the thick of the costers and on to the more genteel Piccadilly Circus. Here fine buildings dominated, as did gentlewomen and men finely dressed. I tried to keep myself in check, to remember there would be other days, but it was all too much to hide my enthusiasm.

'Why, Poneke,' said the Artist, when he saw how distracted I had become. 'Keep your wits about you! Don't want to get run over by a carriage. Not today!'

I must have had a dopey grin across my face. 'It's just… Piccadilly!'

'Ah yes, Poneke. So it is. So it is. Rightly so. But we have work to do today, young sir, so let's try to keep together.'

I murmured agreement, gazing upwards. Then I shook my head from side to side, rolled my shoulders, and followed on.

The Hall was mere steps away, and so different from the surrounding buildings. I knew the design emulated the monuments of the ancient empire of Egypt, and I now wondered at the beauty of those people, for on each side of the first-floor window, standing above all else, there were two well-shaped statues, one male and one female, in the Egyptian style. The Artist inclined his head towards them and proclaimed that they were the goddess and god Isis and Osiris. The figures were tall and well-muscled, fine, harmonious forms. The order of the Egyptians' world showed itself through the other designs around that entrance, too: winged beasts called sphinxes, suns and stars, hieroglyphs I could not give a meaning to. There were papyrus columns holding up a cornice that gave a wonderful symmetry to the whole, and a sign announcing 'London Museum' that drew us towards the doors. I was left with a feeling of helpless curiosity.

As I looked up at Isis and Osiris and their hall of many wonders, I also thought of the carvings of our great houses in my homeland, the ancestors on their pillars, the balance and symmetry of the house with its rhythmic carvings and geometrical woven designs. I recognised a kinship. It felt good to walk through the doorway they guarded. I bowed my head as we entered.

The Artist removed his hat and moved directly towards the stairs, his assistant following closely behind. I hesitated for a moment. I wanted, as had become my habit, to explore everything, to take my time even with the decorative elements of the building. You will laugh at me now, and they would have laughed at me then, but I marvelled at the attention and flair it must have taken to create just one of those door frames. It was a rich country indeed that could afford such effort over an item so common. Yet again I had cause to reflect on our own ancestral houses, sure that somewhere in my homeland there might be carvers who could challenge these English craftsmen.

But there was no time. The Artist was moving briskly, and I was not keen to be left behind. We were at the top of the stairs now, and still he charged forward. But this time I stopped, and I did not care that I lost sight of the assistant's coat tails a moment later. Before me was the most wondrous cavern I could imagine — rendered in paint and plaster, yes, but almost real to my eyes. Here were sharp-edged rocks all piled up and stately like the pillars outside, a formation that defied belief though I knew it could only be copied from Nature. I stepped through and found myself in a forest, where every shade of green and bright flowers invaded my senses. I was a child again, a small boy who slept under trees as naturally as I now slept on a soft mattress. I was a boy looking up in wonder at the light as it filtered through many-faceted leaves. These were different, more luxuriant plants than I had known, so my wonder was fresh. I looked and looked. So I was shocked when I came to a

103

painted wall, and realised that the only thing feeding my reverie was this thin facade. Once I stood back to get some perspective I could see the painting gave a sense of expansiveness, as if the painter had found a way to include the whole world in his vision. But still, now that the illusion was apparent to me, I was no longer a wondering child but a speculative youth who saw that the luxurious forest was made not from living trees but from wood and plaster and fabric.

No other visitors were yet in the building, and I had lost sight of my party completely. Now something else caught my eye and I moved towards the centre of the room. There, surrounded by a low structure as if fenced in, was a great group of creatures gathered together, still and unbreathing. Looking back now, they evoked in me an odd feeling, for they seemed to be lifelike as well as being obviously not-alive, and I was drawn to this suspended animation at the same time as I was repulsed by it. What had been done to the creatures to capture them so?

I knew that all of these creatures must exist somewhere in the world, for I recognised among them those I had seen at the zoo. There were giant cats, and bears, and all manner of birds. Some of these stood among the animals, some perched in trees, yet others cocked lifeless heads in glass cabinets. I looked up into the fabric trees then, and was surprised to recognise birds from my own country: the tui, the kaka, karearea and ruru. None of the birds had a song. I had felt some dazzlement at all there was to see, but now had to adjust to some discomfort at the nature of it.

A creature curled around a branch had me mesmerised when I heard the Artist's voice. 'It's a snake, James. Come, we thought we'd lost you. There'll be plenty of time for looking later. We must get you ready!' He took my arm. 'I promise to give you a guided tour when the exhibition is complete. For now, there is much to do. You will impress all who meet you with your natural grace, but we must be prepared.'

The Artist always had the best ways to coerce me to his purpose.

There were two other rooms besides the one the Artist led me to. Again he promised time to explore later, then he asked me to don my costume and prepare myself for the visitors. I didn't want to increase his consternation — he was quite agitated in his manner, more abrupt in his language than usual. I understood that the opening of the doors meant a great deal to him, that the audience's first impression of his work would mean the success or otherwise of his great undertaking. This first day, he had told me, would tell whether profit was to be made from this venture, or whether his father had been right in suggesting he would never make a life from his work.

I could now brag of some of the British Empire's best education, but still I could not make sense of some of the customs and commerce of my hosts. The Artist had created these wonderful depictions of all the greatest chiefs of New Zealand with his pencils and watercolours, and these pictures now hung in the wondrous gallery in which I, too, stood. The mana of the chiefs was all around us: this would ensure success, surely? If my people resided in London, they would flock to marvel at these images of great leaders. But the Artist did not seem so sure his people would behave in this manner. And if his venture failed, he would find himself again working at the position his father had dictated for him: counting other people's money. Odd employment for any man, and strange that it should be so profitable.

I unfolded the cloak and gathered it around my shoulders, tying it with the muka and wool threads provided. I had flattened my hair with pomade already that morning, and I knew the feathers would not need too much encouragement to stay where I planted them among my tight curls. Even without a mirror glass, I would present a fine figure. The assistant had brushed my shoulders and straightened my neck tie, over which I wore Ana Ngamate's hei tiki, then handed the taiaha to me. As well as the etchings and paintings and myself, the Artist was exhibiting his collection of tools and weapons obtained in New Zealand and Australia. I hefted the taiaha in my palms, turned it slowly, swung it in a slow arc. The weight of it was pleasing. I had not often held one in my homeland, since they are specialised, personal weapons. Perhaps this one had had a name. The Artist then pulled me by the arm to the position he wanted me to take between a portrait of Te Wherowhero and one of Te Heuheu, two of our most eminent chiefs. I held the taiaha in an unaggressive pose. I looked around, and felt a great swelling of pride and wonderment, and sent out a silent mihi of gratitude to all who had offered a strange boy care. Each of my parents, my adopted tribe, even the Pakeha mission and village. I would not be here had it not been for them. I was surrounded by great chiefs and relatives, some close and some more removed, all delicately rendered in picturesque colour. I felt that we would represent our people well to the English men and women who visited us in this magical place. The Artist had created a spectacle: over two hundred pictures of my people and the people of South Australia, as well as many of our most treasured possessions, and me — the living Maori boy in the Egyptian Hall.

At precisely ten o'clock the visitors began to arrive. I felt shy in my function as ambassador, but I was determined to play my role correctly. The first man to approach me was very finely dressed and carried a cane. He had taken a turn about the room, peering at each image through his eyeglass, and when he reached me he stared as if I were a painting myself, beginning at the top, making his way down and all the way back up again. This scrutiny unnerved me, but I withstood it in good humour, and when he reached my face on his second take, I made a small bow.

'Good morning, sir,' I said.

'Good heavens! You speak very good English for a native.' He raised his eyeglass again.

I let my hand drop. 'Yes sir, I was educated in New Zealand and have now begun a fine English education in London.'

'Indeed, you have, have you?' He shifted aside, still staring, as a gentleman with a lady on his arm approached.

'Excuse me, but we couldn't help but overhear. Are you the young chief of New Zealand?'

'Why yes, I am. How do you do?' I lowered my head and shoulders again.

The lady gave a light laugh, waving the handkerchief in her hand. 'His manners! You wouldn't know he was a native if you didn't see his face. And from the Antipodes!'

'We are being rude, Mrs Sands,' said the gentleman. 'We are very well, thank you, young man, but how do you do?'

'I am much improved now that I have made your acquaintance.'

The lady laughed again, louder this time, and I allowed myself a half-smile.

'But you haven't made our acquaintance, not properly,' she said.

'We are Mr and Mrs Sands, of Kensington,' her husband continued. Mrs Sands dropped into a small curtsey this time, and offered up her gloved hand, which I took, bowing again.

The small group seemed well pleased with this performance, and as each new group arrived they asked more questions about my homeland and my current occupation. The ritual of manners was repeated with each new arrival, and it was this they seemed most taken with, as if I had performed some feat of imagination or skill that equalled the fine paintings themselves. They were so curious to me, these Londoners, with their rituals of exchange.

Early in the day a very tall, finely dressed man came through and caused a flurry of excitement. He took much time with the etchings and objects, but did not talk directly to me, standing back to observe my interactions with others instead. The Artist stayed by his side, talking quietly to him as required. The gentleman had other helpers following him, as well as the eyes of everyone gathered. I tried not to stare at him too often myself, for he had a marvellous nose the length and shape of which I'd never encountered, and this only added to his aristocratic air. The Artist told me later that he was the famous Duke of Wellington, well known for his love of the exhibitions as well as for his many achievements in battle and politics, and his appearance boded well for the success of the show.

In general, the Artist appeared pleased with the attention both to his work and my presence. He was seemingly very busy himself, engaging in conversation with as many visitors as I. By late morning we were both in need of refreshment. At one o'clock we had some luncheon and rest at Hatchett's Coffee House across the road.

'I don't want to overstate things, but I think we've done it, James!' the Artist said over a good meal of mutton and bread. 'This morning's audience proves interest in the exhibition is high, and now, with the approval of nobility, the rest will flock. They come out of curiosity, and for that I suspect you are the main attraction, but I hope they linger for the pictures and take more away from the experience than they anticipated — it was a fortuitous day when we met!'

The Artist's excitement was infectious. And it was flattering to be a great attraction in Piccadilly, though I had already begun to think that it was not me they came for but the idea they had of someone like me.

'I am happy for you,' I told him. 'But I am puzzled by their curiosity about me. I am just a person, after all.'

'But such a person! The stranger the better, these days. Your particular charm lies in the unexpected, I think, James. They already have ideas about what a native person should be. They seek an encounter with the savages they have heard about. But you are the educated savage, the civilised. I've seen men, and women, in cages or standing before images of barbaric landscapes. Most of these visitors have, too. But to bring a real native boy here and show that there is very little difference between him and us? This is different!'

At two o'clock we returned to the Hall in good spirits, refreshed enough for the rest of the day. The Artist was now fully in his element. I liked seeing him happy and proud, yet I felt distant from him, too. One might think that this rare experience would bring us together. Somehow it had the opposite effect. As the day wore on I felt myself less and less connected to those around me, as if I were a wind-up doll on a revolving stage, unreal yet fascinating enough to stare at. The visitors came through regularly, and continued to express delight and amusement at the show. And I continued to work hard at my role, as I had committed to do. I felt, from their reactions, that I must be doing an adequate job as ambassador for my homeland.

After a few more hours repeating the niceties and performances of the morning, a particularly rotund man approached me.

'You are the cannibal chief of New Zealand?'

I decided not to take offence at this remark. 'I can assure you I have never been a cannibal,' I said, and leaned forward to imitate intimacy. 'And I'm not sure I should even be called a chief, though my father was.'

The man sniffed and leaned back, as if my movement towards his person offended him, so I stood straight once again. He then proceeded to point his cane at me, using it to lift the tip of my cloak. He sniffed again.

'I have it on good authority that all the natives of New Zealand partake of human flesh in the most gruesome cannibal feasts.' He was speaking more loudly now. 'You can imitate the ways and speech of an English gentleman, but your black skin belies a black soul if ever I saw one. Frederick, look at this savage. They have taught him tricks like a well-trained pet, but I am not fooled.'

A young well-dressed man joined my persecutor and inspected me with the look of one who had eaten raw nettle.

'You are right, of course, Uncle. Nothing can hide this self-evident truth.' And then, as if to prove the point, he reached out and proceeded to pinch the skin of my hand.

I don't know what took hold of me then. Perhaps it was the absurdity of the moment, perhaps the beer I had taken with my lunch, it was certainly something to do with the men's idiocy, but I felt the need to laugh, and allowed myself a grin. A small crowd had gathered around us by then, with a number of pretty ladies present.

'Of course I am but a dancing cannibal,' I announced, 'and would be nothing without my masters.' I bowed, and then began to dance around the men, wielding my taiaha like a warrior, eyes rolling, prancing, knees high. I knew this little performance would surprise the Artist, for up until now I had not gone outside the parameters of behaviour he had set for me, except when I was out of his sight and certainly not in public. The truth was I really didn't know what I was doing. If one of my own people had been there I wouldn't have attempted a wero like this. It wasn't what I was made for, with my English ways and my nose perpetually in a book, but I'd seen it done, and I wanted so badly to teach these bores a lesson. The dance brought out a high spirit in me, so that I began to flick my head and eyes this way and that, taking aggressive positions I had only played at in the past. Perhaps your spirit took me, Papa, for I began to feel my blood boiling with an anger that threatened to take me away with it. But as I pranced around the men, I became aware that the room had become completely silent, that all eyes had turned my way. This cooled me somewhat. In my hot-bloodedness, I did not want to prove their judgements of me.

I resolved to complete my little charade. In my final flourish, I wielded the taiaha high above my head and lunged forward, eyes bulging and tongue fully extended, like we did when we were boys pretending to be warriors at the Mission. My two victims looked terrified by this time — the young man was completely pale, while his uncle was wiping his eyes and forehead rapidly with his kerchief. They were both inching backwards and seemed, by the looks on their faces, to want nothing more than to run.

I lowered my arms and adjusted my clothing. It was all a jest — surely they would understand this? But when I looked up and saw the Artist's face, I was not so convinced. This all took place in a matter of moments, you understand, for I needed to act quickly. I faced my audience and smiled widely, then bowed my deepest, most graceful bow.

'Ladies, gentlemen,' I said in my best British accent, 'thank you for your attentiveness to our little performance today. I am but a young Maori chief's son with a good English education and no experience in the ways of war. Those ways are unknown to me and I wouldn't know how to use one of these —' I raised the taiaha and watched Fat Uncle flinch — 'except in the war dance. These kind gentlemen agreed to take part in my demonstration for your interest. Let us applaud them!' I looked expectantly at my audience, and they looked hesitantly back, unsure what to do until I raised my hands to clap in a demonstrative way, maintaining my most wide and agreeable smile. Finally they seemed all to breathe out at once, tapping their palms together lightly.

'I am harmless, I promise you, and to prove it I will sing you one of our peace songs.'

Well, now I had landed myself in some trouble. I was not what one would call a good singer, but I could carry a tune, so I sang them a mournful waiata tangi, which was not so much a song of peace as it was a lament for those who had passed in battle. The gentlemen and ladies gathered were not to know this, and seemed touched by the tears I managed to produce in the final notes.

'Therefore, dear friends,' I announced, 'don't be deceived by my play. We are a joyful people who like to laugh much more than to fight. In my land, we make friends by hongi — touching noses. This means we share the breath of life.' Here I turned to my former tormentors. 'Let us hongi now and depart as friends.' I gripped the Uncle's hand, holding his opposite shoulder and pressing my nose to his, then repeated the ritual with his nephew. They didn't know where to look, or what to do, so withstood my attentions with as much stoicism as they could muster.

'Ah, now we are family!' I announced, and the room at last broke into rapturous applause. Even the ladies were clapping and nodding and talking all at once, and the most brave of their partners lined up to hongi me, too. My persecutors somehow managed to smile, and I hid the satisfaction I had gained from making them pawns in my game.

The Artist looked my way, but was immediately taken by the arm and drawn into conversation by several of the crowd. I wavered between embarrassment at my behaviour and something else — some kind of awareness had grown in me, I don't know how to describe it, but I began to assess my audience in a different way. Whereas at the start I had forgiven their actions as curiosity or ignorance of my people, I now interpreted the way they stood back or talked about me in my presence as arrogance. They made announcements to each other about my people and my land without ever having been there, as if gazing at even a hundred of the Artist's pictures could tell them what it was really like to be me. Only the boldest asked me questions directly, but those questions seemed posed not necessarily to hear my answer but to observe the novelty of my reply. It was all so curious to me, even though it was I who was considered the curiosity.

૭૭

In the days that followed, things followed the same pattern: I would begin enthusiastically, enjoying my interactions with our visitors, but as the day wore on I would encounter ignorant bores, or simply boredom. And so to relieve the monotony and jest my visitors I became more flirtatious. I began to devise ways to surprise them from their assumptions. But I also began to observe them more closely — how their clothes and manner of speaking gave away their origins, how they judged each other. Later in the afternoon the less well-off members of the public would begin to make a more abundant appearance, and they had an earthy, straightforward manner that would broker no nonsense. If I could make one of them laugh, I felt a sense of warmth and achievement. And it caused them to look at me again more closely, and I fancied I saw recognition in their eyes. I knew it was not completely wholesome to behave in this manner, but by this time of day I was often helpless to prevent myself. My audience seemed so pleased with my exuberance.

One afternoon near the end of our first week the Artist took his leave of the room, presumably to discuss important matters with his admirers and benefactors. My interest was waning, and the only way I could compensate for my tiredness was to pay special attention to the ladies with their soft linens and ribbons and coy ways. I remember bowing deeply (somehow my bow had become more stately and grandiose as the days wore on) to a group of young ladies who were giggling a little too loudly, and then, when I straightened, I noticed someone out of the corner of my eye.

It was his eyes that caught my attention, the blackest eyes I had yet seen on a white man, twinkling fiercely with mischief. This fancy was soon borne out, but first I took in the rest of him. Black hair, almost as curly as mine, but worn down past the collar. A moustache trimmed with a touch too much care. His dress was meticulous but curious, the cut and colour of his waistcoat indicating an uncommon individualism. He stood to my right, observing, bold in his contemplation, one hand in his jacket pocket, the other relaxed at his side, and though he was still, there was something in him that was all movement. Somehow that movement transferred itself to me and I felt a rushing in my ears. I lost my focus on the ladies momentarily and stared. He smiled, lifting one corner of his lips, and acknowledged my bewilderment with a nod.

I looked back at my audience, somewhat flustered, but played out my part, adding a wink or a flourish from time to time that sent the ladies giggling back to their amused consorts. Finally, I was left quite alone, and the dark-eyed gentleman approached me and bowed lightly, the smile not gone from his eyes or his lips.

'How do you do?' I asked.

'I am very well as you can see, and you?'

I don't know what took me in that moment. 'I am very well, but tired of this performance now and hoping for some relief.'

'Do you not live for such opportunities to bring life to the paintings of British dandies?'

I caught his tone and did not know what to do with it.

'Excuse my poor manners. I am William Smith, but my friends call me Billy Neptune: gentleman sailor, adventurer, lover of ladies and fine linens, at your service.' He bowed deeply this time and I bowed low as well, and when our eyes met on the rising motion, it was all either of us could do to hold in our laughter. 'I have heard tell on the streets of the young chief who attends this room in costume. Word is that he is a very entertaining fellow who brings his audience to rapture with his sad stories and saucy manners. And that impolite folks are soon rendered mute by this fellow's dance.'

I bowed again. 'You are very kind. I am James Poneke, son of a chief of New Zealand, as you have already discerned.' It couldn't hurt to make more of this game. 'But I am an orphan and friendless in this city, apart from my benefactor and his family. If I were to have a friend of my own age and inclinations, I should ask him to call me Hemi, the name I was known by as a boy.'

'I have already resolved that we should be friends. So, dear Hemi, what are these inclinations you speak of? My own are so varied and democratic that I am determined they should include yours as well!'

I had never heard an Englishman speak like this. There were plenty of jokers, yes. Plenty who liked to laugh and tease an innocent (or tease the innocence from a person), but Billy Neptune spoke to me as his equal, with a hint of challenge in his voice. Billy Neptune was issuing a question, an invitation, even before the words escaped his mouth. The way he held himself, I would not have been surprised if he fancied himself the son of the sea god he was named for. I could do nothing to hide my awe.

'It is nearly seven p.m.,' he said now, 'and I have frequented the Egyptian Hall enough Saturdays to know the doors will close soon. I can wait for you outside, while you take your leave of your master, and then show you the sights of my city. You will not have seen the London I will show you, young Hemi.'

'No. Indeed. I suspect not.' I looked him over again, and he withstood my scrutiny in good humour. 'Why not, Billy Neptune — I'd be delighted to accept your invitation.'

He stood back, clicked his heels together, nodded, and was gone. I adjusted my cloak around my shoulders, and felt the feathers, loose now, in my hair.

Looking back, I see that this was the moment my second education in the world began.

NINE

The day finished, I removed my costume so as to take my leave of the Artist. Something had changed in his demeanour towards me in recent days: he regarded me quietly and with a different measure of intensity, as if I wasn't quite what he expected. I hoped I had not disappointed him, but rather that my efforts had made his exhibition even more popular with his audience. When I tried to say as much, I could not find a way to address the matter directly.

'We have done well. You certainly have a way with your audience, James,' he said. 'Indeed. Your performance has been surprising, though it seems to elicit a positive response in the crowd. A little bit of excitement is good for business, perhaps.'

I nodded. 'Surely attention means success?'

He smiled broadly. 'Yes, James, I think it may. After this week, all of London will hear of us, and if they visit it should be enough for the exhibition to pay for itself.'

I returned the Artist's smile. 'If you don't mind, I've been invited to view the sights with a new friend who has made my acquaintance during the course of the day, and I should like to go. Please offer my apologies to Mr Angus and Miss Angus for missing what I am sure will be a fine meal this evening.'

The Artist's demeanour shifted once more.

'Do you not think you should return with us? You cannot trust every person you meet — you're still fresh to these streets, and how will you find your way back? There are many dangers. Who is this new friend?'

'His name is William Smith.' I thought it better not to use Billy's preferred name. 'Mr Smith seems very trustworthy and very knowledgeable, and will surely help me home.'

'I do not know the fellow, and I must entreat you again to return with me. We have some responsibility for your wellbeing.'

The truth is, I could think of nothing the Artist might say that would prevent me from going.

'I'm sorry, sir. I do not mean to appear ungrateful, but I have been in London many weeks now, and have not made any friends apart from yourself and your dear family, and even though I am privileged by your company... Well, sometimes a young man seeks the companionship and robust humour of boys his own age.'

He regarded me again.

'Yes, well. I find I cannot argue with that logic. We've all done such things. But do be careful, James. Guard yourself until you are sure.'

◎◎

Mr Billy Neptune was waiting for me under the streetlamp outside the main doors of the Egyptian Hall. I was struck once more by how, even in stillness, there was something about him that spoke of motion. He faced away from me, looking into the street, and puffed on a short-stemmed sailor's pipe, his leg cocked so that he cut a casual figure as he leaned against the pole.

'Mr Neptune!' I called out.

He turned and grinned. 'That's Billy,' he said. 'You should call me Billy.' I noticed then an unusual lilt to his speech I had not noticed before. 'And Hemi — have you ever been to The George? It's not far from here, the one I'm thinking of. There are at least three further afield if you don't like the look of it.'

I had no idea what 'The George' was and why there were so many, but I could make a guess. 'No, I haven't been there, sir, but I'm willing to acquaint myself with the look of it!'

I found myself half skipping to keep up with Billy as he led the way through the streets.

'You'll have to leave the formalities aside if we are to be friends,' he said. I was half a step behind him and couldn't comprehend how he managed to walk so fast, talk and puff smoke from his pipe all at the same time. 'I'm not usually a George man, really, but you seem to have the right bearing for it. I usually head back to Southwark. That's where I stay, that's where my girl is, and many local establishments of good quality. But the day has been long, and you could use the respite, I can see, and when we're done here we shall turn our attention elsewhere if the evening isn't finished with us.'

I liked the familiarity of his talk — his place, his girl, his local establishments. We were from different ends of the Earth but it was as if he spoke my language. I wondered if he would feel the same way if I spoke to him of my home in my native language, but of course it would have no familiarity for him.

'Speak to me in your tongue,' Billy said, only minutes later.

119

I was shocked at him, this new companion who it would seem had the ability to hear my thoughts.

'Ah, don't look so alarmed now, Hemi. I like to hear the sounds of a foreign country and I've been to a few of them.'

'Ae, he tangata mohio koe. Pirangi ahau ki te tino mohio ki to ao ki nga mea katoa o tou ao. He orite pea taua?'

'Aye, that is a good sound, my friend. Reminds me of Tahiti.'

What a strange and entertaining fellow this Billy was.

∞

We walked towards the river but did not cross it. This part of the city was busy with traffic, even at night. There were shows to see — theatres, music halls, halls of illusion and spectacle. Places to eat and drink — public houses, gin houses, cook houses, pie shops, oyster and fish costers. High entertainments and low. Billy gave me a running commentary of each place and its offerings, the kinds of people who frequented it, the costs and likelihood of an excellent time to be had. He bade me protect my purse from rabble and the robbers who lingered at each corner and doorway.

'People are desperate, Hemi,' he told me. 'This is a town of fortunes to be gained and lost in a night, and hunger to avoid with each step or be gained with each mis-step.' He had been working with luck all his life, he said, until he was comfortable enough with her proclivities to fancy himself her match. Sometimes I could barely keep up with Billy Neptune's turns of phrase, but he made such pleasant sounds I was happy enough to relax into his voice. And he was happy enough to use it. To me the language of the streets will always be the swift, soft ramble Billy was prone to embark upon should any opportunity arise. There was a song to him.

I look back now and see what a romantic and foolish boy I was. From that first day Billy told me about the dangers and hungers of his streets. I didn't truly understand him, though I thought I did. I nodded and smiled, or frowned in consternation, but I was so taken by his lilting tongue, by the tallness of buildings and solidness of roads, by the gathering of more people than even existed on all the islands of New Zealand. He could not have torn the blinkers from my eyes if he had shown me a corpse. The filth underfoot and the shadows of the night held only adventure. Looking into my eyes, seeing only his own twinkle shining back at him, Billy must have realised he had the opportunity of a playmate in all things fun and jest but with little comprehension of more serious matters.

So he found The George, and bought me a tankard of beer. It didn't take long before I was overtaken by a warmth that spread to my toes and teased my senses. My limbs and lips were soon soft and heavy. The excitement of the day and the pleasures of the night crowded in. This beer was darker and stronger than anything I had tasted before.

Billy seemed to know everyone. After a while I gathered he might not know every person as intimately as it seemed; he simply greeted each new face as if he had known them all his life. 'All right?' he'd ask a stranger in the most familiar tone, or 'How are you then, Tommy?', even if he didn't know whether his companion's name was Tom. I liked it a great deal, the way he made everyone his own. The ladies liked it too, I could tell, the ones who frequented places such as this. I was a naïve boy, but I knew these were an altogether different type of people than I had encountered thus far. We sat at one long, low bench, right in the middle of the room. The more private booths with their dark wood and pretty glass windows were already occupied. A stream of people came and went beside us, using the table for their drinks, often remaining upstanding. The clamour was spectacular. We had to yell at each other.

'So what do you think of this George then, Hemi?'

'It is a fine place and I am very happy with the drink,' I shouted.

'Aren't we all happy with the drink, my friend?'

'Aye, a bit too happy, I venture.' This from a young man who'd arrived just as a great cheer rose up for a fiddler who had begun to play around the room. 'It's taken me all night to figure out where you were, Billy.'

'My apologies, Henry, I forgot we had an appointment. But look who I have with me! It is Hemi Poneke, son of a chief of New Zealand, on his first night out in the capital city of England. Isn't he a fine specimen of humanity?'

Henry looked me up and down. 'A fine specimen all right, Billy, but fine enough to keep you from your regular responsibilities? I don't know. Let's take him with us to the theatre and see what fun is to be had there.'

Billy placed his arm around his friend's waist. I thought this must be a sign of friendship I hadn't yet encountered in London, but then Billy grinned at me and pulled Henry towards him to kiss him on the lips — a surprising and protracted affair. Henry did not look surprised, but eventually did stand, and wipe his mouth, before draining his glass and offering me a wink.

'Never mind him. Billy is the quintessential show-off.' Henry offered his hand to me, and I noticed it was small and gentle, though it was hardened by work. 'Henrietta Lock. Just call me Henry. It's the way of things, Mr Poneke, that this here gentlemanly outfit makes my life a little easier as often as it makes my life a little harder. Billy mauling me in a public house certainly doesn't help.'

And then I saw it in the shape of Henry's cheek, the way

her jacket hung more loosely around the shoulders. I laughed again, and felt such great affection for my two new friends that I drained my own glass in one merry gulp, shaking my head as I placed it down. Billy patted me on the shoulder as he made to stand.

'You have not known woman until you've known a woman who is confident as a man,' Billy said.

I did not tell him that I had not yet known woman at all. Or that his and Henry's riddles had my head spinning. But I thought they made a fine couple, and though it was unusual, it was not unheard of in my own upbringing to see men and women play at being more like the other. Still I knew it was taboo in the Christian world for a man to be with another man, and this little play of Billy and Henry's had me confused for that reason alone.

Billy pulled me along. 'Come on, Hemi, we'll find you someone to kiss before the night is through.'

I hesitated, and he looked back.

'Why the consternation? It's not such a thing. Not to us who wander the nights. But we won't push you into the arms of anyone you're not ready for!' He grinned again, and I skipped after him.

Henry was already bounding ahead of us, tipping her hat at passing ladies.

୭⊘

The noise and colour and commotion of all the people crowding into the theatre was a different kind of dazzlement from the one I'd experienced in Regent's Park and Piccadilly. The ladies and gentlemen here were not as finely dressed and were much less genteel, but there was something loud and fearless and *understood* in all of it, as if beneath their tumbling yells and jibes another conversation was being spoken, a conversation everyone had the key for, except me. The fabrics they wore were not as fine and their perfume not as sweet; even so, I loved the high colour in their cheeks, and the earthiness of the odour, like the steamy muck of pigs in a pen.

I had the feeling, as we peered over the heads of those in front of us, that my companions were watching me, and when I caught Billy's eye I saw that there was much amusement there. I must have looked quite wide-eyed and impressionable, for I was swept away with the excitement of the crowd. Here was a splendid tribe, not unlike the tribes I had known at home, and I felt warm in the cradle of it.

First we were entertained by a singer who moved in such a sultry fashion I felt redness rise in my cheeks, then by a man who claimed he could cut the singer in half — and, what's more, seemed to do so by placing her in a box. Even after dividing her in two she appeared to live still! There were dancing bears, and more song, and a man who came out telling stories so funny the crowd roared, though I couldn't discern his accent or his meaning well enough to understand him. At that point I needed the privy so badly I could not concentrate on the rest of the show, but I stayed in my place, for I wouldn't know where in the city I was without my companions.

At last the crowd surged out of the theatre. After I'd relieved myself in a dank corner, as I observed others doing, I found Billy in his customary position, leaning against the pole of a streetlamp, preparing to light his pipe. 'A drink!' he exclaimed when he saw me. 'And victuals! I know just the place.'

Henry had her own pipe lit and was busy chatting with a group of young women, but then we were off again, dragging her away, dashing through the streets towards the Thames.

Billy found a waterman to take us swiftly downriver, and we disembarked at Southwark. Here Billy took me by the shoulder.

'Look, Hemi, my fine friend, I know this part of town probably isn't what you're accustomed to. Don't tell your masters we took you here, or they might not like it. Not the prettiest side of town. But I know these streets like I know my heart and I can keep you safe.'

It might have been the first time I thought about Billy's heart and its contents.

'He always accompanies me home after the theatre,' said Henry, extending her vowels so that she suddenly sounded like Miss Angus. 'And then if you two are up for more, he'll continue to corrupt you, no doubt.'

'Argh, Henry, such a terrible friend,' Billy roared. Then they were chasing each other, grabbing and fondling, and I had to look away.

'Perhaps I should return,' I called after them. 'To the Anguses. You two go ahead!'

'No, Hemi, the night is yours. And Henry tires of us. Come on!'

We walked, a jolly group, towards Henry and Billy's residence, which I could see would be nothing like the one I had woken in that morning. The houses in this part of town were much in need of repair, or had been repaired poorly. There was more refuse and filth to step around, the smell of something indescribable but offensive below all the others.

'This is where I grew up, Hemi,' said Billy, 'And now Henry lives here, too. She can keep the room when I have to go back to sea.'

'Or I might return to the docks.'

'Well, there's that, too.'

'I don't know about those sailors though, Jimmy. A girl likes to be left alone from time to time.'

'What would you know about what a girl likes, Henry?' Then they were at it again.

For my new friends I loved this place. I loved the mysteries of it. The warrens of streets, the map in my companions' minds that caused them to choose this alleyway over that, to find their way past fallen brick tenements and fallen men and women. Yet seeing those poor people sleeping out sent a pain to my heart, and I did not understand, nor did I know what to do, so numerous were they. A shadow fell over Billy's eyes when I asked him.

'This is London, young Hemi. The poor are so common it's as if we paint our streets with them. What can you or I do? I've seen this all my life and haven't figured a way to make it better. I'm happy it's not that way where you come from. Here the only thing we can do is look after our own, and hope our fortunes keep us from the same fate.'

I nodded. It seemed inadequate, *I* seemed inadequate in the face of it. I imagine in your time such scenes are a thing of the past, my mokopuna, but in my time, when progress and enlightenment are just beginning, people are easily discarded. And despite myself I let my concerns slip easily from my grasp. What could I do in the face of such immense poverty? I put it away, to the side, in a pocket I wouldn't search for a long time. A hundred paces along I allowed the pleasures of the evening to beckon once more.

Then we were at a door, giving our goodbyes to Henry, and were away, with Billy striding on ahead.

'Another George!' he said, and there we were, indeed, at another inn named after one of the kings of that name, and Billy obtained more beer for us both. It was all a fog to me by now, but I liked the homely feel of this new place, and was

126

happy simply to listen to the talk that went on — English as I had never heard it spoken, a song of riddles. Billy was full of light and energy and movement, but within the hour I had to admit I was not his equal and asked him to point the way home for me. He agreed, and took me back to the bridge from whence I was sure I could find the Angus residence.

We bowed to each other, removed our hats, and laughed.

'This is the beginning of something, Hemi — I feel it!'

All I could do was laugh and wave, though I certainly felt it too. I thought I might follow Billy any place he asked.

◎◎

The night walk through the streets back to the Angus home was most peaceful. That first night I was filled with excitement and fatigue, but on subsequent evenings it was my time to myself — a meditative interlude. Every other waking moment I was in the presence of someone else, either play-acting some grander version of myself at the Egyptian Hall, or in genteel conversation with the Anguses, or in boisterous play with Billy and Henry, some part of me always trying to keep up with their antics and prove myself equal to them. But during those night-time moments when I found myself alone I was able to take out a secret part of myself, the part that was at once mystified and fascinated, and allow him room to breathe.

The novelty of those streets has never really worn off. At night they were different from the day, lit as they were by the odd luminescence of gaslight steeped in fog — a particular magic trick that had me enthralled for some weeks. Every time I stepped outside I marvelled at the impossibility of it, and yet here it was — as if stars had been captured under glass to light our way. And if I came upon an unlit street, for there were

127

many, the black enveloped me like a blanket, the only light an occasional glow from a lamp in someone's window. The fog was too thick to see the stars or moon most nights, and I missed them, but it seemed as if I blended in more, as if this was my city as much as anyone's. Everything was shades of yellow and blue-black, as if no other colours existed after dark. Thus, I myself was the same colour as everyone else, and the shadows took care of the rest. I should have been frightened, I think, yet I felt so comfortable in my own skin there was no fear in me, the tension I carried during the day gone. I certainly saw things, and learnt who to avoid. Learnt who to greet and how to do it in a way that showed I was minding my own business.

You would likely laugh at the things that fascinated me: the bricks, the signs, the advertising pasted around shopfronts. My night was filled with this streetside reading, and with taking in the style and measure of people and monuments and buildings. If I was lucky I would see into rooms as I passed, dim candlelight exposing the lives within. At night I could brush the flank of a horse or tip my hat to a lady without causing alarm. I know they were not thought of as ladies, the ones I saw out on the streets, but they were all ladies to me, all somehow out of reach, and I had no desire to bring them within reach, only to admire, and watch, to listen to the cadence of their sing-song words and insults. I would never speak unguarded around ladies of Miss Angus's standing, and I missed the ease with which women back in my homeland treated me as a brother or cousin.

Other nights, when I did not see Billy or Henry, I stayed home with the Anguses, and we played cards or read, sometimes aloud. I enjoyed these evenings too, even if they had a different set of rules to abide by, and I often puzzled over them. It was the card games I enjoyed most. Mr Angus's favourite was Speculation, which he was always best at, though I was more partial to a simpler game called Commerce, which required the matching of cards in certain patterns or sets to win. When the Artist was home we were able to play Whist, Miss Angus's favourite and one that took the most concentration on my part.

I found much contrast between the two worlds I now found myself living between — the right side of the city and the wrong side of the river, perhaps. The meeting place for these two different groups was the Exhibition Hall, where it was not uncommon to meet both the most genteel and the least. I was a sight and a fascination to them all. At the Hall, they were all on the same side, all home, and real, and I was a figment of their imaginations, as unreal as a character in a storybook. Until I shocked them with the sound of my English-speaking voice, or touched their gloved hands, so that suddenly the boundary between them and me blurred, and they did not feel so real themselves, and they were not quite so sure of the way of things any more. But then, after a moment or two, they moved on. As soon as they were finished with the exhibition, they left the Hall behind, with me contained in it, and their world returned to the correct order. One or two might look behind, or think on it later as they readied themselves for tea, or remark on it over card games in the parlour that evening. And I would go out into the streets with Billy and Henry and watch their world with as much fascination as a child at a magic-lantern show.

TEN

Many mornings, since that first day at the zoo and Colosseum, I had left the house before breakfast to walk in Regent's Park. Often it was dark when I rose, but it was the only time of day the streets were clear of the thick fog of coal smoke that obscured all sights. I slipped past still sleepy houses, dew clinging to my shoes and trouser hems as I began my journey around the park. I loved watching the magic of light coming into the world, as it did each morning for no other reason than the glory of it. Anything seemed possible in that in-between time.

As I walked, a pure sensation of joy would wash over me. At times like that I was aware of my fine clothes: necktie, waistcoat, frock coat, the beaver felt hat that once had been so beyond my imagining. I had done the thing I had always desired to do, and now I was to be a gentleman in a city of gentlemen. It was a fine thing that simply being Maori and clever with words had brought me to this. It was a fine thing, too, that perhaps I gave

London society a good impression of my kind. As more and more people emerged from their houses and I made my way back to the Artist's, I was inclined to observe them in a wholly positive light as they passed by or went about their business — selling coffee and warm loaves, perhaps, which I sometimes took as my breakfast. It was Billy who had started me on that habit, for on occasion we were late enough heading towards home that we observed light breaching the horizon and heard the callers who serviced the first workers.

There was another pleasure to these early-morning excursions, for every housemaid and cook had already started their day. I would often see Miss Herring as I left, and offer her a whispered good morning. From there each house offered me glimpses of women in- and outdoors, starting fires, sweeping, washing clothes or preparing the first meals of the day. What a pleasure it was to look into windows warmed by fires and lamplight, to observe strong women, some stout and some thin, cooking or snatching time to eat their breakfast. I was fascinated by that life below stairs, by the seeming warmth and homeliness of it. Life for them was hard, I knew this, but all the same it felt familiar to me. Somehow these women reminded me of Ana Ngamate, or dear Mrs Jenkins of the pub in Hollycross. It was a solitary, secret pleasure, watching through those windows.

Less than a month had passed since our first day at the Egyptian Hall when the Artist discovered me in my morning jaunt. He was dressed and ready to walk with me, so I could see he had planned the interruption. I felt a dark twist of disappointment. I had outgrown my infatuation with him now that there were so many other calls on my interests, but we passed the first quarter of our walk in pleasant discussion about the city, the new buildings and train stations being erected, the blooming flora of the park.

131

'How are you faring with this new life, Poneke?'

'I am happy, I believe — I am certainly well, thanks to the great hospitality of your family.'

'I am glad. My father and sister are the best hosts, and they like you very much.'

'I do hope so. I would like them to, as I like them.'

'Indeed. You might think on it. I have been meaning to speak with you since your first week at the Hall, the night you went with your new friend.'

Ah. There it was.

'James, be careful. You do not know the kinds of men who run loose in this city.'

'You are right, of course. It's only that — well, you don't know Billy Neptune.'

'Yes. That is the problem, you see. We can only protect you through our connections. How can we tell you what kind of person this Mr Neptune is? You told me before his name was Mr Smith.'

'I understand your concern, but I believe him to be a true friend. I do not think he would harm or betray me.'

'That may be, Poneke. Even so, the association may already be damaging to the show.'

We were circling the park at a quick pace, not the dreamy stroll with which I usually began my days.

'Ah, so that is what your real concern is.' I could not help myself — first he had circumscribed my solitude, now he was attempting to limit my friends.

'Better that you don't assume that tone. I have many concerns, of which the show is one. The other is my sister, who could stand no taint on her reputation should she come into contact with such an unlikely character.'

'I see.' So he might pay his shilling to attend the exhibition, to gawp and gape and poke at me as others did, but not to engage in genuine discourse and offer me his friendship.

'James, you may have your friends, but understand this: they should remain separate from your work with me, and from your stay at my father's house. Do not bring them to our home or our neighbourhood. And be watchful. They may not be who you think — the city streets are dangerous at night.'

'Yes. I thank you. I understand your concerns.' It was all I could manage to remain civil, and I was surprised at my strength of my feeling. I would not give Billy up. Not for the Artist or the exhibition, not even for dear Miss Angus and the generous Mr Angus. I had known Billy only a few weeks, and already he had come to mean so much to me. I should have seen it then, what lay in our future.

The Artist and I made our way home in silence. On our return, we spoke to each other cordially when necessary, knowing that we had the Hall to attend in a matter of hours.

@@

The Artist's work now took his full focus and he had no time to follow through with his earlier promises to encourage me in higher studies, though I took my own opportunities to read from his father's library or find what education the city offered up in its buildings and stores. As a result of the good reviews and income of his New Zealand venture, the Artist was now planning an expedition to the southern regions of Africa — lands that, like my own, were still relatively unknown. And before that a pictorial exhibition tour of other English towns. We were steadily growing our own separate preoccupations, it seemed. I had heard the Artist speak about his work often enough that I was no longer impressed by his talk, and sought something more. Yet I could not find any deeper connection to his interests. He had taken what he wanted from my land, and now sought to do the same in other lands: once his book sold, he would be done with us. As I felt his interest wane, so did my own. I even began to doubt my own judgement, for listening to his opinions no longer held my fascination and I wondered how it ever had. So when he asked me to accompany him on his little tour, I excused myself, pretending that I had much to do to finish my education in London. Had I already grown so far from the naïve boy who had left New Zealand those many months ago?

We were already past the middle of our season at the Egyptian Hall when, one afternoon, a man in a fine but food-flecked suit stopped to speak with me.

'This exhibition has enlightened me a great deal,' he said after some blustering introductions, during which he shook my left hand with his right and attempted to hongi (this now being my customary way to draw in the crowd), only to bang forehead and chin against mine before connecting with my nose. 'Indeed, those continents and islands so far south seem a dark mystery to us here, but your presence suggests otherwise. I am gratified to find that you, like every other native of foreign lands I have viewed or met in person, seem to be nothing more than a man after all.'

I did not know how to take this comment.

'No. You see, what I mean is…yes, well. You are not anything unusual at all.'

I may have lifted my nose hereabouts.

'I do not know what I am about today. What I am trying to say is, you are no savage, no half-beast, or embryonic or half-wild human. They would have us believe the rest of the world is populated by primitive beings not unlike zoo creatures.'

134

'Perhaps I would prefer to be like the creatures of the zoo.'

'Yes indeed, the idea is not so absurd. I have heard it is done in Europe.'

'I did not mean caged.'

He appraised me then, and blew out a sharp, dismissive breath. 'Goodness, no. You are not unlike us. I'll admit, at first I was overwhelmed with curiosity, and I have viewed every native person that has been paraded through London: the Laplanders, the Sioux, the Hottentot Venus, the Pygmies, and the Aztecs, who I do not think were from that part of the world after all, though the poor mites had other problems, evidently. Most of them came through this Hall right here. And I wondered at first, especially with the little black peoples of Africa. I'll admit, I did wonder.' And there he stood, wondering, for another long moment.

'No. No. I cannot agree.'

'With what, sir?'

He seemed so disturbed by his own pronouncements. 'With any of this. You are here of your own free will, are you, son?'

'Yes. All is well.' My story was long and I was tired. I did not know if I was prepared to recite it to this stranger.

'Hmm. It's a puzzle I can't piece together. I feel we are so very wrong in this. But here you willingly are, though I couldn't say the same for the Hottentot or some of the poor misfigured types one sometimes sees.'

'Misfigured?'

'The small, the tall, the overly fat or overly thin. The skin-diseased and mutilated. There are marrying midgets in the next room, as we speak!'

Yes. I wished very much to meet the celebrity Merry Marrying Midgets of Middlesex, whose show had opened only three days previously.

'I can speak only for myself,' I said. 'I have not been mistreated. I receive much in return.'

'Well, I suppose it is a living. I hope it is. But the prodding. Sometimes they seem humiliated.' Here he moved in so that he could lower his voice. 'I have been offered things. Perverse liberties. I was insulted and made it known, but still…'

I could not think what he wanted from me by telling me this, but his unease was certainly migrating to my own skin. Sometimes, to say plainly what one needs to know is the only method.

'What do you want of me?'

'Ha! Absolution!' He stood back, laughing at his own discomfort. 'No, dear boy, I want nothing of you. I apologise for burdening you with my concerns. My brother tells me I am too sensitive a soul by far, always worrying about those less fortunate than myself. It is clear for him that everyone has his place in society, to each his own. Profession, health, wealth, sex and race. None of these, he says, can be changed. We are born to them. We must learn our station.' He began to fuss with his gloves and hat, and it took a good time for him to sort them as he spoke. 'My big brother says I should have joined the clergy, where my do-gooding and guilt would have some use, but I am a philosopher, an anthropologist if you will, if such a thing can be said, a student of men. I cannot see absolutes like my peers.' His wardrobe complete, he bowed, and I returned the gesture.

'You see? Civilised is the only word for it. And patient, and kind, listening to my ramblings. Mr Poneke, you are a gentleman. My name is Antrobus — Richard Antrobus — and it is my privilege to have made your acquaintance this day.'

'Thank you, Mr Antrobus, the pleasure has been mine.'

'No. Not at all. It certainly hasn't!'

I stared. He had such an odd manner.

'That is to say...I mean, rather...oh young man, you must think me strange. I should like to meet with you again. I should like to involve you in some of the scientific discussions of the Royal Society — would you like that?'

'Indeed, I would.'

'I will ensure you receive an invitation to the next soirée — you and your artist.'

Thus he made his departure, not much enlightened about my life, but feeling more well in himself, I could see, from the unburdening.

I had found, over time, that each visitor required a different performance — some happiest with the exuberant play of manners I had devised on my first day, some more intent on a contemplative interaction. I had become expert in reading people, the way they carried themselves, the preconceived notions they liked to test against me. Sometimes I made a game of staying so still and quiet they may have wondered if I were more Madame Tussaud's wax figure than living flesh, and for that I earned a pinch or prod, and once a tickle. What interested me was the freedom with which people told me their own stories. I only had to make the space in front of them, make the conditions right. They had come to view some far-off part of the world in the Artist's paintings, and some other kind of person in me, though in the end I think they came only to know themselves, to understand their own thoughts and see their world or their selves reflected in our images and faces. I was made of flesh rather than paint, yes, and how much better that was. That our time at the Hall would soon finish was good, for I was beginning to lose faith in the wonder of the etchings, and in my own performance.

☙❧

137

At last I sought out the midgets in the third room of the Hall. I had seen them from afar, but our daily programmes were similar, and between the Anguses, the Artist, and Billy and Henry, I had been too distracted to linger and know them better. I was curious, just like anyone else. I wanted to see them up close. But the words of the philosopher Mr Antrobus had stayed with me too. I hoped I would find they were free and happy in their work.

The doors of the Egyptian Hall had closed for the day. The little people would soon depart for their accommodations. I watched them climb down from their platform, which had been furnished with a miniature sitting room and bedroom, and on which they play-acted the life of a married couple throughout the day. I did not know if they were a married couple in real life, but as I came upon them they were arguing as one might imagine a husband and wife do.

'Doctor Shepherd says it is the only way we can keep profits up, Esme.'

'I won't play mother to a younger, cuter woman. She is not a child! And I am not old enough to be her mother!'

'Indeed, but she is smaller, and the customers seem to calculate our age based on our size, you know that.'

They had been walking towards me, and at last I came into their sphere of conversation. They both looked up.

'Well, if it isn't the young native chief from the southern seas!'

'Oooh, what if he is a cannibal, Ernie?' They both laughed and slapped themselves. I had to laugh too, though I knew not whether it was at or with them, since they were laughing at me.

'How are you, young man?'

'And how may we be of service?' I soon learnt they always spoke in tandem.

'I have been wishing to meet you since I first saw the poster for your show. My name is James Poneke, and it is a privilege to meet you. I have never seen people as small as you in my life. It is a great pleasure.'

'Oooh, it's a great pleasure to meet us!'

'We're the smallest people anyone has ever seen.'

'That's why they come to stare, and why we eat well.'

'Oh good. You are well cared for, then?'

'Who wants to know?'

'I don't mean to be rude. Only a man came to question me, and put so many questions in my head.'

'Aye, we know the type.'

'Questions like what?'

'Like, are all your people like you, and are you happy in this work?'

'These are mighty personal questions, Esmerelda.'

'Indeed, Ernie, so very personal.'

'Do you think we should answer?'

'I think we might, if the boy answers likewise. But let us do it over an oysters and eel soup supper upstairs at The Mermaid's Bosom.'

'Ah, most fine idea, milady. Let us take him to our rooms at the Bosom!'

'The Bosom!'

They both looked at me expectantly. 'Say it, boy!'

'The Bosom?'

They fell about laughing then, and when they recovered told me the real name was The Mermaid's Tail, but of course the tail is not the part of the mermaid most sailors are interested in.

What a fine couple Esme and Ernie turned out to be. They were generous with their food, and made me sit on their most comfortable chair when we went up to their lodgings. They liked to make fun of every well-to-do gentleman or mangy dog they saw, they explained, everyone a target for their jokes, not just me, for what was the point of life without some japes? My night was filled with the sound of their laughter, a child's and an adult's laugh at the same time erupting from one throat. And The Mermaid's supper was the best I'd had so far. The midgets reminded me in an odd way of home, unless it was simply the flavour of eel and the constant teasing that made me so at ease.

After supper we drank too much port and talked into the night. No, they were not husband and wife, but brother and sister who had been doing this work since they could walk, and had kept both their parents and three normal-sized siblings well, before the parents died and the children grew up.

'And then we were alone, just me and him, and it's not a bad life.'

'Not mostly. Not now that we have the doctor —'

'— who is not a doctor —'

'— the doctor who is not a doctor. Before him there were some scoundrels. Easy enough to rob the ignorant, but that's why we got educated.'

'And when we saw the doctor with his living skeleton and his three-legged girl, we thought he might be one of the good ones.'

'— because of the horse —'

'Aye, because of the horse.'

They didn't bother to explain the horse, but they did explain the tenderness with which the doctor cared for his two original charges, both of whom died during a cold and particularly choking miasma-ridden winter.

'No constitution, see.'

'Couldn't handle the winter smells and chills.'

'Gawd, it can be worse in summer.'

'Not cold though.'

'Not as cold.'

'But the doctor keeps us well. He does all the dealings and introductions. Only takes a third of the pot.'

'Less than most.'

'Keeps us in the style to which we are accustomed, right missus?'

'But now he wants to add children to our act.'

'The wedding's getting a bit old. Families, that's what people want. Miniature families.'

'Are children used often?' I hadn't had the opportunity to ask many questions. This one elicited only pitying looks.

'Always.'

'Children is best.'

'We make our money on sweetness.'

'Prettiness.'

'Pretty as a piglet.'

'A sausage.'

'A pumpkin.'

'A pussycat.'

'A baby.'

'Yes. Sweet as babies. That's what they want.'

'Aw, look at the boy. Look at his brow all furrowed up.'

'Like a farmer's ploughed field.'

'All of a consternation.'

'It's all right, little Indian boy. You can make a good life this way.'

'Look at how comfortable we are.'

Ernie produced a little tray of sweets then, and I enjoyed the taste of each they insisted I eat.

'You can be our friend. On the circuit.'

'We come through every year or two. We've seen a Maori

troupe before.'

'No, that was Samoans. Or Aborigines.'

'Well, how do I know? We've seen your type. I'd do it myself, if I was normal size, just to make a living.'

'Don't be silly, the boy doesn't want to hear that. He's the real deal. Can't you see? No leopard skin and grease paint for him.'

'The point is, the living is decent. You'll be fine.'

'You might even be happy.'

'Sometimes we are.'

'After whisky.'

I tried to speak over the peals of giggles that erupted from them then.

'I'm sorry — you have me wrong. I am not contemplating this as a life. It is just a way to see the world. It is not my future.'

'Nice for some. What is your future then, boy?'

This was a good question.

'I would like to see more of the world. And learn more.'

'And how will you pay for that?'

I had no ready answer.

'Ah, see. Don't be so quick to dismiss the life in front of you. We could show you how to make a run at things.'

'If you should ever desire it.'

'Aye, what she said. You're a good boy. People can take advantage. We'll look after you.'

'If you need it.'

'If you need it, yes. Think on it, boy.'

'Maori Boy.'

'Indian Boy.'

'Native Boy.'

'Spicy Boy.'

'You like cards, Spicy Boy?'

Thus began our nights of cards, a regular event that took me through the next weeks as the Artist worked on his manuscript for the book and made his preparations for another expedition. Sometimes I would bring Billy and Henry to the game; sometimes I would go alone and meet the midgets' magnificent friends, like the towering Giraffe Man and the Faerie Woman whose deformed back bones had the appearance of wings. Ernie and Esme knew all the freaks of London, they told me with some pride, leaning up for their customary peck on the cheek. The way they gathered all of us to them reminded me more of the old people back home than anyone in London had before.

They weren't always so jolly. Some nights we simply sat before their fire and talked. Ernie and Esme had had a strange and sad life. Yet most of the time they were cheerful, and they took an interest in me — not even in the usual way. They were protective and kind, warning me what sorts of people to be wary of and what sorts of people to love. It seemed I was doing well on this subject. Billy and Henry were my greatest friends, and the Anguses my great allies, and in this strange new group of outcasts and mythical beings I remembered some other part of myself.

ELEVEN

Oftentimes, during the first few weeks of the exhibition, the Artist had shared our reviews over breakfast. Miss Angus and I clamoured to see how the exhibition had been received, though Mr Angus remained resolutely behind his own papers. It was evident that the Artist hoped to elicit more response from his father than he received, so he read the best parts of the reviews aloud. He was particularly pleased to see the response from *The Illustrated London News,* and read us the aspects he found most appealing before revealing that the illustration was in fact of me, depicted quite differently from the portrait he had made. In the *News* I appeared very stately in my costume, with fine features and, from other depictions I have seen, an almost Indian appearance. The Artist's own image of me, made so long ago on the shores of Te Whanganui a Tara, showed an open-faced, large-eyed boy wrapped in a cloak. I couldn't tell which likeness was more true to life. The article itself was very complimentary:

The scenic views of New Zealand are extremely beautiful; and the painter appears to have seen more of the country than any other English artist. The subjects are well chosen; whether the boiling volcano in the centre of the island, or the evening serenity of the Bay of Islands. The carved houses of the natives are minutely delineated, and impress us with their resemblance to the carvings of the ancient Mexicans and inhabitants of Yucatan… There are, also, several portraits of New Zealand belles, a few of whom appear to be as graceful in their carriage and dress as an European beauty.

But the living attraction of the Exhibition is a New Zealand youth, about fifteen years of age, who speaks English fluently, and is a very intelligent person. He excites considerable interest among the savants.

It was not bad, having one's intelligence recognised by one of the most popular publications in the city. Other reviews were equally complimentary, and the Artist took time to read each with some ceremony.

The exhibit consists of truly beautiful drawings of very strange and beautiful scenes. The Artist's work is a triumph of technical skill. To this he adds spirit and expression, and all the requisite 'effect' that Nature herself paints with sun and shade… The Artist is a young man whose genuine zeal in his art is evinced in the number and excellence of the works that adorn the walls of the gallery…

Another portrait is that of James Poneke, a boy whose genuine origin is attestedly a genealogical anecdote: his father, a chief, was vanquished and eaten, about eleven years ago, by some rival statesman. James himself, in proper person, is also to be seen in the room; and in conversation he proves to be a very intelligent lad, speaking English with facility...

They liked to talk about this, the papers: my chiefly origin and the cannibalisation of my father. Somehow the story that emerged from my performance that first day had stuck, and this was the outcome. I suspected the Artist himself shared it, for it elicited so much interest. Whenever I saw the tale repeated, I knew I was paying the price for too much pride and bravado. I did not like it, but could blame no one but myself.

Besides these pictures, which fill about two hundred frames, the Artist has brought home a little museum of curiosities: native weapons, utensils, dresses, carvings, and models of canoes, specimens of birds, minerals &c., which completely fill one of the largest rooms in the Egyptian Hall.

After reading his favourite pieces, the Artist would circulate the papers and we'd read further in detail, for some of them took more than one column. And then I would see the parts the Artist had left aside, the parts that did not praise his work but did examine the people he'd made studies of:

The views in both Australia and New Zealand are most striking from their peculiar character... The chief Rauparaha and his lieutenant have very remarkable faces; fierce, but of a true Caucasian cut: the outline of the face is slightly concave, the features well defined; the nose elevated from the face, aquiline, and as it were, well chiseled out at the tip; the lips thin. These characteristics are the very reverse of those presented by the typical New Zealand face; which, though very superior to that of the negro, is marked by a flattish nose and thick lips, and differs both from the Caucasian and African

*face in having a concave facial outline. The contrast is so great,
between Rauparaha, for instance, and the ordinary New
Zealand face, as to indicate some double and separate origin
for the inhabitants of the country.*

Sometimes I felt I did not know what I was reading; I did not
think I understood it at all.

∞

When I became bored with the Hall and its requirements of
me, and with the restraints of domestic life in the Angus home,
I yearned to be out exploring the streets with Billy and Henry.
They were the cousins I had never had. I should have been more
wary, having experienced so many loyalties cut short by life's
demands, but I knew Billy to be a true brother of my soul, and
Henry was as pure a spirit as I had ever met, despite her manly
bravado. In fact, I thought her much closer to Miss Angus
than would be guessed from outward appearances. Miss Angus
herself was unfailingly kind to me, but was tied to the house
and its proprieties, as her station demanded. I could see it in
her: the little flares of enthusiasm that signalled a keen intellect
and desire for more freedoms than her situation allowed; but
it would have taken an uncommon steeliness to escape the
confines of the roles assigned to her. Henry had that iron in
her, and her position demanded it of her anyway.

I saw my friends every second or third evening, and while
they showed me their favourite places to eat or drink or sing or
hide, their stories came out, piece by piece, and my admiration of
them grew. They had come, by now, to know what would impress
me. Despite my love for all things intellectual and genteel,
it was the loud and gaudy that really filled me with delight:

147

mechanical and moving pictures, tricks of the imagination. The Colosseum's Panorama was only the beginning; we explored the Diorama, the Cosmorama, the Panopticon. Sometimes there were shows by actors or with tricks of light that took place alongside great images of cities with strange names like Timbuktu or Constantinople. At Mr Shrewsbury's Emporium of Wonders we took in a show so ghostly that I was overtaken by shivering. Were they real spirits I had seen? I couldn't believe people made such otherworldly sounds, or that they had devised a way of making images so lifelike yet transparent. I could not shake the idea that my dead people might find me here, so far from home.

Back at The George, Billy thought it amusing that I was so disturbed by the scene. "Tis only the magic of ghost work first devised for the Phantasmogoria!' he said, as if such a word should mean anything to me. 'It's a common enough trick these days, Hemi.' And seeing that this did nothing to allay my fears, he clasped an arm around my shoulders. 'I will look after you should the ghosts come to tickle your soul, my brother.' He pushed a full mug towards me.

Henry was more solemn. 'We all have our ghosts, Billy,' she said. I stopped my shivering and Billy swallowed his grin. Henry was a girl not given to such a quiet, contemplative tone.

'Billy knows about mine,' she went on. 'Father is always there, even though I can't see or hear or smell him no more. He died when I was just a poppet — seven or eight years, I suppose, the second eldest of three sisters and two brothers. It was just his time, my mother says, just his time. But I think she says that to make it better, because he had a family that had only just begun its growing, so why would it be his time already? Perhaps God is that cruel. Common enough, ain't it, Billy? Babies on the streets.'

Her words took me to my own infancy, so long ago now, it seemed.

Henry told us all of it then. There was an insistence in her voice that bade us make no interruption. It was as if, once started, the story had to be seen all the way through. Billy must have heard it before, but he held himself in for the telling. It was the most still I think I ever saw him.

It was a pestilence that had taken Mr Johnny Lock away, and lucky it didn't take the children and their mother too. Something in his lungs. But then his cab work had him on the streets most of the night, breathing in smoke and shivering through the cold. The rest of the family were lucky: Mrs Lock had skill with the needle that kept her indoors with her children. The eldest two were girls, and that meant she could train them up for piecework and they could take care of the three baby boys while she handled the orders. Henrietta was a help with the sewing of clothes and linens, but it was her elder sister who showed precocious talent for her age: Mary's stitches were so fine Mrs Lock was determined to apprentice her to a milliner, for a good living could be made with fingers like those. Henrietta's stitches were clumsy by comparison.

But what did it matter? There were more exciting things to do in life than sit in a house, sewing. So much more excitement to be had on the street. Back in the days when there were fewer children, her father seemed to have more time for a Sunday ramble. He had once taken her and her sister to see a show with puppets and a menagerie and acrobats in red and green and gold — so light, twisting and turning in the air, bouncing as if they had legs like crickets', looping and throwing their hoops and ribbons and balls. But that was not the thing that kept coming back to her for weeks and months and years afterwards. It was the lady acrobat who ran up mid-performance and offered Henrietta a flower that emerged magically from behind her own ear. It wasn't just the magic; it was the way the lady held her and every other spectator with her gaze, manipulated them with her expressions, beguiled them with her sinuous form. This lady was different from any other lady Henry had ever seen.

For two years after her father died, the family had managed to survive by piecework and selling the occasional windfall of flowers or feathers or fruit. But there was never quite enough to fill everybody's belly, and what little they had soon started to be sold away to buy food. Then Ma began to go out for long days and eventually nights. Henrietta and her sisters worried about what their mother must be doing, and how she paid for the soft loaves and cheese or herring she brought home. They hadn't seen oranges for a long time, but here they were in their mother's pocket, and sometimes gingerbread or a pudding. Finally, she came home one morning and told them to gather up everything they had. They were moving to the docklands, to a house in which she had rented two rooms. So they moved to the two rooms and it was more comfortable than what they were accustomed to, but there was a man there too, and he shared the second room with their mother while the children slept by the hearth.

I won't tell you his name, Henry said. He was all right. We didn't pay him much attention and he paid little to us. We kept out from underfoot, and he stayed in the comfort and manner of a married man, with a wife to cook for him and keep him warm, until he was due to leave on his next ship. It was quiet then, for a day or two, or noisier perhaps, with no man to mind. But Ma again took to spending more time away from the house until she returned with more food, sometimes with a new husband too. Those were most often the good times, the times when there was a steady man in the house. Their ma had become single-minded about her business, and it was better than giving herself away on the street or in some pleasure garden, she told them. As long as the men were kind, or at least tolerant, she'd let them come and stay, take their meals in the bosom of a family. Sometimes they took a liking to fatherhood, played with the children, especially the boys. But sometimes they were drunks. For the most part, it didn't matter. None of them stayed long.

Though they did come back. The men were regular. No weddings involved. No, that was only for her first and real husband, Ma said, and God forbid he'd be looking down at her from Heaven now, though if he did she thought he'd understand. And they had other wives at other ports, these husbands of hers — she knew this even if nobody talked about it. Far be it for her to question God's laws, but plenty of women did it, and what's sauce for the goose is sauce for the gander, not to mention all the little goslings.

That was all right, said Henry again, but what was she to do? Mary would find a place, the boys would find apprenticeships, but Henrietta feared her lot in life might resemble her mother's. The infinite possibilities of the world came down to this small space, then, and she wanted none of it. Not the men, not the children. Not a life of service or factory work. She felt herself too clever for that. She wanted freedom and the chance to live off her own ideas. She'd always been uppity and too proud, said Mary, when Henrietta intimated as much. She would soon be a woman, and her choices would funnel into so few alternatives it made her head hurt to think of it. But there were people in the world who could twist their bodies in ways so unexpected no one asked them to follow the same rules as normal folk. There were people who could mesmerise with the right flick of eye or tongue or hair. People who got away with things, who went outside what everyone knew as the way things are.

In the end, something else decided matters. Her mother arrived home in the early hours of a spring morning, and she was not alone. Henrietta heard it outside the door: the low, insistent rumble of a man's voice; Ma quiet and placating. There was movement, not quite struggling, Ma's voice becoming more insistent, the man's taking on a sharp edge. Then he was in the room, striding about, touching things.

'Please,' Ma said, 'you'll wake the children.' All of them in the one bed, Henrietta holding herself still so as not to draw attention or wake the little ones.

'Soon old enough to work,' the man said. He was so close to the bed she could smell the rotten-apple reek of him.

'They do work.'

'Not that kind.'

She heard him move before she felt him lift the cover. It was all she could do to keep herself still. He cleared his throat, hawked and spat on the floor as he let the cover drop. Then he made a sound that was meant to be a laugh but had no laughter in it.

She heard his footsteps recede, her mother opening the door and barring it behind. Ma moved to the fireplace, sank down on the chair. Henrietta's eyes were open at last, but she was shaking so violently she had to leave the bed and sit by her mother's knee.

'Shhh,' Ma said, 'shhh.' Her hand patting Henrietta's head. But the tremor in her voice held tears, and fear, and hatred. They sat like that while light crept into the room, and before her siblings began to stir Henrietta made a decision.

'No,' she said. 'Not ever.' Her mother would know her meaning.

'I wouldn't wish that for you, Henrietta. No. But I don't know if — I don't know if I can stop it. I don't know how —'

'No, Mother —' She had thought on it. Figured out how it might work. Puzzled it out during the long days of her adolescence. 'I think — well, I'd like to go by Henry now. I'd easily get work, a strong boy like me. You'll see.'

Her mother would doubt her abilities until she saw. If a woman could hold an audience in her thrall, then surely a clever girl could make herself out to be a boy. She would trim and adjust her father's remaining clothes, mimic the stance of boys and men in the street, and go out into the world. Her sister was due to leave, and maybe people would assume she had gone too. The world was what you made it. If you could just imagine it. She found their sharpest knife and hacked off her own knot of hair, right there, and her mother cried and slapped her half-heartedly, shaking and laughing until she finally embraced her new son.

She doubted herself, of course. It was an audacious plan. Some people saw right through her, but some bought the illusion wholeheartedly, and gave her work. She was taller than boys her age and just as strong. By the time they started overtaking her in size she had already perfected their manner, and built strong connections of supply and demand. She could sell a mousetrap to a rodent, if she had a mind to it. All you had to do was watch your customer, see behind their eyes what they wanted, what they dreamed of. Everyone but the darkest souls wanted to believe, she said. Everyone wants to think someone or something can fill the hole in their soul. Sometimes Henry was frightening with all her knowing.

'But my father, it's hard not to be haunted by him when I carry him on my back.' She swallowed her last mouthful of ale. 'I like to think he wouldn't be ashamed to have a son like me.'

Henry's voice faded then, but I was still curious about one thing. I had seen Billy gazing on her with as much devotion as I think one person could ever bestow on anybody, and I had a sudden desire to be the recipient of that gaze. What was the thing that made her irresistible to him, even dressed as she was?

'You want to know about us, don't you, Hemi? Everyone always does, those what we tell our woeful tales to.' Billy was grinning now, ready to take centre stage. 'My dearest, sweet Henrietta was known only to me as Henry for as many weeks as it took to build a strong trade between us. You know I make my living by sea, Hemi, but sometimes I bring something a little precious and exotic home to keep me on land for a while, and Henry was regular at the docks, looking for new wares to trade. So last time I come back from the East I brought with me a good supply of bright silks that I knew would fetch a good price if the buyers got the worth of it. I'd heard of this trader who knew a thing or two about the cloth market and had good links to the dressmakers in town. So I made inquiries. This man was known for trading well and trading fair, and when I met him I liked him immediately and decided to make him my friend. Much like you, Hemi. We spent a lot of time together over the following weeks, didn't we, Henry? Even after the cloth was gone and we'd both moved on to other things.'

Henry had a little more colour in her cheeks, and she rewarded Billy with a small smile.

'The strangest thing was happening, though, and it almost made me stop seeing my new friend.' Here Billy paused for effect, and hunkered down in his seat. 'I liked him too much. I wanted to spend all my time with him, and when we weren't in each other's company, I thought of him constantly. I'm not that kind of man, Hemi. I've been the subject of advances. It's something you come across when your tastes are as varied as

154

mine. But I only ever wanted ladies. Until Henry.'

'Watch who you call a lady, sir!' Henry teased, low and soft.

'Then one day he did it. He kissed me, and I didn't push him away, I couldn't push him away. I soon learnt Henry's secret.'

Henry laughed. 'Do not look so surprised, Jimmy. Inhabiting this mantle of masculinity makes me more bold than is acceptable for a woman. I was shy with him, though,' she said. 'First because he didn't know I wasn't a man, and second because he was my first.'

My face must have shown my shock.

'Ah. Fine young Hemi. Just because I behave like a man doesn't mean I have to succumb to their baser instincts. Though I have had my share of fair lovers. Aye, fair. I couldn't resist sharing sweet words and a few kisses with the ones who showed an interest. They liked that I was gentle and didn't require more of them than they were able to give. I liked the softness of them and the warmth of embraces I could never fully reciprocate. I think if I'd had the choice I might have chosen to be fully a man.'

Billy didn't look impressed at the prospect.

'Don't worry, my love. I cannot, of course. But let's not pretend you're going to make an honest woman of me, or that life wouldn't be easier if I could simply be what I pretend I am. And if I don't find the gentler sex abhorrent to my manly sensibilities, why not? 'Tis more harmless than playing with the men.'

'But you don't need to, now that you have your Billy to carouse with.'

'Albeit so, young Billy goat is often away at some other port with a dusky maiden in arms. Poor Henry must make do with local talent.'

I was embarrassed with their terrible teasing of each other.

It was as if their passion would become more ardent if they brought each other to the edge of anger. They had simply brought me to the edge of confusion. I kept seeing Henry in Billy's arms when he thought her still a lad. I saw him succumb to his desire to kiss. I had heard of it, but the possibility had no substance to me before then. I tried to imagine what came after, and Henry transformed to some other boy with a bare, flat chest. But I could not go any further, even in my mind.

When they began preparing to leave, I was relieved to make my departure.

'We'll walk you home, Hemi!'

'No — it is far out of your way. I am accustomed to these streets now. I'll be fine.'

'Are you sure? We can't abandon you to the dark shadows.'

'You won't be. I'll keep to the well-lit lanes, and blend into the shadows if I spot trouble. What use is skin like mine if I can't do that?'

They laughed with me, and were gone.

౷

You know how well I loved to walk these streets at night. But this night I saw everything differently — more enhanced perhaps, certainly more bright of colour. I passed a butcher's just as he was beheading a beast, a scene of horror on another night, and it seemed like a red dance, the lamplight glancing off his muscled arms as they worked, the blood flowing, splashing the floor and his trouser leg. I passed by dark or glowing windows and people on the street, said hello to some, avoided others — the same misery and joy as any other night, depending which part of their evening each individual had reached — tonight it was all glorious to me.

It had been there from the start, I knew, but Henry's story changed everything. Not everything I knew, but everything it was possible to feel. She had opened up a world in which Billy could look at a man and feel love, and act on it. A world in which I could do the same. It was a secret feeling in me, but perhaps there was a way to make it real — just as Henry had changed her fortunes through fortitude and believing other ways were possible. It was euphoria I felt as I walked, euphoria at this world made of more things than I could dream. How many times in my life had I been fortunate enough to see a new world revealed behind the one I thought was real?

TWELVE

The invitation arrived three days after I met kind Mr Antrobus at the Egyptian Hall. He was a scientist of sorts, as he had intimated, and a very close associate of the Marquis of Northampton, due to his extensive involvement with the Royal Society. As president of the society, the Marquis extended an invitation to the Artist, 'and the New Zealand Chief, Mr Poneke, to the fourth and concluding *conversazione*, Saturday, at his Lordship's mansion, on the Terrace, Piccadilly'. This was not far from the Egyptian Hall itself, and we could attend after Saturday's show.

Let me paint a picture for you, since I had never before seen anything like the room I entered, and I suspect you have not experienced such sights either, even from our future. The ceiling was carved in the most elaborate patterns and swirls with heavenly bodies dancing upon it. I could have stared at this for many hours, had it not seemed rude and hurt my neck to do so. All of this was set out in the most dazzling white, offset by gold trimmings on picture and mirror frames, and by brilliantly hued table arrangements. Terrestrial and cosmic globes were placed at various stations, illuminating the world beneath our feet and the heavens above us. I was struck by the density with which the room was inhabited, both by breathing men and their painted and sculptured forms. Along the far wall was one very large painting, in which the figures were greater than life-sized. Even from my position I could see a soldier returning home in his red jacket, revelry and a market all around him. What astounded me most was the feeling that I was looking into a true distance at the painting's centre, and that I was looking into another man's life. Perhaps you have seen such wonders. If so, I hope you can locate that feeling now — of an experience that expands your world suddenly and in ways you cannot anticipate. For this is what the Royal Society soirée did for me.

My new friend Mr Antrobus met the Artist and me soon after we entered. I don't think I've ever seen the Artist so agitated in his manner. He had dressed even more meticulously than usual. I was in my native costume, which the Artist assured me was what the men of the Royal Society would desire. To my delight, Mr Antrobus was as flustered and odd as ever, and introduced us to each man we came upon. It was fortunate that I was so well practised in my manners, and so ignorant of the men assembled, for I did not find myself as nervous and obsequious as my benefactor was.

I can remember but a few of the names we encountered that night now — the Earl of Shaftesbury, for example, Viscount Mahon, Lord Cottenham — but I was, it is true, dazzled by the number of earls and lords and men of God I was privileged to meet. The Bishops of Oxford, and of Jamaica — a place wholly unfamiliar to me then — though these we did not approach except to bow in passing. And then there were the many doctors and learned men, all in various ways like Mr Antrobus — inquisitive, deep thinkers, extensive in each exchange. I pride myself on my knowledge of many things, but some of their conversations slipped past me, especially when they turned to the politics of the day. When they turned to matters of science and technology — well, then I felt myself attune most precisely to their cause. And of course there was art, which seemed to be somehow connected to the great technologies and preoccupations of the Royal Society.

'I keep seeing your eye stray to the Marquis' grand painting on that far wall,' said a gentleman who had been introduced to me as Mr Broughton. 'It is "A Soldier's Return from the War". I like it too — it celebrates the common soldier rather than the general. Quite progressive for the Marquis, though I do believe I heard him discuss replacing it.'

'Why would he do that?'

'Ah, well, it pays to keep up, doesn't it? All that war nostalgia is fine, but we live in a new age, as you'll see tonight. I believe the Marquis has been eyeing up a painting of a steam engine, maybe even a Turner. Not my taste, but he likes to make an impact.'

'Turner?'

'Damned confusing artist. I like my pictures a bit more... pictorial.'

'Yes, you would, Broughton. You like things black and white, fair and square, in straight lines.' This was Mr Antrobus.

'Indeed I do. But a little colour never hurt anyone either, eh boy?' At this he nudged me with his elbow, winked, and flapped his gloves so that the servant might notice his empty hand and bring him a glass.

'There are a great many politicians here this evening.' Mr Antrobus's head bobbed as if he were counting.

'How many do you count, Antrobus?'

'At least ten MPs.'

'MPs?'

'Yes, and even more lords.'

'Keep your eyes peeled for Peel, boy.'

'Don't tease him, Broughton.'

'I don't mind, but what if I do see him?'

'Make yourself scarce.' Mr Broughton bellowed with laughter, then he was off making the same joke to some other men.

The Artist excused himself then, and began to circulate among the other guests. Mr Antrobus watched him go, then turned to look at me intently. 'How are you faring, Poneke?'

'I must admit I grow tired of the Exhibition Hall, and I never thought I would. The Artist plans further exhibitions elsewhere, but I have declined his invitation to attend.'

'I can see why. Such an odd occupation — professional spectacle. But do you not wish to see more of our country?'

'Ae. Yes, I do. But the Artist has graciously accepted my refusal to do it in such a way. He says we are even, all exchanges equal, and I expect he is correct. Utu is fulfilled.'

'Utu?'

'Fees paid. Reciprocation complete.'

'A fine concept.'

'Very important to my people.'

'Ah, yes, the noble race. I would so like to see your people one day, to see you amongst them. In your homeland, that is. I fear we Englishmen get so caught up in our own ways, we do not see the world beyond our borders. Sometimes even when we go there.'

'Why do you think that is, Mr Antrobus?' I did so like the

way this man thought about things, and I wished to draw him out.

'I do not know, Poneke. I cannot understand it, for if I had the means to travel, I would enmesh myself in new worlds as fully as I am able. I would probably "take the blanket", as they say, if you gather my meaning. But I am not the right specimen of Englishman to ask.'

'Perhaps I am the right New Zealander to ponder the question. I think I have been trying to "go native" here, as you say, but I do not know if I see — really see — as I should. I see like a wide-eyed child of New Zealand some moments, like a too-wise elder at others, but for the most part, like the careless, unencumbered young man that I am. Yet at the same time I am valued for my difference, and asked to play it up. Look at me now, in my native costume. I do not dress thus in my homeland. My oddity may, in fact, be the only value I have. The only thing that keeps me from ridicule, at least, at quite the same moment as it leaves me open to ridicule.'

'Goodness. No, I say. Do not think it so.'

'I am not sentimental about it, sir. People are kind. Very kind, in fact, even when they see me as an object of entertainment. I have seen how those with nothing live here in this city. I have something of value, something to exchange. He utu. I have that.'

'I see. Indeed.'

'But I do not know if it is enough. I do not know if it is the right thing. Should a man be valued only for his skin? For the odd phenomenon of his birth?'

'For the stories he tells?'

'Yes, stories have worth. But people don't come for that. They come to look, and they have some pre-made story of their own which they apply to their vision of me, and for the most part they do not ask me to speak.'

162

'No. That would not do.'

'Unless it is to fill a script, like our little friends.'

'Ah, the Merry Midgets.'

'I try to become one of you in my daily life outside of the Hall. But of course I cannot. The greatest performance in the world would not allow me to do so, for my skin is a giveaway, my hair is too wild. Like Ernie and Esme, I can only be what others see, only inhabit what they ascribe to me.'

Poor Mr Antrobus seemed alarmed at the morose direction our conversation had taken. 'Do not feel upset at my pronouncements,' I said. 'I only ponder it as a philosophical question. Can a man escape the fate dictated to him by circumstance, appearance or the prejudices of his fellows, no matter how enlightened they think themselves?'

'Indeed, Poneke. My dear boy, you are quite something. Quite something unexpected.'

'I apologise. I have said too much.' I had said things I had not even known I thought. 'Please let us move on.'

'It is an honour, young man, to be the recipient of such musings. Though I agree, perhaps we can reconvene this most interesting discourse at a later time. Let me think on it some more. It is a question for the times we live in, don't you think? I dare say no man should underestimate one such as yourself, despite your youth and dark skin. No matter how queer your hair!' He chuckled then. 'Come, meet Sir William — your hair is nothing next to his flaming kinks and curls.'

◎◎

We passed the time in pleasantries after that. There was wine and port and rum punch to drink, and very small morsels of food which, I understand, made it easier to eat whilst talking and standing, but there were no ladies in attendance, save for those serving us. The Artist was at my side again, and bade me pay attention to the famous gentlemen in the room for whom he had great admiration. Among them was Dr Dieffenbach, whose own work in New Zealand had inspired my benefactor's travels.

'James, to think — my work in New Zealand has brought us here!'

The Artist pulled me along towards him, but etiquette dictated he wait to be introduced. Thankfully, Mr Antrobus was never far away and saw our need. After he had introduced us, the great naturalist looked me over curiously.

'Tena koe, Mr Poneke,' he said, disarming me. 'Kei te pehea koe?'

'Aue, e te rangatira. Tino whakaohomauri tou reo maku! Engari, he pai te mita o tou reo, ne?'

'Ah, ko taku he. My skill in the Maori language is not so proficient as my greeting would suggest. I know only a little. I have forgotten much already.'

'Ae, as I have. It is a wonderful thing to hear my language again, even briefly. Thank you, Doctor.'

'It means something to me also to see someone from New Zealand. I always hoped to return, but it was not to be.' A small group had formed beside him, evidently attempting to prompt his attention. He looked towards them, then back to me, inclining his head to the side, and nodding. 'I do hope we meet again, Mr Poneke. I'm afraid I must now attend to a prior request.'

He seemed to regret the dismissal, though it didn't upset me greatly. It was clear from the rummaging and clearing at the far end of the room that it was almost time for the purpose of the gathering to be revealed. There were several tables on

164

which mysterious items were placed under covers. A number of gentlemen took their place by each table, and the Marquis was introduced so that he might begin his opening address, primarily regaling us with the splendour and great worth of steam trains — how this new technology would change everything, from the fortunes of the poor to the commerce of the wealthy. Of this I needed no convincing, but I can't say that many of the Marquis' exact words stayed with me, for my enduring memory is of what happened next.

One by one, a series of curious mechanical inventions were exposed, accompanied by a brief lecture on their purpose and workings. First, a group of models illustrative of the history of the steam engine, furnished by Sir Isaac Goldsmid. One was said to be two thousand years old. There were ten of these beautiful models in perfect working order, and I was much gratified by them. The item that excited the deepest interest was the steam carriage, which Mr Pardington, in his introduction, heralded as 'that mighty abridger of time and space'. Every necessary explanation was given by him, at arduous length, though it did improve my spirits to learn that so much of the modern philosophy dedicated to such things is intimately connected to ancient philosophers, nothing being so new in the world as we are inclined to think.

Next, a piece of clockwork expounded on with great excitement by Mr Perigal, and for good reason. The clockwork kept a small glass ball, representing a comet, in very rapid motion, in a curve of a very curious and enchanting figure — a sort of eight-rased star, of which the eight branches had a parabolic form. This was intended to prove that a comet might return along the same path, and continue to visit us periodically, as though moving through a U-shaped curve, continuing ever in the same direction. That we could know so much about the movement of the stars reproduced within me the same feeling as accompanied my first sighting of a steam engine, and Mr Perigal was kind enough to talk to me at some length, even when others had moved on, explaining that as many as five comets have been visible at once in recent times.

'Ah — the wonders of the starry firmament,' he exclaimed as he finished.

I could not stop myself. 'Where I come from, we think of them as ancestors.'

He smiled indulgently.

'But they guide us as our ancestors did. In navigation. In life. I have heard that my people can pinpoint islands smaller than Britain in the great Pacific Ocean with only the stars to aid them.'

I saw him look harder then. 'Indeed, young Poneke. I have heard such things. But it is our job to separate fact from superstition, is it not?'

I thought about what he had just shown me, how fantastic and beyond imagining it had been until moments ago. I thought about his God, and the miracles of his Bible. I did not understand the difference between these and the things I had just told him, but I did not mention this, for the miracle of his spinning clockwork orbs were still dancing in my eyes.

From there, we were offered all manner of models to examine, as well as artworks, and the Artist made a public introduction of me, alongside a small number of etchings and items from his collection. After this I was occupied for some time answering questions and exchanging pleasantries. The more curious gentlemen enquired about my origins, the customs of my people and the march of progress in New Zealand. I told them what I could, but soon tired of these same questions repeated. Eventually, though I couldn't think why, I began to feel quite heavy, as if I were being insulted.

At last everyone dispersed, taken as they were with the next item on the programme — everyone, that is, except a magnificent-looking man of African origin. He had a regal bearing, and wore a stunning velvet top hat, silk cravat and waistcoat, and the crispest white collar. His jacket was a deep green fabric that seemed to reflect crimson in its folds, thus presenting a dance of shades when he moved. But none of this was as compelling as the man himself. I had noticed him from time to time as the evening proceeded, one dark face in a sea of white, and desired to meet him, but had also felt shy of him. It was not that his figure was too imposing and grand, although that was part of it. I was feeling unsure of myself in such company, unsure of my own appearance and what I might say to this fellow. Some force was keeping me from approaching him; oddly, I felt more comfortable with the white men who were so certain of my place in the world and their company.

The fine man introduced himself as Dr Richard Spencer, of New York by way of Nova Scotia. A doctor of science, rather than medicine, a recipient of education and luck and wealthy patronage. A mind as sharp and strong as a sword — that much was immediately clear.

'I am pleased to meet you, Mr Poneke. I found your story most interesting.'

I bowed a little, as if in service.

'You work for this artist, at the Egyptian Hall? He treats you well?'

'Indeed, I am well cared for.' I found it difficult to continue the conversation. I had a multitude of questions about this man, but something unsaid stood between us.

'You do not feel...*troubled* by your work?'

I had not been asked this quite so directly before. My answer, though I did not yet understand it myself, was similarly direct.

'Yes. Yes, I believe I am sometimes troubled.'

'But you still continue?'

'I…that is, I think —'

'I apologise, Mr Poneke, I have made you uncomfortable. Such is my profession, always asking discomfiting questions.'

I mumbled disagreement. He had such a presence, this fellow.

'I do not mean to concern you so — you seem a smart young man. You seem proud, and intelligent. It is why I must ask.'

'Why?'

'I wanted to ask the same of the Ojibway Group who were exhibited at the Hall only two or so years ago. Like you, they seemed…they had dignity.'

'Yes. Perhaps that is why.'

'Why you'd allow yourself to be exhibited?'

'To show our dignity.'

'Yes. I see. I cannot say I am convinced that this is what the exhibition achieves.'

I could not say this either. 'But does it not bring them closer to us, sir? To see that we are like them?'

'Or objects to be stared at. Freaks of Nature. Throwbacks to a different time in what they like to think of as their own history.'

'I do not think—'

'I know. Forgive me my interruption. If I may, you do not think they see you as lesser. Indeed, they often do not think that themselves. But you are there to serve a very specific purpose. I know because I am at the bottom of their evolutionary ladder. I, too, make an exhibition of myself, by attending Royal Society soirées, by giving lectures, by mixing with the great and the good to show how very intelligent and civilised I am. I should not have to, but I am always a representative of my people. Yet I do not know what it achieves.'

168

Dr Spencer's words were like an anchor, such a dreadful weight they held me against the current I found myself adrift on. I could not reply, so he continued.

'I do not know what my display achieves, but I choose carefully where to place myself. Mr Poneke, I am afraid your act does nothing to promote our cause. It merely plays into their hierarchies of man. You are lighter skinned, more like them in form. Of course you are seen as more civilised than the pygmy Bushmen who were shown earlier this year, dressed in animal skins and without such a fine English accent. I assume they do not make you dance.'

I thought of my haka that first day at the Hall. I had been so proud. He watched me shrug, and I felt like he could see all the many ways I had playacted a native boy.

'Think on it. If they do respect your dignity, they will allow you to retire.'

But I could not tell him I enjoyed it too. The attention. The pretence. It was not such a big price to pay for the life I was now leading.

'I have just one question,' I ventured.

He waited. I felt as if nothing could escape that gaze.

'What is "our cause"?'

He smiled, a long slow expression that filled his face in measured increments, and I saw that he measured all his expressions thus. When he spoke, there was some change in his own accent, some relaxing into another tongue, as if he were showing me a door to another world he knew about. 'Boy, my cause is the emancipation of my people. As it will ever be. I do not know what your cause is, but I understand your people have not been enslaved in the same way as mine. Now, when I say emancipation of my people, I mean all African peoples on the good Earth, for as you can plainly see, there are no slaves in the

Queen's England at this time. But I can tell you that slavery still exists in many places, including much of the Queen's dominion, and that her economy relies on it. Sometimes it might not be called slavery, but if you look you will see that that is what it is.' He lowered his voice. 'I've seen what they do with those of us they consider aberrations from humanity. And, young Poneke, what I can tell you is this — no man is free unless all men are free, not even these here noblemen, and certainly not you.'

He stood back, and I watched the stiffening of his expression and posture again. It was like seeing the shadow of a cloud pass over a landscape. I was suddenly so very, very tired. Who were these white men of science and enlightenment? Where was *their* humanity? But these questions tired me also. I laughed — more a snort of disgust than any measure of mirth, and swayed a little under the weight of the doctor's pronouncements. He grasped my arm at the elbow, leaned in and looked me in the eyes. When he nodded it was all I needed — a sign of kinship, acknowledgement. We were brothers in this.

'It has been a great pleasure to meet you, sir,' was all I could manage. I bowed a little. He returned the gesture and the farewell, then he turned, and I watched him withdraw, and felt both relief and a desire to follow him.

◎◎

But that was not to be, and before I left the soirée I was to have all my illusions torn from me without room for doubt. The Artist and I had begun to make our departure when two gentlemen drew us towards them and introduced themselves.

'Good fellow! We did want to meet the Maori chief while the opportunity presents itself. What do you think, eh, of our fine city?'

'I think it well. It is a joy to explore.'

'Indeed. You must be a magnificent specimen of your kind, surely.' He turned then to the Artist. 'Is he?'

'They're a fine people.' We were both tired now, I could see.

'Well, yes, the Maori, I understand, are quickly moving towards civilisation.' This was the other gentleman. 'Very close to the European on the ladder of man, comparison suggests. The stratified society, the collection of wealth. These are all good indications of relative civilisation.'

Here they paused to examine me more closely. I shifted under their gaze. Enough of this now.

'And it is well to be exhibited alive rather than otherwise, don't you think, sir?'

'Well, I suppose. Though I dare say the dissection and exhibition of some ostensibly human subjects does no harm. The savages have no Christian souls. In some cases, we do not have evidence to suggest they are truly human species at all. The head shape, the physical form in general. There are ... animalistic features to the anatomy.'

He had, he went on to say, been involved in some very important discoveries with his scientific work. At this point, I had to concentrate on my breathing. I found I could not process the exact meaning of his words. Even the Artist seemed to have lost patience with the conversation, his eyes trained on the doors. I wanted nothing more than to get away from these men.

'I viewed the Hottentot Venus recently in Paris. Fascinating specimen.' This was the first gentleman again, and I felt compelled to speak.

'But Mr Antrobus told me he saw her at the Egyptian Hall decades ago. That she died soon after?'

'Yes, and now she can be viewed at the Musée de l'Homme. Excellent job they've made of it. Not entirely sure how they managed to preserve the skin tone so well. Unless a paint of lacquer is involved.'

The meaning of this came to me slowly, a nightmare I was waking into rather than waking from. Was this the world I now inhabited, where nothing was tapu, nothing beyond the rapacious hands of these scientific men? None of the wealth I saw around me was enough for them — they had to take everything. Down to our very flesh. And then what? Would they not be satisfied until they owned the very essence of us? Our souls? For what is left once you transgress the sanctity of the body? What kind of savage place was this?

I suspect the Artist could see the rage flaring behind my eyes, because he pulled me towards the door, hastily offering farewells. Outside I bent over and tried to breathe, tried to quell my horror and the wrath that threatened to overwhelm me.

'Pay it no attention, James,' he said. 'You will meet some people like that, yes, but we are not, are we? My God, how damned inconsiderate of them to upset you so.'

I'd not heard the Artist so passionate before, but I was not sure if he was angry for the same reason as I. On the journey home I felt more distant from him than ever, barely saying a word in the cab. What did he know of the things Dr Spencer had shared with me? What did he know of these men who stuffed humans the same way they stuffed the animals of the Egyptian Hall? Was I happy to be a plaything for this Empire, and to enjoy what the Empire offered me in return: was that my entire purpose? It shamed me that I still did not have an answer, that despite the way the doctor had illuminated the choice for me, I was not yet ready to abandon my desire for all the riches my British education offered me.

I could not sleep that night, thinking over each aspect of the wonders I'd been shown, as well as the horrors. These things were separate, yet in my half-sleep state it seemed they all crowded in at the same moment, so that my mind whirred and stumbled over clockwork and mechanical wonders held in place by macabre human dolls. The spectre of human chattel tainted the edges of each shiny new thing. 'Dr Spencer,' I would have asked if I'd been bold enough, 'do we belong in the old world or the new?' But perhaps that was not the right question. Would they let us belong to the new? And was there any way to return to the old if we chose not to pay the price?

THIRTEEN

And so our time at the Egyptian Hall concluded. On the final night Mr Angus and Miss Angus attended and we returned to the house all together, then celebrated with a grand supper of fish, roasted meats and fruit jellies, as well as little bowls of tasty delicacies at every corner of the table. Miss Angus had gone to some effort to celebrate her brother's success, and even her father seemed happy to acknowledge his son's achievement. Two of the Artist's patrons and several other well-wishers were special guests. After the meal, the Artist would reveal the first proofs of his book, which would be paid for by subscription.

'*Savage Life and Scenes* will contain reproductions of my best work from the exhibition,' the Artist told the gathering, 'as well as an edited narrative from my journal of the expedition. It will be released in ten separate parts, which my subscribers can then bind into a handsome volume.'

The guests congratulated him, and there was much discussion

about the content of the book, the central thesis of which seemed to be that the different levels of the transmutation of man could be found among the different cultures the Artist had encountered.

'For instance, the Aboriginal people of South Australia display more savage tendencies than the Maoris of New Zealand, their culture is less developed. The Maoris often have proper houses, which you will see in my etchings, and their arts are more developed.'

There was a general murmur of appreciation from all except me. Though I had become used to scrutiny during the exhibition, this was different. My thoughts turned to the evening of the Royal Society Soirée. I didn't like the Artist speaking as if my people were objects to be turned over under a microscope. He had known me for long enough. He had known me as *a person*. Did he not see that we are all real, individual *people*; that the Aboriginals of South Australia are thus also? That there is no difference between them and me and him?

'And will you make a similar volume from your journey to South Africa?' This from a bespectacled man.

'Yes. That is the intention. I could build up quite a portfolio of impressions of savage peoples. I had the opportunity to meet Dr Darwin at a recent Royal Soirée. I think we may be similar in our thinking about such things, though of course I am merely an artist.'

I could see the Artist was enjoying himself — the attention of the table was his. He could afford the false modesty.

'And what of you, Mr Poneke — what do you think of the book and the exhibition?' This from another guest, who had an accent I couldn't place — German, perhaps.

'It must be different for me than for any other who encounters the Artist's work,' I said. 'For I am one of the artworks, am I not? I was on display, at least. And so I see it from the inside rather than the out.'

'But what do you see from the inside, Mr Poneke?'

'I believe I encountered all stages of the evolution of man in our visitors, from the savage to the civilised nobility themselves, all of them coming in from the streets of London.'

Beside me Miss Angus gave a little gasp. I could sense her holding that breath in. The table paused long enough for my statement to hang in the air, as if no one was sure whether to laugh or take offence. Then the visitors opened their mouths and guffawed, and the Anguses quickly took up the laughter, just loud enough to signal their relief.

'Forgive me, but it is true. One can truly observe all the stages of man in one place — this great city. And I do not mean that as an insult.'

'Indeed, it is the great metropolis, the centre of the world.' Mr Angus began carving thick slices of meat. At the other end of the table, beside me, Miss Angus spooned from smaller dishes as each plate was passed around.

'But when people make London their home,' she ventured, 'do you not think they should all behave like us? Don't they become more civilised, begin to grow towards a higher ideal? That's what you did, didn't you, Mr Poneke?'

Indeed, this was what I had done — had wished to do. Yet now I was confused. I was confused by that word — savage. There was not an image of me in the book, but the Artist had made my picture. Many of his pictures were of my people. And he had categorised them and studied them like his objects and the marble statues we had seen at the Colosseum. If our greatest chiefs were savages, what did that make me?

'I wish to answer your question with a question, Miss Angus,' I said. 'Was I a savage before I came here? Am I still a savage?'

She immediately looked dismayed.

'I am sorry, Miss Angus. I do not mean to cause you discomfort. Perhaps I should direct my question to the gentlemen gathered.'

This I did and a lively discussion ensued. The men seemed very content to discuss the extent of my savagery in great detail, with reference to the latest theories, physical comparisons with other races, and the effect of education. Was savagery inherent, they asked, or was it based on upbringing, society and education? Could a man not of a white race be fully civilised?

Miss Angus and I remained quiet through most of this. She chewed slowly, lips tightly sealed, as she looked into a far distant spot just above the heads of the men gathered. When someone looked to her and made polite remarks on the bounty of her table, she nodded and made her lips curve into a smile. At last, after a dessert of marmalade pudding and fresh berries, she looked directly at me.

'I do not think you are a savage, James,' she said quietly. She stood before anyone noticed, trembling so slightly that only I could see it, and excused herself to the gentlemen, who were preparing to proceed to the drawing room. It was the only time I have ever heard Miss Angus use my Christian name.

I was saddened that the conversation had troubled her and that my conduct may have been part of that, but at the same time her consternation meant a great deal to me. Miss Angus had gone beyond her own boundaries of propriety to speak to me so intimately. So I found that I was not so concerned about the Artist's leaving London as I might once have been. I had friends in this home and in the city. I did not feel abandoned. And I wondered at the young boy who had so admired him. I did not hate the Artist, and yet I could not say I loved him either. I do not think, if he ever did look to me as an equal, that we would now see eye to eye.

He left one morning before dawn, having given his farewells the night before. I did not rise to see him off, but I heard the carriage come and the transit of luggage down the stairs. I could see him impressing the dark peoples of South Africa with his sensitive brush. He had bravado, I give him that, to go where hardly any Englishman had ventured before him. I tried to find within myself some sadness at his leaving, but felt only that same discomfort about our work together. He had brought me into his world as I had requested, and for this I owed him an allegiance. More than that was no longer possible. The Angus household continued to offer me their hospitality, but with the Artist gone and the exhibition now complete, I knew that life had brought me to the junction at which I always arrive, and soon I would need to choose a new path.

꩜

There was something between Billy and me that transcended all those differences that the Artist liked to measure. Just as my father was the sun, and you, my mokopuna, are all the rivers that run on from the ocean of this life, so Billy was the rising and setting of my days and nights. I could rely on his rhythms to be my own. He was not the moon and stars, but the backdrop to all of it, the place where such treasures might be found. I looked up to him, and at night I liked to find myself enveloped in that firmament, right where all the delights of creation might find their way to us.

Not long after the Artist left, we arranged to meet on my side of town and walk down through Hyde Park to the river and Cremorne Gardens. It was early evening, and I expected Billy to arrive at the square with Henry at his side as he always did. He was alone.

'Henry is at home looking after her poorly mother,' he told me. 'But we shan't get up to any more mischief than usual, eh, Hemi?'

'No. How much more mischievous can one get?'

'Well, we are headed to the pleasure gardens, and it was our secret plan to procure you some pleasure.'

'You're both wicked.'

'Indeed, lad, but that's why you like us.'

I couldn't argue with his logic. It was a merry jaunt down through the park and on to Chelsea. I told Billy about the soirée and the Artist's leave-taking and my ambivalent feelings.

'Well, he is a gentleman, that is true, but I never was sure if I was as taken with his drawings as I was with his Maori Chief in Costume. And the exhibitions? Well, there is something odd about them, which is why we go, but I dare say that work isn't any worse than what other jobs you'd have to do on the streets.' Here he elbowed me. 'He was lucky to have you. It made the thing a bit more *authentic* than it would have been if you hadn't been there, a bit more lively. All in all, it was a good trade.'

'Do you think so, Billy? They have given me so much.'

'Well, look at it this way, my friend. You have helped the Artist achieve fame. Now, it's a strange thing to go about town with a Maori boy. Hundreds might have visited you at the exhibition, but you're still a rarity, and in a city like this that's worth something. Life is cheap if your life is just like everybody else's. Don't forget how special you are.'

I grinned.

'Well, don't get a big head about it either, brother.' He whipped off my hat and ran, and I ran after him until we were almost at the gates.

Let me take you into the dream: ornate iron gates curl as if keeping a secret and issuing an invitation at the same time. These open to a softly lit garden in which each tree and clutch of flowers seems placed as to create the most serene and uplifting effect: rows and circles and bowers of greenery — just enough irregularity to hint at wilderness. Freedom. Inhale the fragrance of flowers in abundance, constant in the night air. And ahead, beyond this scene of tranquillity, the coloured lights of the pagoda, where the music has begun but the dancers are not yet crowded. Walk towards the lights and music now, because it is excitement you are after, and tranquillity can be sought later, or shadows, if you are in need of an intimate spot. We make our way along paths lined with stone mythical beings towards the bars and tables where we can buy our supper and some sherry. There's no serenity to be found here among the side shows and shooting galleries, the circus and gypsy tent.

After taking our fill we find the theatre, where we are entertained by marionette and pantomime, and then it's outside again to the orchestra and platform, where the dancing has finally begun in earnest. And while the gardens are impressive in their beauty, it's the crowds who now really astonish, with their gay dress, their pretty smiles, their dazzling skill on the floor. Since we are earnest fellows, Billy and I find ourselves partners with little trouble and then we are swirling them around, though I am clumsy and don't know the steps. Somehow my partner finds this endearing rather than irritating and takes the time to teach me, laughing at my slow absorption of technique. These ladies are more colourful and friendly than other ladies I have met in similar circumstances, but Billy reminds me that I have not been in similar circumstances, not really, and intimates to me what kind of ladies they are. Other than the brightness of their demeanour, they do not seem so different from anyone else. So I think on this a while as I watch and take part, and I cannot think that any one of us here, in this circle, gets along in life by anything other than selling something, and often that something is a part of ourselves. All except the nobility, who have no need of work. Underneath it all is a faraway memory of home, of a world where each person works for the family, and although I found no glamour in it at the time, I wonder, momentarily, if it might have been better. We had no wealth to speak of, not like what I saw every day now, and maybe that made us lesser. And maybe it did not. As much as I enjoyed this new world, here a person's worth was limited to what we might afford on any given day.

Even so, we had all paid our shilling to come to this place to celebrate beauty and take a little joy for ourselves, to not be beholden to anyone else for one night, and I found myself happy for it, and for every penny my dance partner took home with her from such a time. Billy was at my side, urging me to take my lady on. He had been sharing kisses with his lady, and I did not know what to do about this. I felt a great indignation on Henry's behalf, and also my own.

'I'll take it no further, Hemi. But you should see what comes of things with your girl.'

I didn't feel comfortable with it, and when we sat together and she placed her body against mine, I could not respond. It did not feel right, and I told her as much, and wished her well. She said that was a shame, and returned to the platform, where someone would soon find her. I felt no judgement at her profession, and knew my lack of response had nothing to do with any moral objection.

Billy simply laughed. 'You are a soft and gentle fellow,' he said, 'always taking the high road.' He did not suspect my motivations, and nor did I enlighten him.

But they were there, for at each turn about the dance platform one thing had made my heart leap higher: Billy, his eyes laughing into mine, my heart full at his happiness as well as my own. At such times I was two people: one who was simply Billy's friend and always would be, and this other who felt in ways over which he had no control. There was a heat in my chest that spread to my eyes and lips and limbs, and I hoped no one noticed how that flame flared a little in the breeze of Billy's passing. At times like these my thoughts seemed to exert no influence on the rest of me. No amount of logic or clear thinking could snuff out this thing. I did not desire to see either of us burnt, and so I tried to keep it contained, tried to convince myself that whatever this was, it was enough. Our friendship, I thought, would carry plenty of small leaps of joy to satisfy me. Perhaps I would meet a lady one day and love her, and this ardor for Billy would dissipate. In the meantime, I hoped to preserve our friendship just as it was, and so, as the revelry continued, we walked, and took in our surroundings, and took our leave from the harsh streets that existed outside the garden. And somehow we came to a place where Billy could tell me about his own growing up, which was a thing he did not like to think on or talk about much.

'I don't remember a time I wasn't working or hungry when I was a wee lad. But look at me now. At least part of the year I spend in leisure, until it's time to go back to sea. That seems a good enough trade.'

'I remember hunger too — not as bad as you, I think. But one never forgets.'

'No. It's not a thing you ever accustom yourself to. Not a

thing that fades easily.'

'What was it like here as a boy?'

'Wasn't ever as crowded as it is now, brother. We moved here from Leicestershire when I was barely knee-high. There was nothing for us there and we'd heard there was plenty of work in London. Work, yes, but homes, no — lucky to have a room to a single family. My folks died when I was no more than ten, so us children moved into a shared room, but not for long. I was lucky to be the youngest. If I didn't have an older brother already working and willing to take me with him, I would have gone to the workhouse in the end. I started as a cabin boy and have lived more on sea than land ever since.'

'I feel like I've known you much longer than I have. But I know only part of you, since I've seen you only in the city.'

'Aye, Billy Neptune was born on the sea and he's due back there any day. It's time to re-fill the coffers, my friend.'

'But what about —' *What about me.* 'What about Henry?'

He dipped his head. 'I know. I mean to say, I don't know. I have only one set of skills with which to make a living, and they can be employed only at sea.'

'Surely together you could —?'

'For now. For now it is the sea. Even if we were married, that would be the way of it. But maybe one day we will find a way. A trading post, perhaps.'

'In some far-off place?'

'In New Zealand!'

'I don't know if you'll find it very exciting, my friend.'

'Perhaps we'll be ready to settle down by then.'

I couldn't help but smile at the thought of it.

☙

We talked for hours that night. And soon a picture began to form of a life I could barely imagine, a life that made Billy much tougher than I could ever be, and perhaps cleverer too. He'd had to be. And as he talked my admiration of him grew. I told him everything there was to know of me except that which I could not say. My feelings, if shared, would not bring us closer. I knew this as well as I knew anything.

The night bent towards morning, and it was time to break the spell. I stood on the riverbank while Billy found a boatman to take him to Southwark, then began my walk home to the Anguses. On this night it seemed a small betrayal that I should live in such comfort while my friends lived as they did. And my thoughts became morose at the restrictions I suddenly felt at every step. I could not deceive myself for very long, for my greatest happiness was married to my greatest sadness: I knew at last that I loved my own closest friend as ardently as he loved my next closest friend, and because my love for her was as a brother for a sister, I would do nothing to break my bond with either of them. I would never experience what they had with each other.

FOURTEEN

Each night I found my way back to my room at the Anguses' home. Each morning I breakfasted with them, then walked the short distance to the boys' school where my lessons had begun again. But it seemed as if there was a wall between us now, much more than when I was a simple Maori boy wide-eyed at the grandness of their city. How could I tell them? How could I share anything of the life I really lived? It was not just the night world of the city that I had become accustomed to, the streets that they knew nothing of, the fact that I counted among my friends freaks and malcontents who belittled the civilised, just as the civilised belittled them. It was him. I woke each morning with him on my lips, at my fingertips, pulsing to life between my legs. Desire stalked me deep into the night and curled its tongue around me when I woke. Billy, the gravel sound of his voice a rough caress. Billy, those black eyes. Billy, who I would never have. Yes. I understood that. He would never be mine.

But love doesn't care for reality. Each morning he was there with me, in my arms, my desire a heat that would only leave me cold. I kept it from everyone, and it kept me from everyone.

I carried my unease with me everywhere now, and a question building beneath it all. But there were always things to distract a person in the city. Ernie and Esme's season at the Hall finished a month after my time there. I still visited them weekly for cards, and was introduced to an ever-expanding family of human curiosities. All of us shared something — if not the exact nature of our oddity, then the strangeness of living primarily by our differences. We were of one tribe because we were of no tribe. But I had to be careful: my admiration of society and my conditional acceptance into it might have made me an object of suspicion. Though lately it was clear to me, if not to them, that I no longer believed in the Empire the way I once had. I was now too well acquainted with the many layers of humanity in London, how some came out on top only by climbing over others, how it was necessary for common folk to grovel in the mud so that others didn't have to. Still, given the option, I would choose a comfortable life like the Anguses', not the struggle to exist that Billy and Henry had danced around their entire lives.

Though they loved him, everyone groaned when Billy came with me to play cards, for he was far too good, and nothing was more certain than that he would end the evening with their money. He was forgiven as soon as he began his tales of sea travels: India, Canada, the West Indies, North Africa. He was away for three seasons out of four, he told us, though he spent as much time as he could afford in London. It was, he admitted, becoming more and more difficult to leave Henry behind.

Our friends had also travelled to different parts of the world for their shows: mainly Europe and America, where there was an appetite for such things. We were not so lucky as to meet those who came from further afield, parts of Africa or Asia, native peoples like myself. They were often not treated so well, Ernie told me. He had heard that an Eskimo family had not been provided with adequate food, and were soon abandoned when they began to succumb to ill health. Likewise, a troupe of Mexican natives lost two babies to European winters. It seemed that the freedom and relative dignity I had enjoyed were rare.

'It is true, you have encountered the better side of the trade. We've seen it all,' said Ernie.

'I admit the Hall wore thin in the end, but the Artist was good enough to me, and I met with no ill treatment, and the Angus family still care for me. I cannot complain by any measure.'

'Indeed you cannot,' Esme agreed. 'It's not unusual in our line of work to see children stolen away from their families. Ernie and I were once made to perform without income for six months.'

'Fed and dressed, but no money means no freedom.'

'It was distressing. We know what we are. We know how they look at us. It gives us some reprieve, some pride even, to know they pay a price to gawp at us. Let their curiosity and ignorance pay for our comfort, we say. But we aren't pets. We cannot live by feeding alone.'

'I never liked to be looked at.' This from Miss Annie Temple, who was as beautiful as she was large. 'But in the end there was no other way. Who was going to take me on, at my size? Well, someone has now, but when I was a young girl I was told I was too outsized. I got used to it. The staring. I pretend I'm not there.'

'We play up to it,' said Esme.

'But you know they don't really see us, don't you?'

187

'Of course, my dear. We don't seem real to them. On some days I think they don't see us as human in any way. And that is what they come for, ain't it? Doesn't matter what their station in life, at least they are not subnormal.'

'Yes, at least they aren't one of us Subnorms!'

'Who'd want to be a Norm?'

'We probably eat better than most of them. Certainly as well as the middle classes.'

'It's brought us some comfort, this job, if nothing else.'

'Fame? Fortune?'

'Sure, why not. Some of that too!'

We all six of us at the table that night fell into an unusual silence. My friends, for the most part, lived up to their merry name, but I could see they weren't unacquainted with the discomfort I had come to feel in recent weeks.

◎◎

If Billy's prowess at games was begrudgingly acknowledged by the group, Henry's skills were openly welcomed. She was good enough to take on Billy, but she did not appear frequently, since card nights often fell on the same evenings she went to visit her mother and siblings. When she did come, a great cheer went up, for the group preferred to see their money lost to the girl-man, such a charmer she was, and kind too. Billy was cocky, and though he earned their regard all the same, it was delightful to watch his girl take his money.

One night Henry even appeared without Billy, who had other matters to take care of. She winked at me as she said it, and I knew he was up to something and she was wise to it, and it would be better not to ask. It was an unusual pleasure to have Henry's company independently of her mate, and so we sat together and laughed through the evening, Henry flirting with all the womenfolk in the room, who flirted right back, even the ones with husbands in tow. Though she played at manhood well, I still insisted on walking her home under the pretence of providing some protection against the night. She snorted at the very idea, but took my arm anyway. Perhaps she savoured time alone with me as I did with her, for though I considered her among the best of my friends, we rarely had the opportunity. I said as much as soon as we were outside.

'I know, Jimmy. I fancy myself a man at times, but I have not the liberty you two have, and still have family to look after. A woman is never free of the obligations family places on her.'

'Will you and Billy have one of your own, do you think? A family?'

'I don't know. Maybe we will, but I don't see one for now. Not unless we both change our ways and work out how to settle down. We're both strong-willed and we both like to play too much.'

'And you're both charming. I think you're the only one I've seen who gets the ladies fluttering their lashes as much as your Billy.'

'He's terrible, and it brings out the worst in me. A little sugar and spice. But you have your own way with the ladies, Jimmy.'

'No.' Perhaps the answer was too direct, too blunt. Henry peered at me more closely.

'No? It seems to me you could.'

I let my head shake imperceptibly. I wanted to tell someone so badly.

'Is it — do you not like girls, Jimmy?'

I could only look at her without speaking.

'It's all right, you know, among us. Well, well, well.'

'Please don't tell Billy.'

'He won't mind.'

'No. Please don't.'

She let her head drop in assent.

'What's it like?' I asked her. 'With Billy?

'Well, that's private really. Even among friends.'

'I mean, to love someone like that.'

'Oh Jimmy. It's everything, but you've got to find a way to keep on living. The world doesn't stop to celebrate just because you find each other, even if it feels like it should. Billy and I have found a way to be together that suits us both. We're an odd fit, but that's the way it was always going to be, no matter who our mates are. So we're lucky. You might be odd too, in a different way, but I feel like you also must be lucky.'

And in that moment I could almost believe her. But then I remembered who we were talking about, and how that person belonged to her, not to me, and how I loved them both regardless. It seemed like an immense jest of the gods to make it so, and yet I did feel lucky to be arm in arm with sweet, clear-seeing Henry. She would hold my secret, I knew. Or any other troubles I placed in her sure, strong arms.

◎◎

One long, warm night at the end of July, the Merry Marrying Midgets of Middlesex told me they were shortly expected in France for three months, and their good doctor was organising a tour of Germany to follow.

'We will soon be away, dear James.'

'We will miss you, Mr Poneke.'

The candlelight was particularly alluring that evening, warmed as I was by brandy and custard tarts. I felt lazy and somewhat hazy, but their words awakened me enough to make an incoherent noise of alarm and regret.

'But we have organised our own parting soirée!'

'Yes! Not to be outdone by those who get invited to such things by marquises at the Royal Society.'

'Ours will take over The Mermaid's Bosom.'

'It will be quite the do.'

'And you must be there, Spicy Boy, with your friends — Neptune's son and the infamous girl who dresses as a boy.'

'We know they are our kind underneath their disguises of normality.'

I thought of Henry in her guise as a man — and how my little friends considered this normal.

'And the scientist. Mr Antrobus. He can converse with our good doctor.'

'And your patrons if you wish it.'

'All must come!'

'It will be a party like no other!'

I could not see the Anguses attending, but I knew Mr Antrobus had long been curious about my circle of friends, and his philosophies of equality would make him popular among them. Billy and Henry loved to laugh with this lot, so no doubt they would also be keen.

'I can't say I am pleased that the time has come to say goodbye,' I said, 'though I am pleased the nature of that goodbye entails a party. Let us pretend we know not what it is for.'

'A masquerade party! Then we can at least pretend we know not who it is for!'

'Yes, dear sister, a masquerade, though I fear our size may give the game away.'

'Let us invite all the little people of London.'

'And giants too.'

'Yes, and those without regular limbs.'

191

'All irregularities will be embraced with much fervour.'

'And all behaviours too! We do love a fervent gathering, do we not, brother?'

'The earnest Mr Poneke has been one of our most fervent followers!'

They beamed at me, but I could not join fully in their joviality. It was with a heavy heart that I would watch them leave. No matter the day, they always managed to rise, to be cheerful and resolute. Perhaps it was because they had each other to look to.

'Yes, we must celebrate before the wretched Agatha joins us.'

'Now, Esme.'

'Oh come on, Ernie, let a lady have her jealousies. I would rather not be out-cuted.'

'At least you are not to be out-weighed!'

'Why, you cheeky brat!'

I watched as Esme chased her brother, batting at him with her fan. She was not pleased by the addition of a younger girl to their show, though Ernie had intimated he thought the lovely Agatha quite pretty. I hoped for their sakes no jealousies would sour their domestic harmony. And I couldn't help wondering if their departure was a signal for my own journey to recommence as well. I could rely on the hospitality of the Angus family only for so long.

❧

The evening of the party I crossed the river to meet Billy and Henry. The walk would clear my head, for I knew it wouldn't be clear for long once we reached the party. The river flowed as it always did, a mistress to all who lived in the city. That day I needed the busyness of watermen crossing, of sails pulling their vessels past to the docks, of other lives and other destinations.

I was familiar with the putrid smells and everyday drudgery of life on the Thames now, but still it held a powerful magic for me, this great portal to other worlds.

But I was always somewhat trepidatious on the other side of the river; I hadn't yet learnt to decipher the code of those streets. It was better to have Billy or Henry to follow, and tonight I risked calling attention to myself with my costume. I preferred to appear anonymous, a stranger, even if dark and exotic. That way I could watch the crowds with their song-like calls, their petty arguments, their beckoning of sales or repairs: pots, kettles, shoe-black, newspapers, dates, coconuts. I could allow myself to be swept up, only as strange as the streets themselves.

But tonight we were to be conspicuous, for there were my Billy and my Henry, and we three caroused down the street in a kind of dancing circle, swinging in and out of doorways, lifting our hats, calling out greetings, buying apples and oranges from the girls who held their baskets out to us. We were dressed in our finest — not too ostentatious but certainly with a dash more colour than usual, and masquerade eye masks fashioned by Henry. We must have made a sight as we crossed London Bridge again, and found our way to Cheapside and the clutches of The Mermaid's Tail. We were so happy in that swirling moment, a sweet trio, all three of us in love with each other in some way. We would work things out; the world was full of possibility. I had wanted so many things from London, but I had not anticipated that it would give me people I could truly belong to.

And so we were in, and into the crowd, all shapes and sizes, all colours and configurations.

'Hemi! Billy! Henry! The wicked tricksters! Come! We have cake! We have gin and stout and wine!' It was Ernie, carried about on the shoulders of a man who could not have been less

193

than seven feet tall.

There was indeed much food and drink, and Billy and Henry seemed quite comfortable going about arm in arm, even exchanging kisses with abandon. I could only look on, and drink — gin then beer then gin. The music was lively around us, and I was determined at some point to dance like our friends.

'I love this crowd, Hemi,' Henry shouted as she sat down after a jig. 'We can be ourselves here, whatever we are. I do so wish the rest of our world was like this.'

'Aye. All the freaks of Nature at the centre of things.' This was Billy, yelling over a particularly vigorous tune. 'For are we not all misfits of Nature anyway? He's a fool who thinks he is true to type. We're all of us deviants. And not just the people in this room.'

I could not argue with this. 'You are right, of course. But those of us who know it are made vulnerable by those who don't.'

'Ah Hemi, what a blessing to have found you.' Billy nodded towards Henry as she lifted his arm from her shoulder and proceeded to the bar. 'I love you just about as much as I love my girl, and I don't mind saying it.'

Oh, the great swell in my chest. Billy grinned at me so widely and with such warmth I felt it wash through me. It was between us then, this great love. I knew, in my head, it could not be for him what it was for me, but I let myself be seized by what felt like the heat of his gaze. Desire moved through me, and it was as true as anything I had known. Did we not declare ourselves free by our very presence in this place? Were not my feelings as real and just as any of the manifestations of humanity in this room?

Since I had known myself to love Billy, I had known myself to be as defenceless as any human on Earth could be. I could feel it on my skin; the possibility of being flayed by the world and its rejection. But I welcomed it. I wanted only to exist in this sensation, this invisible thing that had so much power. To be damned in it? Perhaps. I did not care. I wanted only to be close, and if I could not have him I would live out the rest of my days with the sweetness of his proximity, the luxurious presence of *something else* suspended in the air between us. Equal parts pain and pleasure. Equal parts motion and stillness. Ah, Billy Neptune, how the shape of your name writes itself on my very existence, even now. But then? I was fooling myself. That night I fooled myself even more than usual.

෨෨

Ernie and Esme were determined to introduce us all to each other, those who hadn't already met. There were, indeed, many more very short people than I had seen before, and many more tall. There was the heaviest man in Britain, as well as lovely Miss Temple, though they were rivals and best kept at either ends of the pub — and not upstairs, Esme intimated.

'It's all right for him,' Miss Temple told me, nodding towards her adversary. 'He's naturally heavier and has much more wealth behind him. I must make a steady practice of my eating to sustain the weight needed to attract crowds. Three-quarters of my income goes to food alone!'

I tried to respond with empathy, but poor Mr Flipp who, it had been explained to me, had a wasting disease and could barely maintain the weight to sustain life, no matter what he ate, stood close by. I felt the enormity of God's jest then, with people of such extreme conditions standing in contrast to each other in the same room, and competing to make a living of it. My own opposite was soon revealed to me, a man who seemed to be nothing special, though he had large eyes and nostrils, and thick black hair. I was making my way to the bar, seeking something wet but not so intoxicating as everything else I had consumed that night. My speech was slurred, and I hated to seem incompetent or ignorant to those I met.

'Mr Poneke!' He slapped me on the back. 'I have so wished to meet you, but I have been busy with my own show. You will have heard of me, no doubt. I am The Bullman of Borneo, also known as The Human Ape. Though so many of us are billed as wild men these days, I sometimes try to distinguish myself through showmanship.'

He had a thick accent that curled around his words, rolling his r's and emphasising each vowel in a pleasing way. I had never heard of him.

'Pleased to meet you, sir.' I managed a sideways bob somewhat approximating a shallow bow.

He returned the gesture. 'You can call me Roberto! I am such an admirer of yours! So clever, to surprise your audience with your "civilised", "educated" demeanour. I wish I had thought of that. But I still dress in my animal skins and tribal fetishes, and grunt when spoken to, and my "keeper", who is actually my brother, must weave a fascinating tale of how I was found living among the orang-u-tan in the jungle. It still draws them in, though. Still earns us a pretty penny. How did you think of it?'

I was confused. 'Think of what?'

'The act, boy, it's ingenious. We all admire it so.'

Yes, it was an act. But I couldn't remember thinking it up.

'I just try to represent my people as best I can,' I said.

'Your people? You mean it is real? How wonderful! How innocent! You sound like such an Englishman, I thought it must be a carefully constructed act. Your dark skin might have passed down to you from anywhere. I myself am originally from Italy, by way of Paris.'

It was now my turn to be incredulous. His game dawned on me slowly. I was willing to buy any illusion, but this was simply a swindle. The man was a pretender.

Billy was suddenly at my side, his arm hooked around my neck. He was in a worse state than I.

'Keep your hands off my Hemi,' he said to Roberto. 'He's a good boy, aren't you, Hemi? The best of men. Not a faker.'

He started weaving away through the crowd, dragging me with him. I looked towards my new acquaintance, and shrugged. We neither of us would miss the other, I suspected.

And then we were amid the throng, swinging around, feet stomping, legs up, knees bent, forwards and back, arms interlocked, laughing. Henry came in and out of focus; I saw Mr Antrobus across the room, deep in conversation with a well-dressed man who alone amongst us all was unmasked. Not that the masks hid the identity of anyone, but they made us bolder and sillier than even the drink. Henry found herself embraced by a group of women, all determined to dance with the pretty boy, or girl, no one seemed to mind. It was a swirling, bacchanalian spree. We were free, unhindered, gloriously alive — no one could deny us our youthful pursuits, and who would want to?

Billy had me in his sweaty embrace, leading me around the floor as if I were one of his blushing maids to be seduced. For a moment it was as if I were, though I had never felt myself so fully man. Everything seemed right, and pure — every kind of person, every kind of desire, every need. Looking up, my vision filled as we moved together, in rhythm, so close that mere breathing filled me with the odour of his heaving body. I was so gloriously submerged in a sea of Billy Neptune, and there were his mouth and teeth and tongue. The next moment I pulled in

197

closer, pushed my body against his from chest to thigh, and closed my open mouth over his, swallowing his laughter in my own throat.

A moment. Less time than it took to count once. I knew immediately, felt his body stiffen and push me away. No, his eyes said, No, the increasing distance between us, No, the stiff turn of his shoulder, and a final look, a final imperceptible shake of the head. Then he turned fully away, and I looked after him, both of us at the same time seeing Henry where she stood, her mouth agape, a startled oh, and something stricken, some look that made me think of the brokenness on the faces of those people, long ago, when I showed them Rua Kanapu's greenstone weapon and they knew that he was dead.

But this was nothing but a stupid mistake. My stupid mistake. I rose, and lifted my arm out to my friend and began to move towards her, but once she understood my intentions she was away.

Billy turned back towards me then, his face contorted, fierce. 'Don't, Hemi. Leave it!'

Then he was away too, after her.

◉

I was swimming through a bottle when he returned — sooner than I thought he would. He took himself to the opposite side of the room, and inserted himself among a well-lubricated group who periodically erupted in cheers. He did not look at me.

Mr Antrobus approached and I tried to maintain a polite and reasonable façade, but it was no good.

'You seem ill at ease, Mr Poneke,' he said. 'Can I help?'

Of course he could not help. I tried to tell him it was

198

just drunkenness, but my drunkenness got in the way and I found myself telling him I had been inappropriate, due to the drunkenness, and offended my friends. He took me to mean I had made advances on Henry, having observed her true identity like every person here, and tried to appease my mood by offering his own tales of embarrassment earned by offensive approaches to ladies. It was no good. I admitted my main concern was that I'd offended my best friend as well as my closest friend, and I did not know what to do to make it up to either of them. Henry, I knew, would forgive. She would understand when given an explanation; she was a generous type. As long as I did not come between her and Billy — and I think she understood there would be little chance of that, given I was altogether of the wrong sex. But Billy? I knew not how he would proceed, and my vision of a future devoid of him was dark and desperate.

'Go and talk to your friends.' Mr Antrobus tried to lift me upright from my slouched position. 'It is all a misunderstanding. And in the morning you will all feel sheepish for it.'

'Yes, yes, kind Mr Antrobus. You are right, of course. I have always known you to be right.'

'It is time I return home, James. Go talk to your friends. All will be fine.' He bowed a little, and was gone.

It was shame that washed over me in waves. Shame not that I had shown my true nature to my friends, though that was mortifying in its own way, but shame that I had betrayed them both by attempting to insert myself between them. Shame that I may have created disharmony between them, when I knew how hard the world had been to them, and how much it meant for them to have found each other. These were the things I resolved I must tell Billy immediately.

But Billy had his own things to say.

'Hemi, you Maori wretch,' he yelled as I faced him. 'Henry

is gone. Can't even find her now. And it's you to blame, you nancy.'

'I'm so sorry, Billy. I lost all sense of proportion and the right way up. Forgive me, let me explain. Let us find Henry together.'

'No. She's gone. Told me to leave her alone. Told me to go away on my damned ships and be done with it. I think, Hemi, I think she believes it's what I wanted. After all, I went for her in trousers.'

I tried then to muster a speech, but we were both too insensible to be clear with each other. Billy pointed a finger at me and prodded my chest a number of times.

'You just stay away from me, Jimmy James. I know what you are. I'd always suspected. Never bothered me, but then you had to go and spoil it, eh? Spoil it for all of us. Where's my girl?' He swung around and lurched towards the door, and I thought he shouldn't be alone, neither of them should be alone on the streets in that state.

But then my friends Ernie and Esmerelda were taking me by the hand, and I followed so that I could sit and listen to them. This was a celebration for them. It was their goodbye. They had been good to me, good to everyone they came into contact with, and I had been neglectful of them this eve. I told them how I would miss them, how they were the most successful, independent persons I knew in the business, in the world, and wished my friends and I were as settled as these two. Then I crumpled.

'Do not cry, little Spicy Boy,' said Esme, stroking my forehead. 'You must be strong. For how will we leave London if we have you to worry about? Reassure us you will look out for yourself.'

'Yes, dear friend. You are family now, and we will be back in London in a year or two. We will expect you upstairs, here, at The Bosom!'

'Do not make us wait, Indian Boy.'

'I do hope I will see you next time you are in London,' I said, 'though I know not where I will be.' I knew nothing any more. 'It has been one of the delights of my life that I have made your acquaintances, for you have always treated me like whanau.'

Their eyes widened a little, a question.

'It means family.'

I held them each by both shoulders, pressing my nose to theirs for long moments.

'Get off with you!' said Esme, but her eyes were watery, and she pulled a handkerchief from the pocket she kept tied around her waist.

Ernie put his forehead to mine and held me by the arms. 'Be what you are, boy, and don't let anyone make you what you are not.' He was gruffer than usual.

It was a shame, I thought, as I watched them make their rounds of the room, that I did not know what I was. They knew who they were, and what they were about. How to be true to something if you were not well enough acquainted with it? I felt I was nothing, after all my parading in London. My friends were leaving or already gone, or perhaps would not want to see me again. I was bereft, and I had begun to see it was not just people I was missing, but my own centre.

FIFTEEN

My future, I have prolonged that last chapter of my story, for I do not wish to get to the next. I dream that your world is more enlightened, more innocent, more simple than the time I live in. When men speak of the march towards progress, I see a time in which equality and liberty sit alongside peace and harmony, when violence is not seen as a means to achieve goals. Does not the Bible speak of the lion lying down next to the lamb? I find evidence in all the wonderful inventions of London, the societies of art and science that busily produce new worlds, and if the Empire is truly great, will it not outlaw tyranny and make all men and women equal? Why else would the Queen have been given dominion over so much of the Earth? Perhaps the sacrifice and desperation of those who now live and work in filth so that others might be comfortable is worth it; perhaps such lives will not be necessary within a few generations. It brings my heart some peace to know that you, my future, live in a time that has eradicated abuse and exploitation.

So forgive me, for surely you will not be accustomed to such scenes as appear in these pages, and the truth is I am a coward to them myself. Now, as I lie here writing, it seems as if I have been running from this, in one way or another, all my life.

I was nearly home when Antrobus found me, and called my name aloud. He was behind me, several houses back. I recognised his voice the instant I heard it, and I knew it could not be good, the reason he was suddenly here, in my neighbourhood, in the hours before dawn. It amazes me how one can know in an instant, even while intoxicated and exhausted, that the world has been utterly changed. I felt a lurch in my lower belly, a strong urge to empty my stomach and my bowels.

'Poneke, wait, it's me — I'm afraid I need your assistance most urgently.'

His words were oddly careful despite the panic I detected within, as if he were using them like walls to protect me from what lay on the other side. I hunched my shoulders against them, and turned.

Everything I needed to know was in my friend's stricken face, his rolled-up sleeves, the way he wrung his hands, binding them tightly and turning them over each other.

'Quickly, please, Hemi.'

He had not used my first name thus before.

Then he was away, with me trying to keep up and not trip over. At a fast pace we returned through Marylebone and Soho to the river, and followed along its bank until we were within four or five streets of The Mermaid's Tail. Mr Antrobus guided me towards a formidable grey stone building.

'I'm afraid it's Billy, Hemi. He will not move, but he has made his accusation and must come away now.'

'Accusation?'

'Oh, Hemi. It's Henry. There were young gentlemen. They saw him, Hemi. With Henry.'

'They saw —? What did they see?'

'It is better the story come out between us all, as soon as you have him away.'

I was still at a loss. I felt like I had left something very important behind, something on which all our fortunes rested. I followed Mr Antrobus, who brought me to the entrance of a magistrate's house, and a manservant let us through. No one seemed pleased to see us at this late hour, including Billy himself, who was red in the face and rigid, holding his hat in his hands. I had never seen him in such distress, and where was Henry?

'Go now, young man, with your associates.' The magistrate was stern, and dressed only in his dressing gown.

'If I may, sir, I'd like your assurance charges will be laid.'

'I can give no such assurance. I will consider the matter in the morning and assess the…situation. The gentlemen involved will be questioned. You have identified them.'

His tone was dismissive but Billy was not satisfied. 'Sir, I demand —'

'You demand? I do not think you are in the position of demanding. You have intimated to me yourself the circumstances in which you and your…*lady* were set upon. Unconventional, to put it in polite terms. I have given you my word that investigations will be made. I thank you to leave now. Good evening.'

The magistrate left the room, and the servant moved towards Billy, who looked as if he was ready to follow the master to his private rooms. He ran his fingers through his hair. I went to take him by the arms, but he shook me off, eyed me viciously. There was such a slick pool of hatred in that look.

Finally, Billy came out with his head down, and did not look up or acknowledge me once.

'Where is she?' The question was directed at Mr Antrobus.

He could look neither of us — Billy nor me — in the eye, but looked to the side of our legs as he spoke, as if reading a passage on the road behind us.

'I'm sorry, Billy.' He paused too long and I knew the next part would be terrible. I couldn't breathe until he spoke again. 'They took her away soon after the police separated you from the others. She was — I don't know if there is anything that can be done for her.'

'Doctors.'

'Perhaps. It doesn't look good. A very good physician, perhaps.'

'The best. For Henry. Only the best.'

It was in that moment I knew what I had been missing, and for the second time felt my bowels loosen, the gagging urge to spill the contents of my belly. No. Not gentle Henry. I did retch then, spilling sour bile into the gutter. No. It was a cruel joke, surely.

'There must be a mistake. She was… Why —?' But I knew there had been no mistake, just as surely as I wished that none of this were true.

Billy looked fiercely at the ground beneath his feet. When he spoke, his voice was knives. 'I thank you, Antrobus — I will reimburse you for your assistance this evening. Please do me one further favour. Tell him to stay away from me.'

I tried to speak again, but nothing coherent came.

'No!' This time he was louder. 'Tell him.' Then he lifted his hat to our friend and strode away.

Mr Antrobus looked bewildered, opening and closing his mouth and making no sound. I watched Billy. His walk was that of a man holding a fresh wound to the gut.

When we could see him no more, I spoke.

'What happened to Henry, Mr Antrobus? What happened to Henry?'

His face crumpled inwards. But he promised to tell me as soon as we could find a coffee house. I was dizzy and confused, which made me docile, and Antrobus himself looked much in need of refreshment. We stumbled along the street until we found a place and, with coffee in hand, we sat. He began to tell me then, carefully and with much hesitancy, what he had seen, and what Billy had told him, before they parted ways.

Out into the night from The Mermaid's Tail, Billy had looked for Henry on all the streets she might take, and was relieved to find her on Puddle Dock, looking out over the Thames. Few people passed that way this hour, and the spot was beguiling for its privacy. She had been crying, and he ran to her, explaining the mistake, trying to blame the drink and the atmosphere of freedom and debauchery the soirée had brought out in everyone. *Hemi is just that way,* he'd beseeched her, *but not I, my love. You are the only one for me, sweet Henry, and maybe we should make that official.* Henry laughed, for she could not go about the world dressed as a man if she was married to a man, and she'd become much accustomed to her garb and her way of life, and was sure she did not want to give it up for anyone, not even Billy Neptune, though she was touched that he'd made the proposition, and she would consider it.

They embraced then, with fervour. It was a sweet relief to both of them, and hadn't emotions run a little high, and wasn't it wonderful, truly wonderful, to have each other. Henry's cap fell off as they kissed, Billy ran his hands through her shorn hair, and they laughed more, and fell about, for it was a delicious thing to be these two against the world, and to make their own rules as they wished, and to confuse others who might come upon them.

A group of gentlemen did come upon them then. But what these gentlemen saw they did not judge as wonderful. They took no delight in discovering two men upon the ground against a wall, one straddling the other, both engaged in the most repulsive and lascivious behaviour. The gentlemen were all young, freshly home from school and determined to prove themselves as they moved into the world of adulthood. There was a part of them that was fascinated by what they saw, but not one would dare admit it, and each knew the price required for membership in the great nation and class to which they were born. They worked as a group then, moving towards the couple, tearing one from the other, laying into each with fists and knees and feet. Two would hold one of the offensive pair, while the other pummelled him. Billy and Henry were insensible and helpless within minutes. But then Henry's beating took on a different tone as her waistcoat came loose, the buttons flying off, her shirt torn away. Breasts, small but clearly female, exposed to the men. Beautiful breasts, and they had seen but few, and they were already aroused by the passion with which they were administering the beatings, and by the vision of two men embracing. A woman, clearly a wanton woman, was a different matter, for only a whore would dress as a man and engage in rude acts upon the street. As if of one mind, they all knew at the same moment what their next act would be, for the evening had become a proclamation of twisted manhood.

They moved with desperation and excitement, fuelled by violence, and in doing so abandoned their beating of Billy, who roused quickly enough to surmise their intent. He had seen much violence in his life, and the night had already been infused with the fear of losing Henry, and he would not have it.

Six men? They could each of them go to hell. Mr Antrobus, too, was heading towards the group at speed. He had come upon the scene soon after the young gentlemen arrived, and had been trying to ascertain how best to help his friends, whether to run to the police or whether his own voice might bring some sanity to the gathering. 'Stop!' he now yelled, but his voice was lost to the group. Coming closer, he yelled again, 'Please gentlemen, no!' But already the boldest of them was unbuttoning his trousers. Each of the group was either preoccupied by his goal or by the small, yelling gentleman approaching them.

While Antrobus distracted them, Billy ran in from the other side, imagining that, with enough momentum, he could ram one body against the others, causing the close-standing group to collapse. His plan worked by half. He pushed the biggest of them, who in turn toppled two others before the ringleader, now with pants around knees, was ploughed into. But rather than falling away from Henry, as Billy had hoped, the gentleman fell towards her, causing the two men holding her to scatter, dropping Henry's unconscious form to the stones below.

The young man landed on Henry, swiftly forcing the sharp edge of a paving stone into the back of her skull. There is a sound bone and brain make when crushed by rock, said Antrobus, and I hope that gentleman never forgets it. I hope it haunts him until the day he dies.

'Gentleman?' I was repulsed by what Antrobus had told me, pulled in so many directions at once by guilt and outrage and shame. I was drowning in blood and piss and sweat, the reeking effluvia of those wretched streets. And out of this I grasped at only one word: 'gentleman?'

Mr Antrobus let his head fall in assent. He was spent. He had nothing left to offer me, had only his own brokenness to attend to now.

It was perhaps the easiest thing to hold on to out of everything I had heard. Educated young men of a higher class, the best the Empire had to offer. Even while I allowed my anger to boil and burn out every other emotion, I knew that again I was missing something. Something I was not seeing, was not feeling. It would be months, and I would be leagues away in a different world, before I allowed myself to think of Henry. Really think of her, and feel her absence, and the way this absence had been forced upon the world. But that day I put her away carefully, tucked her under a soft cloak. Poor, sweet, tough Henry, whose form I still see on long nights, her face obscured by the remnants of a masquerade.

SIXTEEN

It would have to be done immediately. I had long needed to face the Anguses, to make amends for my behaviour. Now there was no time. They had been aware of my nights out, and, I was sure, had already begun to lose faith in my goodness. My declarations of taking night rambles in order to observe the people of London were no longer taken seriously — they knew, surely, that I had become a creature of the night myself and that I was not above drunkenness. Gone were the days of walks in the park and mutual delight in the strange and wondrous excitements of the city. Mr and Miss Angus had been too kind, and too polite, to openly criticise me, but with the Artist gone, and my behaviour becoming ever more erratic, I had left them little choice.

I had not seen Billy in weeks. Henry was still alive, but barely, Mr Antrobus had written soon after the incident. Her mother would not let Billy see her. He blamed me as well as himself and was inconsolable. I should stay away.

Mr Antrobus and I met at the coffee house once more, so that he could bring me up to date on the magistrate's decision regarding Henry's assault, and to say goodbye. There was to be no further investigation. The six accused had been questioned, and all described the same scene: a young woman dressed as a man, playing the fool, the ensuing confusion and fight. Billy had exacerbated it — he'd been very aggressive — and in the scuffle Henrietta Lock had met with an unfortunate accident.

'I see,' I said. 'But surely—'

'Mr Neptune has asked for the matter to be reconsidered, but his voice means little compared to those of the six who all vouch for each other. If he pushes any further, he may find himself implicated.'

'But she is alive! Surely there is hope?'

'Not for Mr Neptune. Miss Lock's mother blames him and will not let him see her. He wants to pay for doctors, but has not the funds. Her family would not accept his assistance anyway, so I called on them with our own family physician, and told them only that I was a witness so they would not think me Mr Neptune's accomplice as the police did. The doctor found nothing new that could be done for her, Mr Poneke. She will either recover…or she will not.'

I could not think of that. I could not think of poor Henry. So much life in her every step. I could not think of that life gone out.

There was little else to say on the matter, and we shared a mournful meal together.

'I will leave soon,' I said. 'I'll take a ship. I do not think I can stay in London any longer.'

'I will miss your acquaintance, young Hemi, but I understand your need. This has been a difficult time for all of us.' It made

211

me sad to see my friend's shoulders hunched so, his hair and beard comparatively unkempt. 'I myself would likely embark on a similar route if I had the choice. But no, my place is here. I have found an excellent pursuit to divert my attentions in the Borough itself. I will be contributing my time to more charitable acts, beginning with an alms house in Hackney. I have the income to go without employment, but no longer do I have the will. I must be useful to society, not just philosophical about it.'

I had never before seen Mr Antrobus so resolute and articulate. 'I will miss you, dear friend. You have always looked out for me, and have only my respect in return, though I do not know any more if that has great weight.'

'Oh, Mr Poneke —' But then he could speak no more, and I could see I'd embarrassed him, and the weight of what we needed to say far outstripped our ability to say it, so we sat with our coffee and watched the men entering and departing, and did not speak until we took our leave a long while later.

෨෧

The next evening I found myself again at the supper table with Mr Angus and Miss Angus. As usual, Miss Angus enquired of her father's business, a regular conversation that rarely deviated from convention.

'Father, I feel like I have not seen you this week. I trust that all is well?'

'Yes, my dear. As you know, the work rarely stops. We can barely keep up with demand. Transport is the great technology of our time, no matter what the printers and architects say. And you?'

'You know my days do not deviate from the path before me,

but I see little of Mr Poneke these days —' here she looked to me — 'neither morning nor evening. I fear I may become too bored with staying home alone and will need to call on other friends more often.'

'That is a good idea, daughter.' Mr Angus continued almost wholly preoccupied by his plate.

'Don't you think it strange, Father, that we hardly see our friend?'

He murmured assent, but continued to carve at his meat while he chewed. When he looked up, I could see that Mr Angus was avoiding the inevitable questions that should be asked of me at this juncture. He was a wily businessman, I had been told, but I believe Mr Angus was the most gentle and generous of benefactors. Finally, he placed his fork on his plate. At the same moment, I found my tongue, though I had no idea of the words I would speak.

'Sir. My dear friend, Miss Angus. I have been a terrible guest, and I have no excuse. You have given me so much, so many nice things. The very best accommodations, and a seat at your abundant table. I don't expect you to understand or to forgive my poor behaviour. All I can tell you is that I came here to learn and to discover, but the things I discovered were not what I expected. Where I come from, it is customary to pay in kind, yet I have nothing to repay your generosity. And I can only apologise for that.'

Mr Angus had started to grow red in the face, to look about him in distress.

'Nonsense! What nonsense! You, dear boy, are our guest. And my son used your services for his great exhibition, for which I imagine there was no payment other than my generosity. A young man will be a young man, I dare say, no matter where he comes from. I know my own sons made their mother miserable with their wanderings as soon as they were of age. I am lucky I have my daughter to keep me sane and in good company. But we worry about you, young James. We are not convinced you are quite as strong as you think you are. Find your purpose!'

'Yes, James — we worry about you so.' It was a relief to hear Miss Angus give voice to her thoughts. I had been avoiding this conversation for so long, yet I finally understood how much better it is to air that which goes unspoken. 'Someone may take advantage of you. You are still so young and new to England. Father wonders if you had a goal, a profession to work towards, perhaps?'

'Yes, a professional goal! We know you love your books, but what will you make of your education? What shall you be?'

What should I be? I had had so many dreams. Writing and teaching, a job that would necessitate more learning. None of that mattered any longer. I had a task to fulfil, a pact to keep. He needed me, even if he thought he did not. And I would do it for Henry. I had done nothing else.

'I want to go to sea.'

Had I not been so serious I would have found the expressions on the faces of my companions comical.

'But you do not like the sea, Mr Poneke. And your books. I would not have thought that your studies fitted you out for sailing.' Miss Angus was the most practical and thoughtful of women.

Mr Angus regarded me as if considering a new design for a carriage.

'What do you want from the sea, boy?'

'I wish to see more of the world, and if I work on one of your ships, Mr Angus, I know that I will be earning my way and returning your favours.'

'You see, daughter, there is nothing to be done with him.

214

He wishes to pay his own way. And so he shall. I don't know about this talk of natives and savages. I have never met a man as civilised as young James Poneke.'

Miss Angus was upset, I could tell. She looked at me as if taking a few steps backwards to consider a painting from afar. Perhaps I was not what she thought after all. I was sad to disappoint her, and to take myself away from her acquaintance, but there was nothing I could do to fill the chasm that had opened between her world and my own. I could not tell her what trouble I had encountered, or why I must leave. I did not want to sully her pretty view of the world, or the little respect she might still hold for me.

It was easy, with the aid of Mr Angus's contacts and enthusiasm, to make the arrangements. On my final day in the house I went out and bought Miss Angus an armful of blooms from a flower girl, and arranged them in a great bunch, and left them for her in the front room, with a card of my own design, a poor sketch of three figures — a rotund man, a young lady with a pretty parasol, and a youth running towards an enclosure of giraffe and elephant and lion, trees towering above all but the giraffe. It seemed so long ago, yet it had been only months. I was but a child then, and it was the happiest day I could remember, and Miss Angus was a true and generous friend to me, despite the entire worlds that stood between us. I imagined her coming upon the gift, and I hoped that it would warm her.

෧෧

I followed my heart onto that boat even though Billy had turned away from me. I followed my heart onto that boat, even though it was not where I really wanted to be. But where I did now want to be I did not know. Henry was our due north and without her we were adrift.

Billy had let his pain turn spiteful, so I kept from him my small interference in our destinies. He was simply offered a job by one of Mr Angus's shipmasters and took it, and was none too pleased to discover my presence on the boat. 'Don't get in my way,' he sneered. 'I won't rescue you if you find yourself in trouble.' Later, after a restless night in adjacent hammocks, he addressed me more forcefully. 'This is no place for you, Poneke. You shouldn't have come.'

'I didn't come for you,' I replied, but he didn't hear, or he didn't believe me.

'You must be happy, James.' The use of my English name was as sharp as if he'd used his fists. 'Now that Henry is out of the way. I'm all yours now, eh, me old mate?'

He wasn't being fair. He knew this was a way to puncture my guilt.

'Don't, Billy,' I said. 'You know I love her as much, as much as —'

'Don't even dare suggest you know anything about other people's love, Poneke. I can tell you right now you better shut your mouth.'

'You're not the only one affected, Billy.'

'You don't know a thing about it. I've got no warnings left for you.'

'I'm sorry, Billy, I'm so sorry.'

'I don't want to hear your voice. I don't want to know you exist. Do you understand? Get away from me.'

But I stood there. I must have thought he would see me, see the friendship we had before it all changed, understand that we could go back to it, that everything else was a terrible mistake. I thought I knew something. I thought we would be stronger if we stayed together. When he moved to leave, I stepped forward, lifted my hand as if to touch his arm, and said his name.

He swung wide. The blow landed on my cheek, and I was so shocked I simply slumped, the pain throbbing in. Billy. My brother.

'Why did you follow me? You disgust me, the very sight of you. If you hadn't—'

I fell back, looked up at him from where I lay.

'If I hadn't what?' I was angry too. Angry at him for being so unfair, angry at him for pushing me away. 'I didn't push those men on her! That was all your own doing, William Smith.'

He glared at me, raising his fist once more, but I was still a pathetic heap on the floor. He dropped his fist and spat, then turned away. I could see him properly then, the devastation behind the fury. He would keep going, I could see, and if necessary he would destroy everything in his path. And I didn't care, in that moment. To hell with him then, I thought.

◎◎

The ship work was never-ending. It was the work of men who were as strong and thick and callused as rope themselves. Soft skin was no match for the pulling and tightening, unravelling and knotting of ship rope, especially wetted by salt water. Calluses had to be grown by working the skin raw and then beginning again the next day. My days indoors in contemplation and bookwork made me useless for this, and London had already infected my lungs. I wheezed and coughed and carried on like an old man, especially at night, in the cold or smoke. I thought the time at sea would clear them and make me stronger. And I suppose it did. I toughened over the first few weeks, though my joints swelled and complained relentlessly. The men soon gave me the lowest and weakest jobs when they saw I had not the

217

brawn for ropes and sail work. I dealt with the waste buckets and endless cleaning. I was the cook's slave, carting and peeling and cutting any rot from saltmeat or biscuit. When the men found the food not to their liking, it was me they took it out on, for no one challenged the cook. They had a go all right, but they kept it within reason, for the captain was never far from hearing, and he was Angus's man, and Angus had given me his protection. Just as well, for if I had been one of the other men, I would have sneered at me as well.

Billy all but ignored me. He had the strength and skill to be one of the most sought-after midshipmen. He barely slept. When he could he took a double watch, and when he was not working he ate and slept without stopping to talk. We saw each other each day, but kept up a pretence that we did not. After weeks had passed, I tried once or twice to speak with him, but he would barely acknowledge me. My attempts were tentative, childish.

'Billy, did you see the stingray leaping in a school off the starboard side this morning?'

'Ah, leave me be, Hemi, I have no interest in your visions and I am not your friend. When will you get this in your head? I have nothing left.'

'But I need nothing from you. I only intend —'

'I know of your intentions, Hemi. And I have no love for any man now. Stay away from me. I am worthless. But then so is every other man here. Perhaps you most of all. All I have is the work to get lost in. I recommend you should think upon the same.'

He was right. I was worthless. I should not have come, but I had thought that if I followed him here, away from the dark city and all that had happened, I could remake a friendship with him. We could be comrades in it, our pain. But I was not

218

worthy of the guilt Billy needed to hold close to his heart. And he knew it punished me to watch him and not be allowed to offer comfort or gain it for myself.

@@

A ship is its own island with its own rules. I was sick for so long on my first journey I paid little attention and hid behind the Artist's coatskirts. On the *Perpetua* I had no such protection. There was only so much scuttling about I could do before it became expedient to prove myself a good man, though I had not the heart to pull out my comic tricks and witty turns. Instead I turned to my coloured brethren, the ones who, like me, were treated with some suspicion just because of the look and sound of them. Be us black or brown, Lascar or Oriental, it takes a bit more for those with dark skin to make the right impression, so we found ourselves often at the edge of things together. This took me even further from Billy, but it was something to be in the company of men who knew what was on the other side of the invisible wall that Englishmen like to construct around themselves. We were tributaries of the same river, orphans of the same Empire. Twins Nabarun and Nabendu, from India — no one could work the masts like them. Jonathan, a different kind of Indian, he said, with a Creole mother and an American grandmother. Man could sing in four languages and speak in three. And of course Song, our cook, as diminutive as he was fierce. He called me Sháozi — his Spoon — for it was to him I reported.

'My name is Song,' he said on my first day. 'Remember it means strong.'

When I laughed he began hitting me across the shoulders with his heaviest ladle. I tried to shrug out of his way, but succeeded only in giving him my arms to bruise.

'Why are you laughing, idiot boy? You're worth nothing more than this spoon.' And there it was, my new name as far as he was concerned, just another tool in his kitchen. I soon came to learn that it was best to keep to Song's good side.

'How do you think a Chinaman gets to be a cook on an Englishman's ship?' Nabarun whispered to me at our first meal. 'Song has magical hands. Can turn the dullest meat and most rotten grain into an Oriental feast. The captain will have no other.'

'There's strength and then there's strength.' Nabendu, his brother, grabbed my upper arm, causing me to flinch. 'Mind him, and all will be well for you here.'

So I did. It was not magic, I soon learnt, but the spices Song carried at all times that made his food so palatable. By the end of the week he did not seem to mind the little rhyme I had concocted — the Strong Song, I called it.

'Very funny, Sháozi. But keep working hard or I'll get a new spoon.'

And then there was Ethan. I come to him last because still I feel the pang of him fresh. Ethan, the greatest of us. He saw me perhaps even before I saw myself. He knew me. How can I convey what it was that we shared, we misfits on that boat? We were all adrift from something or somewhere, and should perhaps have felt more different from each other than we did. What did it matter to me when Song called me Sháozi or Jonathan sang one of his many vicious lullabies? Why did it feel like home when Ethan placed his wide hand on the back of my neck? Why, when we laughed, was the laugh different from any I had caused or given in London? They made me remember things, these men. When we told our stories, they may as well have been the same story.

'The soldiers came that night.'

'I ran away from that place and hid.'

'It was better to leave than to stay and slave. But I shouldn't have left them behind.'

We thought ourselves cowards and traitors. We thought we could not go home.

But Ethan was on his way home, at least to his home ocean. Although we planned to stop at several ports in the West Indies, his island, Jamaica, was not one of our destinations. I knew how I would feel if we were headed towards the Pacific: how the skin recognises its home winds, how the ear catches the song of people so much like one's own. Home does not always mean land. Ethan had fled the Caribbean Sea, he told us, just as any black man or woman with the opportunity would. Slavery, despite the movements against it in Britain, was still common in most places, if not officially, then by default. What do you do with a displaced people who still need to eat? Slave labour is still slavery. But men such as him, men with the strength of gods, could find other masters, and some semblance of freedom.

'We should call you Song!' I exclaimed at this, earning myself a ladle beating when we prepared the next meal. Sometimes my mouth is quicker than my thinking.

'Don't mistake my size for the strength of our cook,' said Ethan. He knew where best to place his loyalties, though he grinned and winked in my direction.

It was this band of unlikely brothers who kept me afloat as we sailed.

SEVENTEEN

I was Song's boy, but I was often given other tasks. Cork the decks, check the holding blocks, the shackles and lines, sand and paint wherever it was needed. I washed the lower decks constantly. Mitchell was chief mate, and had taken me on reluctantly, so he worked me hard, and looked at me with hard eyes. It was not unusual for him to give me more work than it was possible to complete in my watch, and then to make me continue until it was done, berating me for my weakness. 'We'll make a man of you,' he'd say, grinning as if he was making a joke, though it was clear his remark contained no good humour.

This continued for many days, until a rebellion rose in me that I could barely suppress. I'd worked a long day and was hungry when he told me to slush down the foremast. The hour was late and my watch was long over. I wondered if I could talk my way out of the task. My tongue had rescued me from many tight spots before, but he took me as insolent.

'Excuse me sir, Mr Mitchell. My watch is long over.'

'I'm not accustomed to repeating myself.'

'It looks like it will be a fine day tomorrow — I can start early —'

'You've got cheek, haven't you, boy?'

'I'm sorry, sir. I mean no disrespect, only I have so much pain in my joints and I haven't eaten in many hours.'

'Are you an old man, boy? You look fine to me. Back to work or I'll show you how I deal with lazy boys.'

I was more than this, I knew I was more than this. I couldn't drop it.

'I am in no way lazy, sir —'

'I'll give you rope's end for answering me back.'

'But —'

My hesitation was enough. He blocked my escape and began flogging me with the bight of a thick rope. There was no one else about, and I was defenceless. I didn't know whether it would be worse to try to run, or to stay where I was and take what he dealt me. I crouched down as he laid into me, hoping it might satiate his fervour to punish me. The sting of that heavy, wet rope. Burns that stung more fiercely than anything I had encountered. I tried not to yelp, but the pain of it. Perhaps he liked that, I thought, before he finally gave off.

But the next day he was into me again.

'Bring the marlinspike, boy,' he ordered, and when I did not fetch it fast enough, he lifted the rope again.

'No, sir.' I could not take another beating so soon. 'I will complain to the master. You cannot continue to beat me so.'

'You've got a posh accent for a darkie, but there's no way I'll let you get to Captain Hide. You can try, though, if it pleases you, boy.'

His face was contorted in a sly grin, but I took the bait

anyway. My choice was to stay where I was and get beaten or to attempt to get help and be beaten.

I'd taken only four steps when his fist slammed into the side of my head. He hit me at least three more times about the head before I fell, and when I was down he kicked me several times before other crew members were upon us, holding him back. Blood was flowing from my nose and mouth. I remember no more after that.

Until Ethan. I opened my eyes as he placed me in a hammock.

◎◎

One is often occupied by two people. All the while, as I recovered from my beating, and laboured and found my sea legs, another of me turned over everything that had happened, wallowed in melancholy. The condition I now found myself in was completely apt. I mourned the light I thought I'd seen at the Empire's centre at the same time as I mourned my friends. I felt suddenly old, the excitement of discovery like a dull and shrivelled skin around parched animal bones. I did not know if I would ever feel that thrill of the new again. Though physically Billy inhabited the same ship as me, I finally came to see that the friend he had been had passed into another realm, out of my reach. I still thought about him and, when I could stand it, Henry. The journey was a penance; the blisters and cold and nausea small reminders of unworthiness — mine or the world's, I did not know. Mitchell was my punishment.

It was Ethan who tried to draw me out when our rest times coincided. He wanted my story, all of it, and in exchange he offered his.

'You know, Jimmy,' he said, for that is what they called me, 'of all the hardships in my slave days, the thing I always found

224

the hardest was how it don't make sense. One man looks into another man's eye and don't see nothing there. I couldn't work it in my head to give it sense. It was that almost turn me crazy.'

I thought of the deep welts on his back. We'd all seen them exposed on hot days, and each time I wondered how they'd been made and how a man could survive such a thing. It looked like he'd been flayed, the skin pulled back and fused open. There were ridges and valleys, flesh that never quite regained its natural colour. And when he'd seen me looking, he'd told me to touch it. *Don't be afraid, boy, but pray this is the closest you ever get to a proper whipping.* It made me feel better about my own bruises. It's odd how another man's pain can be comforting.

'How did you get out?'

'Sold to a ship. I didn't really get out. Still slaved to a ship. They traded me from one to the other. Kept my head down, and they thought me trustworthy. Do that long enough and they start slipping, start giving you small freedoms. If I was landlocked, those small freedoms would mean nothing, but at port, if you get your timing right, you can be on a different ship going in a different direction before anyone notices anything amiss. And then it became unfashionable to mention slaves in some parts of the world, like England. They like their niggers invisible, don't like to be reminded of the source of their money. Everything they got is still dependent on the backs of slaves. So no one accused me of anything other than stowing away, and someone my size can earn his passage even as a stowaway — they not gonna throw me off when they can use me good.'

I told him my own small story of adventure and woe. All but my feelings for Billy, which were something I had not the language to reveal. I told him of my people, our fierceness at the bottom of the world.

'Sometimes I do not feel I am of that world,' I told him.

225

He laughed. 'What are you talking about, Jimmy? How can you not be? It all over you — the way you look, your laugh.' He looped a great arm around my shoulders. 'Little Maori boy who fancies himself an English gentleman. What do you see in them, boy? They but insipid imitations of real men. Waxy ghosts. Ghoulish niggers. I think that's why they steal us from our homelands. I think that's why they can't look at us proper. We only show them they own weakness.'

I remember that deep voice. The sureness of it. The deep swell of it. I began seeking him out.

'And what of women, Ethan? Have you a wife?'

'I've had women, but not a wife. I don't know there is one for me, to tell the truth of it.' He looked at me then, too long. Just a moment too long. 'What about you, Maori boy?'

'Well, as you point out, I am hardly even a man yet. I've had a time or two, but hardly anything you'd take note of.' I was alarmed at how British I suddenly sounded. The intimacy of the question had caused me to fall back on my longest syllables, my most formal language. Ethan nodded, and turned to his work, began climbing into the rigging, his muscles working under a sheen of sweat, the evening light glancing off just so.

I became his disciple, watching my new friend far too often and at too much length. And when I saw him look back I didn't trust it for a long time — I thought it might be my own feelings clouding my perception. A look that lingers too long is not enough to mean anything, and yet I wanted it to.

And Mitchell still kept his eye on me, and gave me the rotten jobs that came up, though he had been admonished for the beatings that kept me in bed for three days and no longer lifted his hand to me. There were so many reasons I should have avoided looking at anyone for any length of time.

Then one supper time I happened to sit directly across from

Ethan. Such moments were rare. As was my custom, I stole glances, reminding myself not to stare too long. We talked to the other men at the table, laughed a bit, chewed and drank, and looked. I watched his lips as he chewed, the way his throat flexed to swallow. And that was when I saw it: his eyes ran slowly down the length of my face, lingered at my neck, and rose to meet my own again. It was a caress, the way that look played over me. And I knew. What had seemed an impossibility slowly became imaginable, probable even, if only I could cross that space between us. I came to know my own desire in my recognition of his. Ethan looked at me the way a cold and thirsty sailor might look at a long hot mug of coffee spiked with whisky.

After what had happened with Billy, I had thought my feelings unnatural. I told myself again and again that they should go unheeded. Except they felt as natural as breathing and eating and sleeping, and here they were again, even when I thought I'd put them down. Ethan looked to me and I looked to him, and what passed between us was more intoxicating than all the wonderful shows of London put together.

A ship is its own island. But it is a small island with many people. Days pass into weeks. At last, as a warm day turned over into night, we found ourselves above during a late watch, while everyone else was dozing or busy at stern. Recognition of our opportunity was as swift as his movement towards me. He took me, firmly, by the shoulder, pushed me behind the foremast, took a handful of my hair and drew my head back to expose my neck.

'Like this?' he whispered. 'Will you be made a man like this?' And the heat of his mouth was on me, his hands feeling the shape of my body underneath my clothes. The man-stink of him rose in my nostrils and caused a low rumble from my throat.

He grunted and pressed himself into me. I felt his need as if it were my own, but then it was my own. I didn't know what came next, but he did. He gripped my cock and wet his own and found a way underneath to enter me. I'd heard of this. I knew it could be done, though it seemed impossible. He worked me slowly and I found a way to relax, a way to let him in. At first a hurt, and then a release. Such a release. We both felt the letting go and then he worked me harder, his hand on my cock the whole time until we both shuddered and whimpered like two men who had found deliverance.

It had been mere minutes. We untangled and I laughed. His great hand was on the back of my neck like a balm, my head bent forward as I adjusted my clothing. He said something quietly, but I did not hear it, for I looked up and saw a man emerging from the lower decks. Like ice water dousing the heat that had spread through my body: Billy, looking right into my eyes.

◉◈

After that Billy continued to avoid me, but I felt the sting of his disapproval. He couldn't be jealous, he had made that clear, and he'd said he didn't care either way what I did and with whom. Now I saw that these declarations were untrue. Or at least they seemed to me to be. At first I felt smug in my bravado: I had something that even the worldly Billy Neptune did not. But as the days passed, without the all-too-brief comfort of Ethan's touch, I did not feel so proud of my circumstance. Now the weather had turned turbulent and wet, and I was still the boy at the bottom of the pecking order, still not tough enough to hold my own. Lucky for me Song's fondness for his handy and tuneful Sháozi kept me out of harm's way as much as

228

the Captain's protection. And time passed. The moment with Ethan seemed like an hallucination. I dared not mention it to him, though he once brushed his hand across my backside in passing, and another time walked straight into me, our bodies colliding so forcefully we carried each other as bruises for days. Our liaison had been like meat to a hungry peasant, and neither of us knew if there could be more. I'd risk too much, I knew, if I allowed myself the appetite. But I was also not strong enough to fight it. There were quick, rough moments. Stolen gropings and silent moments on moonless nights. No opportunity for privacy. Billy would not tell our secret, but we both worried a more spiteful crew member might witness our coupling.

Finally the evening came where I found myself at starboard, all alone I thought, washing and hanging the Captain's clothes as best I could. A noise behind me.

'You are alone.'

'As always.' Even now, I could feel my heart speeding at the sound of Billy's voice, blood rushing in my temples.

'Not *always*.'

'What do you want of me?'

'You shouldn't. If you got caught —'

'We won't. We're careful.'

'Hmm.'

'I did not think you cared.'

'Neither did I.'

I turned. 'I wish —'

'Best not to do that. Work. Stay safe. Make landfall and a commission. And the same on the way home.' He was moving to leave, but he hesitated. 'I wish it could've been different, Hemi. I wish a great many things.'

'Yes. As do I.' I wished, more than anything, that he was my friend again, like on that first day. Just a lad making a new acquaintance. All the world a bright stage. The show barely begun. As I thought this, I watched him leave, and I couldn't figure out how things had become like this, all dark and twisted, but I saw how life was always this way, ever since I could remember, and I tried to believe, very hard, that it could surprise me with its brightness again, that one day I would find another moment that was purely good and untainted. I tried to believe this, but I couldn't, because sometimes when you stand in the shadow you cannot remember the feeling of sun on your skin.

You had once been my sun, Papa, and if I live long enough to meet you, my descendants, I know you will be the same. But on that wretched ship the only warmth came from my band of friends, our misfit crew within a crew, especially Ethan. And I was drawn to him the way the bird and lizard are drawn to bask in sunlight. Perhaps I fuelled his heat in turn. We found each other. Storms had churned the seas for days, and we took our chances, out there in the wet and grinding darkness. The blunt pleasure of our hard bodies. Everyone preoccupied with getting their tasks done and taking shelter; no one to see us, or so we thought.

But the shadow that came was Mitchell. He was waiting for me as I returned to the lower deck after my watch. Finding him there, knowing he had been waiting. The light going out from the world.

'I saw you, boy. We don't tolerate no dirty buggery on this ship.' He had me by the shirt, he was dragging me through the dark. The night watch was minimal — two of his lackeys came as he ordered, tied me spreadeagled to the deck.

'The Captain. Ethan—'

'The Captain said I should take care of this. You had his protection until he learnt what kind of boy you are. We'll deal with that negro well and good. Reliable that way, we are.'

Nothing can prepare you. The assault.

'I take care of everything on this ship, boy,' Mitchell spat in my ear. He used the end of his rope, his fists, his feet; he enacted what he had witnessed. For some time, I lost consciousness. When I became aware of myself again, I was no longer tied tightly, though my hands were still bound to a rail on the forecastle deck, where the rain lashed at me. There was nothing to me any more. I was blood and bruise, a wet smear, rocked in the callous arms of a ship that had never been a home. I had become darkness. I had become Henry. I was the long and hideous starless night. Take me, I prayed, that's enough now. End it.

So it was no surprise, later that night, when I was awoken by a roiling boat, all splitting and roaring, no surprise at all.

◎◎

When we go in the sea it is a warm sea. I think it's going to be cold the way the English sea is cold. So cold you don't know yourself. I think, as we go down, it will be pain the way ice can sometimes burn. The moment it comes for me I see the great waves coming as if the gods have called a halt to proceedings so that I might see it happen, one slow moment at a time. This is it, I think. This is what all of it has come to. And then I realise I don't want this death, not here, so far from everything I love, in these alien waters, on this white man's ship. But Billy is here somewhere — I think of him and I think of Henry and Ethan. I think of all of my friends in London. And then I think of my mother and father and wonder if I will be reunited with them now. All of it I see in this frigid still pocket of time.

But the sea, the warm sea, and I am deep sunk in. A babe in his warm bath. Oh you, my mother. Oh you. There is no breath in me and no breathing to be had unless I breathe water. No longer the pain. We all come back here in the end, I think, and I am lazy and languid and ready for the ocean to take me. Not my ocean, perhaps, but are not all these bodies of water the same blood? If I sink under, will she not take me home? Will her currents not take my bones to where they need to be? I think of what lies beneath, and a cool stripe of fear runs through me. The waves wash over, but then the wooden rail I am strapped to bounces back up, pulling me with it. My bound hands lift me just high enough to breathe. The binding holds me, even when I have no strength to hold myself. I lose control of my bowels.

I am full, then. Full of sea in my ears, my nose, my mouth, my eyes. Full under my eyelids and between my legs. I am as much sea as I am man. I am the ocean, but the ocean will not have me.

Soon enough, she spits me out.

Underneath, a hard, sharp surface. Then sand, and still. The current calm in this high spot. The black night claims me. And just like the sea the black night is warm and I am alive. I can stand, water about my middle, pieces of boat knocking together in the close distance, and God knows what else, causing me to call out. Hello? Hello! Is anyone there? The moon and stars give just enough light for me to see the jagged edges of planks and masts and broken barrels, the thick slumped forms of bodies unmoving. I want to run towards them, I want to claim them, but my own limbs sink me down now, thick and useless. It is all I can do to keep my head up, my arms held above by the buoyancy of the rail. Hello? Ahoy! There is something here to stand on! A reef? A reef! Come towards me if you can hear me! Hello?

There is little strength in my voice. Shame comes in and takes what's left.

I don't hear others. How the earth has managed to rise up under the sea and ground me I don't know. But I stand in the sea, in the night, and wait.

EIGHTEEN

When I wake I know it has been daylight for many hours from the way heat sits under my skin. The sun is high, not at its zenith but high enough to have been beating down on me for many hours. It is a miraculous thing that I haven't drowned. I have stayed upright only due to the bindings that had me hoping for death. And as I wake I wonder again why I go to so much effort to keep this breath moving in and out of me.

I know I am in trouble. My bones are on fire. My joints swollen and unbending. My eyes, when I force them open, sting as if a thousand tiny jellyfish have settled there. There is water all around and yet the skin on my lips curls like woodchips in the fire. There is no moisture in my mouth. Only a lump of unmovable tongue.

The sun is hot, the water warm. But I am cold and ache. I do not know how much I can move or make sound. Perhaps it will hurt less if I can stop taking air into my tender lungs. It would be like sleeping. I could do that. But ah, no. The lungs want air, sweet even when it hurts to take it in. And I would have to fight my bindings to sink under anyway.

I do not know if anyone else has survived the night. If not, it means Billy and Ethan are dead. I don't have the energy to mourn them. All my attention concentrated on the pain in my body. No matter that I would like to let the sea take me under, when a small wave brings salt water to flood in my nose, my mouth, my eyes, I still struggle up. Up. My own body my enemy.

There is a constant roaring, which I come to understand is simply the world. The sea is the world's voice, roaring: she is mad, she is sorrowful, she is forcing me to live through this. She won't take me under because I am not finished yet. Live, she says, even if you have not the will. You survive. You are marked by it. That is who you are.

I don't know who I am, I tell her. Shhhh, she says, shhhh. I let her rhythm take me, but she is wrong.

And then rising up, slowly, other sounds.

It is a long time. Men's voices yelling, but not loud enough to hear. The rhythm of oars. The rise and splash of paddling the sea. Fishing? Salvaging? Coming in. Receding. And then closer, closer. Shhhh, I say, listen. Shhhh. But the bubbles take that last sound, the water rises around my ears, I can feel her closing in. Soon we will go too far, me and her; soon she will engulf parts of me and there will be no return. But a hauling, a lifting, a dripping sodden heavy load in the bottom of a boat. I am up. And I shiver so hard the pain takes up a rhythm like a beating drum.

@

Under. Deeply. Sweetly. Shhhh, I still hear her. The bed swims. Henry bends over me, Billy behind her, entering her the way Ethan entered me. The men then. Oh Henry, no! Shhh, she says, I let them take Billy this time. Not me. Not me any longer. I am so tired, Jimmy, so tired of this rotten world. They think they own me, all of those men. As if my cunt and arse and belly are theirs to implant as they will. As if I have not a mind or eyes or wits of my own. I am a queen, you hear me, Jimmy? Ridiculous men! And then she is a fire, rising up to join the sun, searing every part of me. I love you, Jimmy, but you are still a stupid man. A banshee rising, and I laugh with her. Go, Henry, take every last one of us with you. Sear the earth. Make them feel it. Every last stupid bastard. She reaches out — a touch that scorches. Oh, Jimmy. You were one of the good ones. Back when it mattered.

It is black for a long time. And then there are dreams repeating and going nowhere. I am repeating and going nowhere. And the sheets are wet and cold. And I am burning with it.

I am under a tree and so is Nu. And my mother. But I no longer know them by the cavities where their eyes should be. Do not worry, child, my mother says, Nu will watch you. But she has no eyes, I say, and my mother cannot hear me. But how will Nu watch me, mother? I keep asking and asking. Finally, she speaks. It's always about you, Hemi, isn't it? You know what happened to the rest of us? Stop thinking about yourself, son. The rest of us are dead. You should be watching for your sister. She has no eyes of her own, you know. If I had known you would be such a koretake, selfish son — we could have left you there. You like being left, don't you, boy? Yes, mother, I say. Yes yes yesyessshhhh. The waves, the salt, the terrible moment before you take the next breath.

He is last to come, and that is how I know. Billy grinning,

235

Billy laughing, the sound of my heart. I found her, he tells me, I found Henry! He is dressed in his finest, just as he was that first day, at the Hall. His energy is back in him, and if I close my eyes now I think I will lose him forever. Don't leave me, Billy. I am blubbering and retching all over myself. Look at me. I became a wretch the moment I met you. No, Hemi. You became a prince.

∽

At first, blur and pain and sweat. Days of it. Someone forcing water or broth between my lips. Spilling it back up until finally my stomach accepts what is put there. Slowly. Slowly, I come to understand again what I see, what I can feel: the dimensions of a small room, a bed of nothing more than cloth sacks over dry palm leaves, the light outside so bright through the door, the moonlight more bearable but no cooler. Always so warm. And people. A man. A woman. Children who seem unfettered in their touching. A language I cannot place that sometimes sounds like English. The roar of the sea. Their many kindnesses. My shame. The roar.

∽

Eventually, my swollen tongue shrank to a size that allowed me speech. I am Chames, I said, no, Chimmy.

Chimmy? Chames? She was a big woman, wrapped in light, colourful cloths that looked so cool. I knew they couldn't be, but I had to reach out.

No touch, Chimmy Chames.

Hemi. Chust Hemi.

Chustemmy?

236

He-mi. Please, call me Hemi. Even this — too much effort. I fell into a deep sleep. And woke some time later, the smell of spiced food in the air.

'He's Chimmy Chames Chustemmy, he says.'

'No. Er, sorry. My name is Hemi.'

'Is it now?' This man, dressed only in tatty short pants, but cutting an elegant figure with his fine-muscled physique. 'Get me shirt now, Rebekah. And somethin' to fan him. I sit with him a while.'

The fanning was like all of God's angels beating their wings.

'I never seen no man sweat like you. No black man. No white man. No brown man like you. Where you from? Who your people up there in England?'

'No one now.' I couldn't look down that dark path. Not yet. 'I'm a New Zealander. A Maori.'

'A Mahwrrri?'

'A native of New Zealand. It's an island. In the south.'

'Don't know it.'

'Where is this?'

'I'm Robert, my wife Rebekah. This our own place. Our very own.'

'Thank you for letting me stay. You have been so kind. You have children. You don't need another mouth…'

'Didn't eat more than a drop. Fishing's good right now.'

'Thank you. A good house.'

'Our very own, made with our own hands.' Rebekah spread her fingers, palms up, as if to demonstrate.

'Jus a two by four.'

'Oh? Where are we?'

'Close to Speightstown, close to the sea.'

'Yes. The sea.'

'All good things come from the sea.'

'Them which don't come from the trees. You feed him?'

'What do I look like? A nursemaid?'

'You found him, you feed him now. I got better things to do.'

'Don't vex me, woman.' But she had already gone. He looked from the bowl to me. 'We pleased to have you, Hemi. Here, you can feed yourself.'

I nodded my thanks. The bowl held fish and a yellow-orange fruit. I did not think I had the strength or the hunger, but as soon as I tasted the fruit I salivated like I never had before. Sighed and slurped at the food.

'Slow down! You make yourself sick.'

'What is it?'

'Mango. And flying fish.'

Fish who could fly. I thought I had seen such things in the days before the storm, but I had no idea where I was. An island, perhaps in the Caribbean still.

'What island is this?' I sucked at my fingers.

'Ho! You don know what island you on? Suppose not. Found you half dead on that reef out there. Not far from land but ready to drown. This is Barbados, boy.'

So we made it. I made it. 'Is there anyone else?'

'I haven't seen 'em. Not since we were out there. Didn't think we'd find any living, but there you were. Flotsam and jetsam coming in off the tide, though. Got enough planks to add to me house. When we find the time we look for others.'

Then I was the only one?

'Storm and tide coulda taken 'em anywhere. We are nowhere here, a small cove. Maybe the others found their way to the towns.'

I fell back on the bed, exhausted by the act of eating and speaking.

'You rest here.'

I managed a thank you before sinking under again.

⊚⊚

I had been lucky, I saw that. Not just that a family had found me before I drowned, but that they kept me alive, and allowed me a precious bed and all the time I needed to recover. Robert fished and fixed the house; Rebekah sewed and yelled at the many children who found their way under her broom. Half of them weren't even hers, but belonged to neighbours who still worked the fields. Came to her every day because she was one of the few who managed a living off land and sea. Robert fished enough for the family and market, taking the older boys with him each day. They were luckier than most, didn't owe a landowner for their plot, didn't have to go on doing the slave work.

'I refused.'

'Always been stubborn, you.'

'Well, you don't mind now, do you?'

'Almost starved the first years.'

'But we didn't.'

'Our eldest won't even touch fish now.'

'Is all we ate for a long time. I never was much of a fieldworker, but the ocean feels like I can tiptoe across it and make fish dance on my fingertips.'

'That you can, Robert.'

'Found this place. Nothing but a spot no one paid attention to in those days. Can't grow anything here. Difficult to get in and out of if you don't know the tides well enough. So we made a home.'

'Nobody else owns it, or if they do, they haven't figured out it's theirs and we owe them rent.'

'It's only beach. Could be swept away any minute.'

'But it's our beach. And the wreck of it'll be our wreck, even if the pickneys have to hold on by their pincers like crabs after a storm.'

'We all just crabs in a storm, ain't we Eemi?'

'I know I am.'

'We couldn't do it any more, could we, Rebekah?'

'No, Robert. No more.'

'Our first two were born slaves. Just a good thing we tough, and quiet, and get away from things as quick as we able.'

'You got to be strong but not so strong, as that they notice you.'

'Strong enough to survive.'

'If things hadn't changed we might not be here now, though.'

'Mmm-hmmm. I think I woulda died just looking at another field.'

'Mmm-hmmm.'

I loved the sound of Robert and Rebekah's voices, the music of them. It was the second sound I collected in those islands after the ocean roar that had berated and lulled me in equal measure. Their song was more a balm on my beaten soul, a gentle rongoa, a medicine. But even without saying it aloud they spoke to me of other beatings in the days before their freedom. I could hear it in their voices, even if it was just a space now, an uninhabited place where that other life had been, the things they'd tried to scrub out. My night terrors were nothing to the terror they held at bay through force of will and stubborn adherence to a squatter's code. I told them what Ethan had told me, what he had shown me on his back. 'I don't know why they can't see it, most of them,' Robert said as we bent over his nets, me trying to help him mend with my shaky hands. 'Can't see us, can't see we is them, can't see what they do to us they do to themselves. Says so in their Bible even. Still they don't see.'

But talking about Ethan conjured him up, and I couldn't think about where he might be, what might have happened.

Robert and Rebekah were gentle and indulgent with me, their strange castaway, and in return I offered them all the stories I could conjure of my homeland and the great white northern city where each of their former masters had their original homes and families, fortunes and good merchant names. The hardship and insecurity of my friends' lives was easier on them than long hours working for one of the plantation owners. No one was going to put their children in the field, they told me, whatever the cost. It was a comfort to watch the rhythm of their lives proceed, the children running in and out, eyes wide at the bedraggled stranger in one of their beds. Soon they grew bolder, climbing over me when it suited the game. Eventually I became steady on my feet, and began to think again of other things. Home. Not London. I did not know what to think of the city any more, I did not know what it meant to me. But home. How I longed for something I had never had. A place of my own. A place that was simply mine. A place to rest. Perhaps, a family.

On the sixth day after I awoke, the bodies began to wash up. The clouds had been threatening for days, and with the winds and currents out of sorts, Robert stayed home that morning and found himself netting bodies instead of fish. I wasn't yet strong enough to walk far, but the bodies continued for three days, just one or two at a time. On the final day I went down to greet my brothers out of some sense of duty. I shouldn't have. Ethan was there, grey and blue and bloated, only half of his face and one of his arms intact, but I knew it was him. Such a strong man. Taken trying to save the ship, no doubt. And yet I survived. The koretake one. I retched and hobbled about, trying to help Robert bury him until he told me to go back to the house. I was no help. I was getting used to that. But Ethan deserved better. He was better. He should have been the one to wash up living. I was nothing but an empty begging bowl, the scrape of algae muck on the underside of a ship. I understood this, deeply, as I returned to the house. It took me a long time to go that short distance, my eyes on the azure horizon. I didn't know what Ethan had been to me, I didn't know what it was possible for him to be for me, but he had been so wildly present in the world, so substantial, so splendid. So beautiful. My world was so much smaller without him.

∾

As soon as I was able, I told the family I would be on my way. I had nothing to offer them, no way to pay them back. The best I could do was remove myself so that I was no longer a burden.

'You stay as long as you like,' said Rebekah, attempting nonchalance, though her eyes were so hard I knew they hid softness.

'You no burden,' said Robert, and the boys ran around me in circles while the girls garlanded me with coconut leaf.

But they knew as well as I did that the island had no place for me, stuck as I was between worlds. And they had mouths enough to feed, despite their protestations. I would accompany Robert to market at week's end, and from there find my way to Bridgetown. 'You'll find a ship there,' he said, 'and plenty of first mates looking for a ship's boy. But think on how to read them. Be wary. Be mindful. All sorts of evil makes its way to our ports. This the ass-end of the world, with plenty of shit flowing through it.' Rebekah made her customary sound of agreement, lips together humming, and in that sound was everything she

242

had to say to me and more. She already considered me one of her brood of strays. Rebekah could say so just by the way her voice lifted and flowed. Then she turned to her work, growling at the children who got in her way. I was not a child any more, and no amount of wishing could make Rebekah my mother.

As we walked, Robert warned me again of the treachery that might await a swarthy boy like myself at the port, but there was no other way home but the tiresome journey north, so that I might take the tiresome journey south again to New Zealand. I helped him as much as I was able at market, and then it was time for him to depart, and for me to follow the road south to Bridgetown. I did not want to say goodbye to Robert. It was as if all the goodbyes in my life might overwhelm me. I am done, I thought, done travelling all these real roads but living all these imaginary lives, none of them real and lasting.

Take me home, I beseeched the gods, though I knew not which gods I was beseeching; take me home, this time thinking of my mother and father and sister; please help me find a home, directing this last at my ancestors. It was perhaps the first time I had really turned my face homewards since I was a very little boy indeed. But despite all my praying and weeping and wringing of hands as I walked that long, dry road to Bridgetown, I had only a vague idea of what my home might look like, of who I might be in that place. All I could do was point myself in the right direction, propel myself forward and hope that somehow I might land in the place from whence I came.

NINETEEN

Thus I found myself at port. A port can be a hard place, but I had been here before, staring into a rough unknown, dependent only on my wits and my humour to get me through. I hoped that it would work for me this time, as it had always worked before, but Bridgetown was a place much used to cheap or even free labour, harsh conditions and brutal discipline. For all my bravado and manufactured confidence, I was still young and soft, and not worth much to anyone. I spent a long day going from ship to merchant to ship, offering my services, then a long night doing the same while avoiding fights and heavy men with too much of a glint in their eyes to have no ill intentions. The following day saw much of the same and, when Rebekah's provisions ran out, the beginnings of hunger and thirst. My fever was back upon me, as well as the ache and swelling that seemed to have set itself into my bones. At least it was a pretty place to live out the last of my pitiful days, I thought. Bright coloured and sea tainted. So many shapely men and women — the locals, not the grimy, red-faced sailors. I don't know if I spoke these thoughts aloud. But I could barely keep myself upright. There was no way a captain or first mate would look upon me as an attractive proposition.

I wondered if I might see survivors from the wreck of the *Perpetua*, and from time to time I thought I did, though I had not the energy to catch up with them. I was fading with thirst when a shadow fell on me and, looking up, I thought I saw a boy my own age, for the light fell behind him and I could make out only his silhouette. But when he moved I recognised who it was that had found me.

'Sháozi! Here. Drink.'

Song thrust his canteen under my nose, and I gratefully took as much water as I could without draining it.

'You look sick, Sháozi.'

'Mmmm. So much better now, Song. Where is everyone? Where is Billy? And Nabarun and Nabendu? And Jonathan? I know where Ethan is, Song. Can't tell you, though. Not enough of him to tell you about.'

'Quiet, Sháozi, you make no sense. Rest now.'

'But Henry and Billy. They'll be all right, eh?'

'Who is Henry? I've seen only five who made it through. No Billy. No Nabarun and Nabendu. No Jonathan. It's good to see you, Sháozi. I thought you were dead for sure. We'll get work, go home soon. After you rest.'

Song stayed with me through another night, then left me under a tree while he went looking for a ship. He came back with food and a position for us. It wouldn't be easy, he said, I must pretend to be strong.

After his saltfish and bread and a good deal of fresh water, I

245

felt strong enough to feign good health. We boarded the *Eliza* before noon.

☙❧

The homeward journey was not eventful, and for that I was grateful. Simple drudgery was acceptable to both Song and me. Without proper positions, we took on the least popular watches and most disliked tasks, and kept our heads down. Eventually the crew learnt our story, and some relayed that a week prior they had encountered a few of our crew looking for a way home. *Perpetua* had sunk, they were able to tell us, and the shipmen they met held out little hope for other survivors. They had used the rowboat before the ship was torn apart, and had little control over where the sea took them through that long night, but made it to Bridgetown the next day. As far as they knew, there was no captain or first mate. We did not know what had become of our friends, save Ethan. We did not know what became of Billy.

As you might guess from my state as I write this, I did not recover. I dragged my sorry carcass from job to job, and though the crew weren't soft on me, they gave me space and sometimes more time in the hammock. We'd survived and with that kind of luck no one wanted to risk the wrath of the sea gods that had saved us. Song did what he could to carry my slack — that man could work. I know I owe him, as well as others, my life.

We came onto the Thames on a fine day. I could smell London from much further upriver, the dirty old whore. Oh, it bites, I know. Where is my respect? But no, London was now an intimate friend who had made me pay for every dalliance, every bright spot of joy. I held an affection for her that was marred by the pox on her neck, the holes in her stockings, the rank odour of her underclothes. But still she excited my passion, both familiar and new. Still I hungered for a taste of her. Still she could dress herself up in her finest rags, eyes flashing, exposing flesh, making my heart beat a little faster. I was sick and pathetic, full of melancholy for Ethan, full of raging pain for Billy and Henry. But London, the seductive wench, she still held me in thrall.

I was a fool, I knew it to my core, and what's more I suspected I brought ill-luck to all who loved me. I had lost so many. The ones who remained untouched were protected by their station in life, their place in the society so carefully constructed by people like them. Even though the Artist was already abroad on another jaunt, he and his family were now the closest people to my heart. They and Mr Antrobus. How I wished I had not abused their hospitality so. Yet I knew I might still ask the Angus family for assistance, at least to find my way home, and that I was forever in their debt, and that somehow I would find a way to return their kindness.

And so it was. Mr Angus sent a cab for me as soon as he learnt of my arrival. It was a miracle to them that I had survived the sinking of the *Perpetua* — they were already mourning the loss of me and the ship, as well as most of the crew. Miss Angus was overcome to see me again, and both she and Miss Herring have nursed me these many months in the room Mr Angus so generously provides. His other sons are grown and gone, he says, so I must be a son to him now, and at last I am content to be whatever he wishes, for without them I know I would be dead.

Mr Song and I parted ways soon after the *Eliza* docked. He is as good a friend as I have ever had, but his family and his home are not in London, and he meant to continue his journey as soon as he was able. Before we parted, I grasped him in a foolish embrace, which he withstood stiffly, and he told me to be well and, finally, not to be a spoon for the rest of my life, and we both laughed with such gusto that we surprised ourselves, and tears leapt into the corners of my eyes.

The carriage came and rattled my bones all the way to the Anguses, and after they drew from me my story and sent me to bed with broth I slept for three days. When I woke I could not rise at all, and Miss Angus fretted and sent for the physician. He says I have the worst rheumatism he has seen in one so young, and there is little he can prescribe but rest and a good invalid's diet. I am bone-sick. Sick to my bones. I can barely hold myself upright.

But you, my future. You have given me reason to hope. To look towards a time when you have come into being, when everything that troubles me is in the past. Mr Antrobus sits with me often, and tells me of the great philosophies of men, and the developments of humanity that are already in progress. I see that we will move away from judgement and prejudice, the things that hurt Henry. The things I saw etched into the backs of Ethan and Robert. We have enough to deal with in the strength of Nature's whims, the strength of the storm and ocean. Oh yes, I have come to respect that.

Listen, my dear, my future. Listen to what I have to tell you now. These last days, Billy has come. Yes, my sweet Billy. At first I thought him a ghost, but no, each day he is here again. He tells me to get well. Tells me to grow strong, and I think I shall. All this time I thought I was dying, but now I understand it was my heart that was broken, not my body. Billy can make me live just by coming here. He sits beside me in the afternoons; sometimes he even holds my hand. He doesn't say it. That he is here is all the evidence I need of his forgiveness.

But no one sees him come and go. When I mention him,

they look at me as if from a long distance, as if they are trying to make an assessment of me. Miss Angus places a hand on my shoulder and tells Miss Herring to fetch a cool cloth. I don't know how he sneaks past them, but I know he is real.

Billy and I, we go through these pages on the days he visits, and he tells me where I have it right, and where I remember it wrong, and where I have surprised him. He reminds me of all my different guises, the names of streets and places I have forgotten. When we get to the parts about him and Henry, he even smiles. Dear Henry, we say in unison. Sometimes I cry while he watches me, but he doesn't shed tears. I visit her too, he says, and I believe she will get well. I believe she will rise from her sickbed again, just like you. But will I, Billy? I ask. And where shall I go then?

You can go anywhere, Hemi, he says. You have been around the world and tried on all the different faces you might inhabit. Now you get to decide, Hemi. Decide who you are.

Wanderer, freak, sailor, philosopher. Native boy in English costume, English boy in native costume. Exhibitionist, lover, clown, Maori boy. Man of the world. How grand. Perhaps it was all real, after all. Perhaps all of those people really did spill out of me. Sometimes it was as if the world demanded it of me. The world demands so much. Perhaps, though, all that time I was simply a boy trying to find his way back into orbit around the sun, my papa.

And you, you in that bright future, you give me hope. For I know that in your time the Empire has become everything she pretended to be, that the march of progress has transformed all, that no one is hurt unjustly, for you must be so beyond that now. I know that progress and civilisation have brought about the golden age we were promised; that men tread lightly; that women and children are free and unburdened by man's hunger;

249

that the place of one's birth and the colour of one's skin has no bearing on the way the world walks upon you, the way you walk upon the world. I choose to believe that the cities of splendour and advancement I held so close and dear to my heart were no great illusion after all; that we do unto others; that the animals from the zoo are uncaged and thriving; that my father led his people to safety; that Esme and Ernie are the queen and king of a realm in which no one is not normal; that graceful and strong Ethan's back is as smooth and unmarked as the day his mother birthed him; that you are listened to; that no muskets were brought to Aotearoa and so my mother and sister lived good, long lives; that no one sleeps on the streets of any city; that all people are liberated in nations who think themselves great; that we no longer use violence to say what we need; that we are as noble as we always made ourselves out to be; that we are better now, that we are better now. For I could not bring you into a world that is no better than this place.

I went from the untamed savage land to the great dome of civilisation, and I fell in love and I grew afraid because none of it was the right way up. But they saw me, too. They saw me looking at them through the savage eye and they felt themselves known. And that would not do. It will be better for you, dear future, and it will all have been worth it. I know you are made of tougher stuff. I know you won't let them off easy. Hold rank, my descendants. There will be peace upon this world. Generosity and goodwill. And what a collective sigh all the peoples of the world will exhale almost at once. This thing we call Civilisation? How great they say it will be. How magnificent. And if it is not, give them the savage eye from me.

AUTHOR'S NOTE

All of the characters and events in this novel are fictional, though I have borrowed some basic details from real people and real events. While I have attempted to faithfully reproduce the particularities of London, circa 1846 — when trains were a new mode of transport, gaslight was only just becoming common in homes, waste was still sent untreated to the Thames or was collected in cesspools, and omnibuses were still too new and expensive to be easily accessible — some of my descriptions may stray into earlier or later time periods.

In keeping with the time period of Hemi's story, te reo Māori words and sentences do not have macrons. Such an omission would be inadequate and incorrect for contemporary Māori language, but we felt the use of macrons to be anachronistic in what is ostensibly the diary of an 1840s Māori figure.

Hemi/James/Jimmy Pōneke's story was initially sparked by the life of Hemi Pomare/James Pomara, about whom very little is known. The most comprehensive description of Hemi Pomare's life can be found in the article on pp 252-253, first published in the *Times* and reproduced in the *New Zealander* on 15 May 1847. I reproduce it here so it is clear that the rest of this story is entirely made up. This novel in no way represents the real historical figure. It appears Hemi Pomare's life was more extraordinary, adventurous and tragic even than Hemi Pōneke's. I have not attempted to encompass that real life, because it is not mine to recreate and because I am unable to do it justice. Hemi Pomare's real life was a jumping-off point from which I began to imagine the fantastic adventures of a young Māori man in early Victorian London, and for that I am deeply grateful to him. Soon after the court case described below, he died, without ever returning home. In the nineteenth century, this was the fate of many Indigenous people who lived in heavily polluted London by choice or by force.

English Extracts.

THAMES.—On Saturday, Mr. Richard Mitchell, the chief mate of the ship *Eliza*, from Barbadoes, appeared before Mr. Ballantine, to answer a charge of assaulting James Pomara, a New Zealand boy, whose history is a very extraordinary one. The case was opened by Mr. Hinde, from the firm of Beddome and Co., solicitors, who said the boy was 15 years old, and grandson of the celebrated New Zealand chief Pomare. His father was killed and eaten in a native fight, and his mother died when he was very young. He reached Sydney in an English ship, after a variety of adventures, and was educated by his guardians. He arrived in England last March, and was taken great notice of by some of the leading persons in this country, and was introduced to Royalty itself in Buckingham Palace. His protector was Mr. Caleb Angus, a merchant and shipowner in the city. The lad expressed a wish to go to sea, and was placed aboard the *Caleb Angus*, a ship named after his protector, the captain being instructed to take very great care of him, and see that he was properly attended and provided for. The *Caleb Angus* was wrecked at Barbadoes, and Pomara narrowly escaped with his life, and was thrown ashore with nothing but his shirt and trowsers on. The lad after visiting Grenada and St. Vincent, where he was taken into the service of the harbour master, and after under-

252

going many hardships and adventures, which had more the appearance of a romance than the occurrences of actual life, was shipped on board the *Eliza* for England. The lad was exposed to much ill-usage on board the *Eliza*, was frequently assaulted, and his unprotected state created no sympathy, as it ought to have been done. The lad was then introduced into the witnesses' box. He was attired in a midshipman's uniform, purchased for him by Mr. Angus, and his intelligent open countenance prepossessed every one in his favour. The particular assault complained of was committed while at sea. The lad, who suffered much from rheumatism and pain, was treated very roughly, and one day he was directed by the mate to take a marling spike on to the main yard. The lad was directed to wait a minute by the man on the yard, and the mate called him down again, and after abusing the lad, said he would give him a rope's end, and gave him a severe flogging with the bight of a thick rope. The lad threatened to complain to the master of the ship, on which the mate said he would prevent him doing that, and after striking him with his fists about the head and face, kicked him severely. Pomara said he would make the mate suffer for his ill treatment when he reached England, and the mate beat him again, and caused the blood to flow from his nose and mouth. Pomara was disabled for some time afterwards. The lad's statement having been confirmed by a seaman, Mr. Pelham after cross-examining the witnesses, addressed the magistrate for the defendant, and submitted that the boy was insolent, and that the punishment was not excessive. Mr. Ballantine said the law did not give any power to mates of ships to correct any one, and he considered the defendant had been guilty of a very cruel and attrocious assault on a friendless lad. It was not surprising that mutinies were sometimes heard of, when such cruelties as those complained of were practised. He fined the mate £5 which was instantly paid. The lad Pomara will return to his native land with Mr. Eyre, the new Lieutenant Governor of New Zealand.—*Times, Nov.* 29.

From:https://paperspast.natlib.govt.nz/newspapers NZ18470515.2.11

This book is also not in any way about the artist George French Angas, and makes no claim to know what kind of man he was, but I could not resist borrowing from the fantastically revealing title of his book *Savage Life and Scenes in Australia and New Zealand: being an artist's impressions of countries and people at the Antipodes, With Numerous Illustrations*, which is a fascinating volume in its own right. Both the exhibition at the Egyptian Hall and the production of *Savage Life and Scenes* show much about the society in which the real Hemi Pomare would have found himself.

The Royal Society soirée scene is also taken from real life — many details of the attendees and items on display are taken from newspaper accounts. However, the interactions and conversations are invented. In addition, the first epigraph is a quote about Hemi Pomare from the London newspaper, *The Daily News*, and reviews of the exhibition at the Egyptian Hall, are borrowed almost unchanged from papers and journals of the time.

Mr Angus, Miss Angus and all the other characters are products of my imagination, although it is known that George French Angas's father was a merchant carriage- and ship-builder, and that in 1846, George, if not the others, lived at Upper Gloucester Street, Dorset Square, London.

Other helpful sources included:

The Shows of London by Richard D Altick (Belknap Press, Cambridge, Mass., 1978).

The National Library and Alexander Turnbull Library for access to British newspaper archives and an original copy of Angas's Savage Life and Scenes.

The historical works of Judith Flanders, Lee Jackson and all the wonderful Victorian London historians and enthusiasts on Twitter — your serendipitous articles and observations made this book richer than it might have been.

NGĀ MIHI —
ACKNOWLEDGEMENTS

Writers supposedly work in isolation, but creating a book is a collective effort. I am deeply grateful for the many ways this book was supported by different people and different groups. *The Imaginary Lives of James Pōneke* would not exist if it weren't for the various forms of encouragement I've received. Whether it was a grant, feedback or personal tautoko, these contributions enabled me to sustain the writing life, keep thinking about the story and gain a little more confidence. There were many times when my steps faltered. There were many times when support from the following allowed me to *just keep going*.

Ka nui te mihi ki a:

Creative New Zealand, Randell Cottage Writers Trust and the Beatson Fellowship for financial support. Also, Commonwealth Writers, for the surprising gift of an international prize. Two wonderful people who made it possible for this book to find a home in the UK: Scott Pack of Eye & Lightning Books, and my agent, Charlotte Seymour at Nurnberg Associates. It's a gift to be working with people who look beyond borders to seek stories that expand our worlds. And Jane Parkin, for always generous and careful editing, as well as the whole team at Penguin Random House NZ. I am lucky to work with such insightful people.

Ngā mihi hoki to my very special readers, Moana Jackson and Victor Rodger, and my writing group. I have been immensely fortunate and privileged to have such astute eyes on my work.

Finally, to my whānau, especially Lorry, Kōtuku and Aquila. I am immensely proud of you. Thanks for your tolerance and for being my eccentric, hilarious and never-boring home.

No reira, ngā mihi mīharo ki a tātou katoa my writing community, my cultural community, my families, for all the kaha.

ABOUT THE AUTHOR

Tina Makereti writes novels, short fiction and personal essays. She co-edited *Black Marks on the White Page* (Vintage 2017), an anthology that celebrates Māori and Pasifika writing, with Witi Ihimaera. In 2016 her story 'Black Milk' won the Commonwealth Writers Short Story Prize, Pacific region. Her first novel *Where the Rēkohu Bone Sings* (Vintage 2014) won the 2014 Ngā Kupu Ora Aotearoa Māori Book Award for Fiction, also won by her short story collection, *Once Upon a Time in Aotearoa*. In 2009 she was the recipient of the RSNZ Manhire Prize for Creative Science Writing and the Pikihuia Award for Best Short Story in English. She has presented her work all over New Zealand and in Frankfurt, Taipei, Jamaica and the UK. Tina teaches creative writing and Oceanic literatures at Massey University.

www.tinamakereti.com